Bryce Anderson • Misha Burnett • Simon Cantan

Dave Higgins • David Kristoph • Richard Levesque • Russ Linton • J.S. Morin

Christopher Ruz • Meryl Stenhouse • Graham Storrs • I.A. Watson

# ALL THESE SHINY
# WORLDS II

—————— The 2017 ImmerseOrDie Anthology ——————

Edited by:

creativityhacker.ca

# All These Shiny Worlds II

# Acknowledgements

Stories are included in this collection by permission of the authors.

"A Rough Spirit" by Dave Higgins. Copyright © 2017 Dave Higgins.

"Alter Ego," by Russ Linton. Copyright © 2015 Russ Linton. First appeared in *Empty Quiver: Tales from the Crimson Son Universe*, from Fictional Work.

"Bodies of Evidence," by Jefferson Smith. Copyright © 2010 Jefferson Smith.

"Borrowed Lives" by I.A. Watson. Copyright © 2017 Ian Watson.

"Digital Commander," by J.S. Morin. Copyright © 2017 J.S. Morin.

"Merge," by Simon Cantan. Copyright © 2017 Simon Cantan.

"Out In The Dark," by Meryl Stenhouse. Copyright © 2017 Meryl Stenhouse.

"The Apprentice Appears," by Bryce Anderson. Copyright © 2017 Bryce Anderson.

"The Earth Ship," by Graham Storrs. Copyright © 2009 Graham Storrs. First appeared in *The Absent Willow Review*, from Absent Willow Review Publishing, LLC.

"The Lancer," by David Kristoph. Copyright © 2017 David Kristoph.

"The Silk Of Yesterday's Gown" by Misha Burnett. Copyright © 2016 Misha Burnett.

"The Traveller," by Christopher Ruz, published previously as "Hercule and the Doctor." Copyright © 2011 Christopher Ruz.

"Without a Care in the World," by Richard Levesque. Copyright © 2017 Richard Levesque.

*For every reader who takes their leisure on indie worlds,*

*And for every author who toils alone to create them,*

*We dedicate this collection to all of you.*

*May our worlds collide all the sooner.*

# Contents

# Introduction

Last year, we embarked on an ambitious mission: to gather a collection of stories from the ranks of indie authors that would demonstrate the breadth of styles, the quality of writing, and the vast horizon of possibilities being explored outside the traditional publishing marketplace. We hoped it would serve as a one-stop shopping solution for any indie reader who wanted to find a new group of authors to dive into, and as a proof they could share with their not-yet-enlightened friends about the high quality of work that can be found in the hinterlands of indie publishing.

But given such lofty goals, we were surprised to succeed as fully as we did. In the sixteen months since *All These Shiny Worlds* was first published, over seven thousand people have given it a home, and in that time it has never fallen out of the top thirty fantasy or SF anthologies on Amazon.

We are humbled by the kind words in all the reviews, and we are delighted that so many have found so much to enjoy. So delighted, in fact, that we decided to do it again. And just like last time, we brought our biggest stomping boots to the selection party.

Unlike many indie anthologies, the ImmerseOrDie anthology series follows the same tough-love principles as the book review series that inspired it. Thirty-seven authors who have survived an ImmerseOrDie review were contacted, and each was asked to nominate one additional author who they felt had game. The resulting pool of approximately sixty authors were then invited to submit their best story. Not their most recent. Not the one they've had the hardest time selling. Their best. Then those stories were thrown into a pit along with seven underfed, cantankerous judges, and nobody was allowed out until only the strongest stories were left standing.

The result is the collection you now hold in your hands. *All These Shiny Worlds II* may be second in the series, but it is just as strong, just as varied, and just as engaging as its older brother. But there *are* differences. This time out, only thirteen stories made the final cut, compared with fifteen in the inaugural edition. And while that first collection leaned somewhat toward fantasy, this collection corrects the balance, leaning back the other way, toward science fiction.

But as I sit here now, reviewing the final roster of stories, I am struck by another difference. This time around, the stories seem "smaller." Not in terms of their length, but in terms of the deeds they encompass. A complete family history conveyed in a simple visit to the salon; a power struggle played out between village urchins; a difficult night in the life of a garbage man. These are not the grand, sweeping tales of power and ambition that are the usual stock in trade of speculative fiction. These are the stories of the people who populate those worlds. Maybe I should have called it *All These* Tiny *Worlds*.

Rather than being tiny in impact though, it seems to me to be quite the opposite. These stories somehow manage to make their worlds seem that much bigger. That much more fully packed and clearly drawn. If the author knows so much about the tiny details of their world shown here, then surely that means the rest of their world is filled with even greater detail and thought. Even bigger hearts and richer tales.

So if you like a story you read here, don't be shy. Click a link and check out more from that author. And if you like lots of them, we've even put together a collection of some of the best novels by the same group of writers. *The ImmerseOrDie Science Fiction Smackdown* has eight complete novels, all in one convenient download, all for one amazingly low price, and all carrying the same promise as this collection: guaranteed not to suck.

But enough from me. Time for you to get on with the job you came here for.

Happy reading,

*Jefferson Smith*
*May 2017, Saskatoon*

# Out in the Dark

## Meryl Stenhouse

*Editor's Note: For all our accomplishments, the majority of even our own world is more question than answer. Less than one drop in twenty of our oceans have been explored, scarcely an eighth of all species have yet been found. One day, robots may do much of that for us, but some of the tasks we might send them to perform in the great, silent darkness are less noble. And a lot more terrifying.*

It was always stifling on the engineering deck. Add to that the stink of sulphur from the overflowing scrubbers and you had something reminiscent of hell; hot, sulphurous and full of the moral flotsam of society.

Brady had the floor, and he had hit his stride, going on about the rights of man and mutiny and freedom and all the Asia-Pacific nations who would welcome men with our skills and knowledge. And I guess it sounded good if you were facing six or ten or twenty years in this submarine, and the very real possibility of never going home again.

Brady finished his rant to cheers and stamping feet. I just shook my head. Three weeks into a six-year stint and he was already looking for a way out. The men who made it were the ones who put their heads down, and the ones who got lucky.

As the cheers quieted and people started to group up, my neighbor turned and gave me a friendly smile. "Mitchell."

After a moment of hesitation, I shook his hand. "Dawkins." I stood to go. I wasn't in the habit of making friends, or doing anything except hiding out in Environmental, which was a restricted area.

Mitchell stood as well. "So where'd you do your training?"

"Townsville."

"Yeah? We all came through Singleton. Wondered why you didn't come in with us."

"I've been here a while."

"Well I've been here three goddamn weeks and this is just bullshit. All this crap about productive member of society and paying your debts. My lawyer told me to go for the armed forces option. Six years instead of twenty. But six years in this tin can is going to feel like twenty."

"You get used to it."

"Yeah? So how long are you in here for?"

"Life," I said.

"Jesus. Never heard of anyone doing life. Even serial killers only get twenty. What the hell did you do?"

"I killed a city." Bald truth. My own special tagline. There was a particular sequence of expressions that people went through when I said it. Confusion. Doubt. Surprise. Then comprehension washing away all other expressions.

Now he knew who I was, and there would be no more friendly exchanges. Isolation, peace. Just the way I liked it.

Schaffer, the sub-engineer who ran the deck in the absence of officers, jerked his hand down. I didn't need him to tell me the scrubbers were playing up again. My nose was quicker on the mark than he was.

Heading down to the underdeck, where the enviro systems bubbled and stank, I caught snatches of conversation, words like *freedom* and *escape* and the dreaded word, *mutiny*. Dreams. Just dreams. There had never been a successful takeover in all the years of the submarine prison ships. Oh, there were rumors, but no one had actually confirmed that a missing ship had escaped, rather than being destroyed. And then there was the *Annabelle*. But blowing up in Sydney Harbor wasn't my idea of freedom.

The problem, the issue that most of these mutineers forgot, or just didn't understand, was that the men chosen to captain these ships were also here for a reason. This was their out. Four years captaining a prison ship meant an honourable discharge, whatever you had done.

I didn't know what Vandermark had done, but if he was an example of the type of man who captained these submarines, it was no wonder no one escaped. On my first day on the *Augusta*, I had reported to his office and he'd told me the score. Then he'd broken the fingers on my left hand.

They healed in a few weeks, but I'd gotten the message. Keep my head down and do what I was told. So I did. Unlike the rest of the lower decks crew, I was a skilled technician with years of experience. Normally I would be in a prison topside, somewhere like Boorang or Jetts Bay. But after New Wellington, everyone knew my face. I'd never last there.

It wasn't my fault. All those deaths. The technician on the shift before me hadn't noticed the readout from the pumps. And the system that should have alerted me to the failing pumps, didn't. I was just the last man in a long line of people cruising through their days on autopilot.

If I'd read the hourly analytic report, I'd have noticed the falling pressure in the coolant tanks. If I'd performed a manual feedback check on the pump system, I would have seen that the flow rate was too low. If I had done either of those things, I would have known the pumps had failed. Would have known that the backup pumps weren't enough. Would have hit the emergency button, and pumped air in straight from the umbilical.

Then the pressure wouldn't have dropped, and the dome wouldn't have cracked, and the water wouldn't have come sweeping into New Wellington as the air bubbled out.

Criminal negligence. Manslaughter. Not murder. But it didn't matter. When you killed that many people, the name you gave it was irrelevant.

It was fitting, somehow, that I spent my penance down here. A few inches of steel between me and the ocean, and every night dreams about the water coming in, salty and cold, choking me with icy fingers as I screamed.

---•---

There was a ping on the radar. The first we knew about it was Halifax coming down to Engineering. He was the chief engineer, and we hadn't seen him since day one. He hauled me out of my bed after four hours sleep to manage the port turbine. While I coddled it, he prowled about, barking at people and listening to the updates from the bridge.

Something had been spotted, out there in the dark. The ocean is a big place, and there was no reason we couldn't avoid it. That was the main goal of every captain of every defence submarine. Keep the hell out of the way of whatever is out there and come back intact. The fact that we were all awake meant that we'd tried to avoid it and failed. It was coming after us.

And that was the big problem. We didn't know what it was. No one knew what was out there, because no government would admit to placing defence measures in the ocean. We were at war, but it was a war that nobody talked about.

The news talked about our defence network protecting the country from invasion. But that was just spiel. The submarines were populated by men who just wanted to do their time and come home alive. Who avoided whatever came out of the sea and attacked our coastlines.

You'd wake up in the morning to read about a coastal town decimated, or deserted, or burning with cold, wet fire. Boats that foundered off the shore and disappeared under the waves as people watched from the docks. Whales eviscerated and left to float in on the tides and foul the shores. New Zealand's east coast fenced off and crawling with green death.

I wondered how many times one of our defences saw something on the radar heading for the coast, and turned tail and fled, as we were doing now. Hoping that whatever was out there would move on to slower prey.

We ran before it for hours, and knew it was gaining. Halifax sweated and shouted as if somehow that would make the engines go faster. I sweated and watched the port turbine founder as the heat sinks failed. Something had clogged the inflow pipes, and the cooling water was not getting through.

Halifax was easy to track down. I just followed the shouting.

"We need to shut down the port turbine."

"Don't be stupid."

"It's overheating. If we don't, it could seize, and then it's out until we hit dry-dock."

Halifax grabbed the front of my coveralls and lifted me off my feet. "We are not shutting down anything. Keep that thing working, or I will shoot you myself."

He dropped me and I stumbled and fell. Schaffer took a step towards Halifax, as if he might intervene, but then turned aside.

I watched the engine as it foundered, the readouts showing a textbook picture of an overheating turbine. The temperature difference between the outer shell cooled by the water and the inner core grew larger and larger and I chewed my nails to the quick, waiting for the shriek and grind of a catastrophic failure.

Then Vandermark was on the intercom. "Why is our speed dropping?"

"Port turbine's not running well," barked Halifax, glaring at me.

"Well get it running. Our tail is gaining."

"Yes, sir."

The connection bled to static. Halifax stalked over to me. "You heard. Get that turbine running."

"I can't. Something has clogged the cooling lines."

"Well flush them!"

"I have. It didn't work. They need to be cleared manually."

"Then you'd better get out there and do it."

"What?"

Halifax pressed the intercom button. "Sir. Dawkins says the turbine can't be cleared from inside. We're shutting down engines and sending him out to fix it."

"Make it fast. We've got about twenty minutes before our tail catches us."

My guts went cold. "I can't go out there."

"Suit up," snapped Hawkins. "If you don't get that turbine back online, we're sitting ducks. Understand?"

I backed away, looked around for support. "I can't."

"You damn well will."

I shook my head and backed into the wall.

Hawkins grabbed me and dragged me to the lock. He flung open a locker and grabbed a suit.

"I can't." My throat was so dry I could barely speak. "I can't go out there."

"You're going. Put it on."

I pulled it on with shaking hands. My arms wouldn't work properly. Then Schaffer was behind me, yanking the suit up over my unresponsive body. Hawkins was pulling two tanks out, and a mask and regulator. Schaffer leaned down and I flinched.

"Come on, mate. I don't want to die out here."

In his eyes there was a child's fear of the dark. I looked away. I didn't want to die, either. But he had no idea what he was asking me to do.

Everything went black around the edges as Halifax dragged me to the airlock and shoved me through. The door had barely closed before he keyed the outer lock. I scrambled for mask and regulator as the water rushed in. It pushed me off my feet and washed over my head. Condensation speckled the inside of my face shield, and the sound of my sucking breaths drowned out everything else.

The speaker in my suit helmet crackled. "Move it, Dawkins!"

He was asking the impossible. The lock was a gaping black hole out into the ocean. I grabbed the diver propulsion vehicle handles and fumbled with the power. The lights came on and I let it drag me through that awful hole.

The *Augusta* drifted. I made my way down the smooth hull. All the outer lights were off, and the dark waters surrounded me.

The DPV pulled me along the hull in a circle of light. Tiny motes danced in the illuminated water, but beyond that the ocean rolled away, an endless, starless sky.

"What the hell are you doing?" Halifax's voice sounded tinny and far away.

Then the port turbine appeared in my lights and I saw a great black ribbon of something stretching back along the side of the *Augusta*. Oil?

No. It *moved* in the water, undulating like weed in a current. Alive? Adrenalin rushed through my system and I dove away. But the thing didn't follow me.

"Dawkins!"

"Sorry." My voice rasped in my throat. "There's something—I don't know, a worm thing—caught in the intake."

"Get rid of it!"

I didn't want to touch it. But I moved forward, to where it came out of the intake pipes.

The light shone off metal and wire. A man-made thing, slightly thicker around than a man's thigh. I reached out a gloved hand to touch the skin. Rough polymer skidded under my glove.

The head of it was buried in the turbine's intake valve. It was hard to get a grip. I tugged and tugged, with no apparent success, but finally it gave. A final tug and the body came away. The ragged end bristled with wires and the jointed metal skeleton stuck out in shiny fingers.

"Dawkins. Report!"

"It's stuck in the pipe. I'll have to dig it out."

"Do it." For the first time ever I heard panic in Halifax's voice.

I let the body fall away and dug the head out with a screwdriver, piece by piece. It was wedged well into the pipe. At the head end I found a set of metal teeth bigger than my hand. The edges were razor sharp, and sliced through my glove. Blood bloomed in the water.

"Dawkins!"

"It's done." I shone a light down the pipe, saw the intake valve at the end, clear of debris. "It should work fine."

"Good. Now get back in here."

7

The DPV dragged me back along the side of the ship, with me silently begging it to hurry. The airlock was in sight when a roar trembled through my bones. I swung around. The turbines had fired. The *Augusta* started to move.

I screamed into the mic, begging them to stop.

Over the roar of the submarine came a sound like whalesong. But there were no whales anymore.

A woman swam out of the darkness, mouth open, singing. Bubbles foamed up in front of my face plate. She passed over me, her cold face frozen, the sightless metal eyes, mounded breasts on a metal chest. The waist tapered to a narrow cylinder with a turbine at the back, covered in the long dark tendrils of black worms.

As the song washed over me, my DPV went dead. I pressed the button frantically, with no response. She ignored me completely in her pursuit of the submarine.

A worm drifted past and I grabbed it without thinking. The water dragged at me, and I wrapped both hands around the black body.

She swam to the *Augusta*, and the song went before her, and killed it. The engines drifted to a stop and it began to list, slightly, then drop towards the sea bed.

The woman followed the *Augusta* for a moment, and then, as if satisfied it was dead, continued on her way. I looked behind me, waiting for the escape hatches to pop, for the little bubble vessels to emerge from the foundering submarine and float up to the surface. But the *Augusta* continued to sink, dark and dead.

Terror kept my hold on the tendrils as the water roared around me. How much air did I have left? My frantic searching revealed a hatch on the siren's belly. The drag made it difficult to climb up the worm, but at last I grabbed the handles, turned and tugged frantically against the pressure. The hatch popped open and air bubbled out as water foamed in. I dragged myself in quickly and pulled the hatch shut behind me.

I knelt on the floor for a moment, water sloshing around my knees. I was in a tiny maintenance room. There was a ladder leading up to the floor above my head, and around me on the walls were banks of upside down control boards.

I pushed myself to my feet, shaking, and pulled the regulator out of my mouth. My lungs seized in a coughing fit. The air was thick with fumes. With my arm pressed over my mouth, I stumbled over to the boards. My tank was running out, and this air was not fit to breathe.

Menu after menu flicked past. There—maintenance. Surface and rotate. I keyed the command and the woman turned and swept towards the surface. I fell, tumbled into the wall on the other side. Then we broke the surface and she rolled, and I rolled, smacking my head on the floor.

Now I understood why the boards were upside down. For maintenance routines, she lay on her back and they crawled in through her belly.

There was something gross and sick about such an intimate act.

When she stopped moving I crawled to the ladder and dragged myself up. The room spun around me and spots dotted my vision. I pushed on the hatch and shoved it open, leaning out into the cold air.

Water splashed over me, but I didn't care. I breathed deeply, clearing my head and my lungs. We were low in the water, and the swells were over my head. I already knew we were nowhere near land. But I had a vessel now, and I was confident I could move her to wherever I wanted. Somewhere that would be grateful to have a skilled engineer, and didn't need to know about the death of a city. Some Pacific nation, like Brady had said.

Brady, who was facing a slow death by asphyxiation, or the choice of a quick suicide. I rubbed my face, and my hand came away shaking. The corpses from my dreams marched in my head, but now they wore the faces of men I knew. Had known.

What could I do? Beyond the metal breasts, the full, silent mouth pouted at the sky.

Why do this? Why make a weapon in the shape of a woman? My imagination conjured up a room of weapons developers, laughing at the idea of making a siren, a killer of ships, and sending her out to hunt, both beautiful and deadly. Pointless. The men who died to her song would never know.

It was contempt. Contempt for the worth of our lives. Fuck them. Fuck them in their safe little laboratories, building fear and sending it out to prey on us.

I dropped down the ladder, hauled the door shut behind me and went to learn her systems.

———— • ————

The *Augusta* appeared ahead of me, a blip on the screen. It had settled on the sea floor, head down and still. I cringed at the thought of what I might find inside.

I brought the siren as close to the *Augusta* as I could, and hauled on my depleted tank. I hoped there was enough air to get me over to the airlock and inside. Then what? I had no idea. But I would do something.

I swam through the dark water to the side of the submarine. The doorlock turned easily. The hatch opened and I slid into the inner chamber of the airlock. But when I closed the door behind me and pressed the button to open the inner door, it stayed shut. I pressed it again, then scrabbled at the latch for the manual override. It was stuck fast. I pounded on the hatch with my torch. No electrics, no pumps to get rid of the water. I looked at my air gauge. A couple more minutes of air left.

What could I do? I turned to leave, then heard the grind of metal. The hatch opened, and water rushed through, dragging me with it, tumbling me onto the floor of the submarine.

Someone dragged me to my feet, and I looked into Halifax's eyes. They were bloodshot, and a deep cut on his cheek had bled down his neck. Men surrounded us, pale shapes in the gloom.

"What the hell did you come back for?" said Halifax, bemused.

"To rescue you."

Halifax started laughing, but stopped, panting. The air was thin. It made my chest hurt.

"You've just come back to die, then. Better take that tank and go."

"Hell he will!" Someone shoved me, then I fell, felt hands clawing at the tank on my back. I shouted and shoved at the desperate men. Then Schaffer was there, and Halifax, hauling people off me and pushing them back.

"It won't do you any good." I shrugged out of the straps and the tank thudded to the floor, splashing in the water. "There's only a couple of minutes of air left." I grabbed Halifax. "What happened to the other tanks? I need to get outside and get the ship moving."

"Gone." His mouth twisted into a grimace. "Once Vandermark realised the escape pods were as dead as everything else, he sent his officers in to take the tanks by force. They took off, left us to die."

"Oh." My mouth had gone dry. My great plan relied on a scuba tank. But, wait— "The bubbles are still here?"

"Yeah, but they won't deploy. Dead as everything else."

Dead, or powerless? "The reactor?"

"Dead."

"Batteries?"

"Working, as far as we can tell, but nothing's getting through."

Electromagnetic pulse. We had power, but no way of using it. How much of the electronics were fried? Surely some parts of the submarine had been protected.

"Okay, I'm going to—" What the hell was I going to do?

I shivered. Halifax and the remaining crew were going blue as the cold seeped into the submarine.

I couldn't fit them all into the siren, and I had no way of getting them over there without scuba gear anyway. But the bubbles would float. I knew they would. I just needed to release them. How much power would it take?

"Get everyone into the bubbles," I said.

Hope blossomed on the faces of the men. Halifax grabbed his arm. "Can you get them free?"

"I think so." It wasn't just the air that made me lightheaded. The lives of these men were in my hands, and the sweat on my skin was like fire and ice. "I need your help though. You and Schaffer. We have to disconnect one of the batteries."

That might sound like a simple exercise, but leading the two men down into the battery store, I wondered if my idea was going to work. There was nothing portable about a submarine battery. They were huge, big enough to power the submarine for forty-eight hours in case of reactor failure, and bolted into the frame.

In the battery room, the readouts were all dead, as I expected. I hurried past the big main batteries, taller than my head, to the little backup battery that powered the server systems and the emergency lights. It was a mere forty-five kilograms of metal and liquid and plastic, ungainly but small enough to move through the ship.

It took us a while to remove the bolts that held it in place, and longer for me to find the gear I needed. I sent Schaffer and Halifax on ahead, lugging the detached battery between them.

The chill had seeped through the walls. No longer hell, just the cold touch of death. I tripped on something soft as I came out into the top deck.

Schaffer's voice came out of the darkness. "Watch out. Body back there."

I flashed the torch beam down before thinking, and saw a man slumped on the floor. Dark blood dripped through the grating. The stars on his shoulders winked in the light.

"It's Vandermark!"

"Yeah." Halifax's voice floated back to me. "You sound surprised."

I flicked the torch beam up again, and stepped over the body. "What happened?"

"I'd say the officers felt the same way about him as we did."

I didn't mention the fact that Halifax was technically an officer. I wondered, in that moment, what he had done to get sent down here.

Faces appeared out of the gloom. A group of men huddled around the hatch of a bubble.

"Can't get in?"

"No."

I could hear them panting, taking shallow breaths as the air thinned. "All right. Let me through. Put the battery down there."

I handed my torch to another man and got to work. In the silent submarine, the creak and groan of the ocean came through the walls, interrupted by the shuffle and cough of the men grouped down the corridor in front of the inert escape bubbles.

The pods were designed to activate on a critical failure. But they were designed on the assumption that the emergency power was still working, and that the electronics hadn't been fried. I stripped the panels in front of the pods, pulling out boards and wires right down to the connection plates. Then I hooked up the battery and leaned in to apply the live wires directly to the connection. The pods had been inert when the siren had sent the EMP into the ship. I prayed that they had been shielded, that this would be enough to wake them, that their circuits hadn't been destroyed by the pulse.

I pressed the live wires to the panel and felt the jolt as they connected and then the pod went live, the lights blinding us. Men down the corridor cheered as the hatch opened.

"Get in!" I shouted. They needed no urging from me. The hatch closed and then the pod fired, shooting out from the submarine on a blast of air. Through the porthole I could see the bubble of light float upwards.

We worked our way down the corridor. Thirty-five men, three men to a bubble. Bright globes of light shooting upward toward the surface. Men breathing fresh air and living.

We struggled to drag the battery to the last hatch. Torches dropped from hands gone uncooperative with exhaustion and lack of oxygen. Schaffer held the torch for me as I peeled away the circuitry to the plate and applied the leads one last time. The lights blazed in, shooting shadows into the dim ends of the corridors. Halifax went down on the grating with a meaty thud. Schaffer and I struggled to get the big man through the hatch. Then we hauled ourselves into the bubble, and it closed behind us. I fell to the floor, unable, uncaring. We shot away from the ship and slid gracefully upwards.

In the beam of light below us, through the transparent side of the bubble, I saw the *Augusta* lying nose down on the sea floor beside the siren. I thought about the men who had built her, the government that had commissioned her, sent her out to prey not only on our enemies, but also on ourselves.

Schaffer and Halifax were sweaty, pale, eyes red-rimmed in pinched and worn faces. This was the face of our country. In the swell I could see the other bubbles floating not far away.

Something came back to me, from the days of sitting in a control room, reading poetry instead of caring for the lives of people in my charge. Something about a two-headed bird, pecking itself to death, and being content to die.

The current would take us north. Papua probably, and from there maybe to Indonesia or the Philippines. Somewhere we could hide, and not end up back in a submarine, fighting a war we couldn't win.

Pushing myself up was an effort, and pulling the heavy air tank out of the locker nearly put me down again. Halifax stirred as if to stop me, but what could he do?

The hatch opened to a blue world. Light above, dark below. Yin and yang. It wouldn't be Halifax who stopped me.

I sat on the lip of the hatch for a long time, putting my breather in, taking it out, sucking in air like a man breaking the surface for the first time in years.

The waters closed over my head. The beam of light from the bubble was my pathway down to the ruined sub and the siren.

My siren. My weapon. She could destroy a city, too. We were well matched. A pair of murderers who might just make amends for a million quiet, watery deaths, if such a thing could be done.

Hadn't I started it already? Hadn't I saved a hundred men?

Maybe I could do it by zones. A cargo ship saved for the docks and warehouses, which had been the first to flood. A coastline swept clean of bioweapons, for the central district, where men and women had been caught on the walkways by the rolling, crashing water. A coastal community protected from the monsters that crawled out of the sea on metal tracks, for the residences, and a hundred thousand drowned children.

*I'm sorry.* "I'm sorry." The words didn't feel right. Not yet. Not with the debt still unpaid.

I brought the siren to the surface to refill the air tanks, then turned her toward my country. In our wake, the bubbles rocked and spun on their way to freedom.

## About The Author

Meryl Stenhouse lives in subtropical Queensland where she curates an extensive notebook collection and fights a running battle with the Lego models trying to take over the house. When not avoiding stealth bricks she can be found at the computer, avoiding writing. She has stories in *Aurealis*, *Metaphorosis*, *Extreme Planets Anthology*, and *Not Your Average Monster Vol. 2*.

For more information, visit www.merylstenhouse.com.

# Alter Ego

## Russ Linton

*Editor's Note: Most stories are told in third person. "John went to the party." It's a simple voice. Direct. Some guy who isn't you or me did something. Let me tell you what he did. Other stories are told in first. "I kicked his ass." Simpler, and even more direct. I did it, and now I'm telling you what I did. But some stories are quieter; hidden between the louder voices. This kind of story is told in fourth.*

Jackie asked to dye her hair orange during the summer of seventh grade. Her father stared, mouth half-open, eyes seeing through her for what seemed like a long time. But he finally agreed with a silent nod.

She reached up and wrapped her arms around him and squeezed. Frozen in whatever mental fog gripped him, there were too many heartbeats before she felt him caress the back of her head. He'd probably never expected her to ask for something so, well, crazy, but he had to know she'd at least considered it.

A few years ago, her father had decided to give her an allowance. Even then, at ten years old, she'd grown tired of living in a weed-choked laundry basket of a house slated for a dust-bunny breeding program. After long hours at work, her father was exhausted. Most often, he'd drop down on the sofa with a beer and tune out everything but the television.

She understood.

So, she started cleaning; learned how, after a few dozen shrunken t-shirts and pink socks, to do the laundry. The dishes. She even conquered her fear of the vacuum cleaner. Sure, she'd screamed the entire time, racing around the house as if she held a live animal, but she'd gotten the job done. After that, she took on the lawnmower, an even scarier monster. But she was brave. Brave, because that's what Ember would be.

Once she'd saved enough money and gotten up the nerve to let her dad in on her secret desire, she raced triumphantly to her room and launched into the air. She always clung to the moment when her feet left the ground, pretending she could control the thermals, change their density to let her tiny frame float. She never could, of course, but she landed on her bed, giddy with excitement about her coming change.

Above her, the ceiling was papered with news clippings and magazine pages. There, in those spaces, Jackie did fly. One of the pictures in particular always held her attention.

Ember, the flame-wielding Augment, soaring through the skies of Chicago on a pillar of fire.

Her costume was made of thick, shimmery material which could withstand the intense heat. A heat that could set the air on fire, burn through the outer shell of a battle tank, and melt guns into puddles.

If Jackie could have any power, it would be Ember's.

But the fireproof costume didn't explain the hair. Ember's mask covered her entire face. A sleek visor, sort of like a medieval knight, but no holes for her eyes. Behind that, a brilliant orange mane flowed in a stripe down her head. Her powers kept her from frying her head, Jackie thought. Precise control of the heat. Too bad Dad hadn't also agreed to the mohawk.

"Are you ready?" Her dad stood in the doorway of her bedroom, keys in hand. He was trying to smile, but his eyes were worried. He always looked like that.

"Yep, yep!" She leapt to her feet on the bed and bounded toward him.

Excitement coursed through her and she knew her face was plastered in the world's goofiest grin, but she didn't care. And exactly like she hoped, he snatched her off the ground as she got to the door, his distant expression transformed by her joy.

"Are you sure you want to do this?"

She smacked his shoulder. "Of course I want to do this." He laughed and lowered her to the ground. "Besides," she added, "this is your fault."

The distant look returned. "Why do you say that?"

"You're the one that watches Ember all the time."

"Do not." He forced a smile.

"Do, too! Every time she's on the news you can't look away." She poked a finger in his chest. "Somebody has a crush."

"Come on, now." He started down the hall, fidgeting with the keys.

"Admit it! You do!"

"Stop. Let's go before I change my mind."

They hopped in the truck and made their way into town. They stopped at the grocery store first. Jackie complained, but Dad was right, they actually did have things like hair coloring kits. But the shelf held only an autumn sort of red, nothing like Ember orange. She even asked a bald, sullen looking employee if they had the color, exactly like that, "Ember orange." He shook his head and went back to pushing a ragged mop across the floor.

They tried several stores and were about to give up when Jackie spotted a salon. She'd never been in one. She and her dad both went to the Clip Shack, which she didn't mind. The stylists were always excited to see her. She felt a bit like Ember those days—a touch of the famous Augment's celebrity. She swelled with pride as they fawned over her, the only other girl in the place. The excitement always waned when she asked for something "easy."

"A phase," they'd say sympathetically. "She'll grow out of it."

"Aren't there any boys you like?"

Gross. Ember didn't like boys. At least, Jackie didn't think so.

The salon looked fancy. With cursive letters on the windows, she couldn't even read the name. The posters with models pointing their chins at the sky made her cringe. Their hair was all silky and smooth and perfectly colored.

"There!" Jackie pointed, before they'd driven past.

"Are you sure?"

She nodded.

When Jackie and her father walked in, they weren't staring down a row of barber's chairs facing little TVs looping *Sportscenter*. She didn't even see any chairs. Instead, there was a reception desk decorated with smooth, turquoise stones all down the front and a blank, brown wall behind the desk, displaying the same cursive lettering as the windows. A girl with perfect hair, like the posters, and razor-sharp lips and eyebrows pulled herself away from a cell phone.

"Welcome to Santé. Do you have an appointment?"

"Nope." Jackie said before her dad could speak. "I want my hair colored. Maybe you have a kit?"

"We don't sell 'kits'," the girl's sky-pointed chin dipped to her collarbone when she said the word. "But we might have a stylist available." She rose and disappeared around the wall. Jackie walked toward the partition, swinging her shoulders like the receptionist.

"Jackie." Her dad sounded stern, but maybe partly amused.

"What?"

The receptionist rounded the corner with another girl behind her. She was young, and her hair was silky too, but a broad swath of it was deep purple on one side and shaved tight to her scalp on the other. Somehow, Jackie thought, the snooty receptionist had found the right person.

"Hello." The girl extended a hand and Jackie took hold. She wasn't much taller than Jackie, but the tight lines of her jeans made her legs appear endless. Her white sleeveless t-shirt hung like a shredded rag and black lace peeked through the holes alongside bare skin.

Jackie realized she'd been staring when the girl raised her eyebrows. "I'm Becca. You are?"

Becca didn't paint on her eyebrows or her lips. The natural lines suggested perfection enough. That and her smile made Jackie's cheeks flush.

"This is Jackie." She felt her father's hand on her shoulder. "She wants to color her hair."

"That so." Becca eyed Jackie and tapped her lip with her finger. "I can probably help you out. What were you thinking?"

It was the finger on her lip. Jackie couldn't erase the image.

"Well?"

"Ember orange," said her father. Becca's face twisted in confusion and he stuttered out an explanation. "Like the Augment, Ember."

"Ah, so this is like an 'I'm not fucking around' orange?"

Jackie nodded.

Her father choked out a reply. "Yeah, you could say that."

"Got it. Come with me."

Jackie followed, her father close behind. At the corner, Becca wheeled and brandished a finger in his direction. "Girls only," she said with a wink.

Her father raised his hands in surrender and half-smiled. "All right. But no mohawks."

Becca ran a hand through Jackie's hair and pursed her lips. The touch made her scalp tingle and she swore she could feel it all the way down to her toes. "Yeah, no problem."

They entered an open room with stylists' stations peppering the space, each made up of a floating wall with mirror and fancy wooden cabinets facing a barber's chair. Everything matched the earthy tones of the reception area. At every station, stylists hovered around their customers, silver blades flickering between their fingers. This was not the humming assembly line of electric clippers like the Clip Shack. Here, women spoke and laughed. A few sat alone reading magazines, oblivious to strange bubbles mounted to the chairs and floating over their heads. Jackie almost asked what they were, but she hoped she wouldn't have to speak. Normally, according to her teachers at school, she didn't have a problem with speaking, but Becca had left Jackie tongue-tied.

Becca motioned to a chair, and Jackie sat.

"Sure you don't want a mohawk?"

"No." Jackie wished Becca would stop smiling, but at the same time, she knew she'd miss it. "My dad."

"Yeah, I know." Becca pouted and whipped an apron around Jackie's neck. "You'd look kickass with one."

Jackie felt her cheeks flush and she checked the mirror in time to watch them blossom. A hand lightly touched her chin and kept her from hiding her face. Those unadorned eyes were examining her again and Jackie looked up at the ceiling to avoid contact.

"Orange, huh?"

"Yeah."

"Cool. Let's get started."

From that moment, Jackie was lost in a world of odd sensations. The warm water from the faucet as Becca washed her hair was exhilarating, but not nearly as much as the pull of slender fingers along her scalp. All the while, Becca hovered over her, her loose shirt dangling open. Things stirred inside Jackie—things that made her drive her stubby nails into the arm of the chair.

Next, they returned to the station, and Becca brushed on globs of dye that looked nothing like orange, but Jackie didn't protest. Becca worked while wrapping strands of hair in foil slips, like leftover pizza. Her playful side tucked away, Becca took to her job with a laser-guided stare. So focused, Jackie finally started to relax. All the staring and examining had been part of the process, she told herself. Checking her hair out, not her.

"Your mom cool with this?" Becca muttered as she brushed on more of the dye.

"My mom's not really around." Jackie didn't normally tell people this —it was really none of their business, but despite her awkwardness around Becca, she felt she could trust her.

"Oh, sorry."

"Not a big deal," said Jackie. She had an urge to sound grown up. "Long time ago."

Becca nodded and fixed on a palette of foil. "What's it with this Ember chick? You into Augments?"

"I guess. Well, not really." Augments weren't a "girl thing" and Jackie was always stumbling with what to say when people asked. If Mrs. Curren, her history teacher, were to be believed, they were weapons. Living weapons created by the world's superpowers. Only boys thought weapons were cool.

As she watched a skull-shaped ring on Becca's finger move in and out of her field of vision, she thought of how stupid she was being. Becca wasn't about to pass judgment.

"I just think she's, well, great," Jackie sputtered.

"Great, huh?" Becca sounded unimpressed.

"Well, my dad thinks so, too. He's always reading about her, watching her on the news."

"Not creepy," Becca mumbled, lost in her work. Jackie waited to see if she was going to apologize, but she didn't, so Jackie took it in stride.

"No, nothing like that. He's got a crush." She stopped at telling Becca about the news clippings on the ceiling of her room. How half of them had come from the trash Dad set out late one night after he'd had too many beers. The next morning, Jackie found the box full of pictures and stories by the curb. So carefully clipped and kept flat with crisp edges, they felt like something he cared about. He never asked what happened to the box. Even when he saw the clippings on her ceiling months later, he still didn't say a word, only stared.

Becca nodded, biting her lip as she applied another stroke. "Okay, so, he's got a crush. What about you?"

"I don't know. I sorta get her, you know? She's always standing up to the rogue Augments, helping people. I want to be like that." She almost added "when I grow up", but stopped herself.

Several more coats of color went on before Becca pulled out of her work to ask another question. "So, say Crimson Mask and Ember get in a fight, who wins?"

Now Becca was being stupid. Crimson Mask was maybe the most powerful Augment ever. "They don't fight. But if they did, Ember all the way."

"Yup," Becca barked. "Girl power, baby." She extended her fist for a bump then slumped back to examine her work. "Okay, I think we got it."

"Now what?"

"I clean this up, you get to sit and wait," Becca said, gathering her supplies. "I'll be right back."

Jackie felt the tension drain from her body. She almost wished it had stuck around.

She didn't have to wait long. Before she knew it, Becca was back and they were at the sink again, rinsing her hair. Fast and efficient, the earlier exhilaration was lost and Jackie began to feel anxious about seeing her hair free from the foil nest. When they got back to the station, Jackie stood in front of the mirror.

"Can we dry it?"

"Let it air dry. I promise, you'll love it."

"Oh, I love it now!"

Becca moved up behind her, gathering Jackie's hair into a sculpted ridge. "Yep, that would be hot. Want me to talk to your dad?"

Jackie felt her cheeks burn again. "No, thanks. He'll need to get used to this first."

He'd been shocked when she returned to the waiting room, but not half as shocked as when the receptionist rang them up. Jackie spread her allowance on the counter to fill the silence, and he eventually paid the difference, even leaving Becca a tip that earned them both a wink. This time, Dad blushed too, and she understood.

Later that day, when the breeze from the open windows on the jeep and Jackie's rushing around the house jumping across the furniture or leaping onto her bed had dried the last strand of hair, she dropped next to him on the couch and shook his arm to pry him from the glow of the television.

"Well, do I look like her?"

Jackie didn't understand why his red eyes grew damp. He took a swig of his beer before answering. "Yeah, baby. Just like her."

## About The Author

In the fourth grade, Russ Linton declared the goal of becoming a "writer and an artist" when he grew up. After a journey that led him from philosopher to graphic designer to stay-at-home parent and even a stint as an Investigative Specialist with the FBI, he finally got around to that "writing" part which he now pursues full time. Russ wants to take readers on a journey through his eclectic imagination and dabbles in both science fiction and fantasy. He writes for adults who are young at heart and youngsters who are old souls.

For more information, visit russlinton.com.

# The Silk of Yesterday's Gown

## Misha Burnett

*Editor's Note: Lust, fear, and rage. These are the emotions that can wrest control from our conscious, higher selves and reduce us to our ancient, animal natures. We do not tell ourselves stories while in the throes of such experience; we only exist, preverbal, without conscious narrative and responding solely by instinct. Then, as the heady soup of primal chemicals are washed away, reason returns, and with it, the narratives. No, there are no stories while in the thrall of the primitive, but there are stories about our time there. And they are the most primal of all.*

Look, I don't *have* to be here.

My lawyers don't want me to be here. I've got my own reasons for talking to you, and I'm going to make it quick, say what I have to say, and get out of here. Then I'm getting out of the country, going down to the Caymans for a while. A long, long while. I've got a jet waiting.

What I say doesn't leave this room.

I mean that. You don't tell your wife, you don't tell your partner, you don't tell your god damned cat. *One word* of this gets out and I am going to have this department in litigation for the next hundred years. You're going to be selling your guns for court costs. And I will see you, personally, in the most brutal jail in the state, in the general population. Is that clear?

No questions. I am going to tell my story and get out.

That's not negotiable. *None of this is negotiable.*

I've got the Governor's private cell number in my phone. Last week I had margaritas with three US congressmen. I am not somebody that you can mess with.

Are we clear? Absolutely, crystal clear?

Good.

You're not going to find Marci.

I know you're looking for her. It's on the front page of the goddamned paper—my wife is missing and the cops are looking for her. What I'm here to tell you is that you're not going to find her, and you need to stop looking before you find... something else.

I'm not saying that she's dead. I don't know that. I think she is—hell, I *hope* she's dead. I loved her more than I've ever loved anyone. More than I ever will love anyone again. And every night I pray to God that she's dead.

But I don't know. I didn't see her die.

I saw enough to know that you'll never find her. She's... gone.

I don't expect you to believe me, and I don't care. Like I said, I'm going to speak my piece and get out. After that, whatever happens is on your head.

You've been poking around in my personal life enough that you know about the Storyville Club, and I'm going to assume that you've been warned off doing any digging there. That's okay, because it's got nothing to do with what happened to Marci. Well, maybe not nothing, but it's a dead end as far as her… *disappearance* is concerned. All asking questions about Storyville is going to do is kill your career. It's a place for public personalities to do private things and there is some serious leverage to keep it private. Swingers, mostly, very, very exclusive—I'm sure you've figured out that much.

I met Marci there, okay? She was someone else's guest, and she left with me. We started hooking up regularly. We had… similar tastes. Complimentary, I guess you'd say.

We got close enough that I married her. I—

I loved her. Not just her body, not just her style, but *her.*

She's an artist—*was* an artist. I set her up with the gallery. It lost money, of course, those places always do. But it made her so happy. It wasn't just something to keep her busy when I was out of town—she *worked* that gallery. She had a real eye for talent and signed the best local artists. It was a career to her, not just a hobby.

That's where she met them, at the gallery.

It was an opening, the usual wine and cheese bash. I wasn't there that night, I was in LA signing papers. But I heard all about it.

Ta—*Christ*, I can hardly say their names.

Tam and Robin. Linn. Married couple. Swedish papers, although Tam was Welsh originally and Robin was Scottish. Or so we thought at the time.

Beautiful couple. Breathtaking. Tam was the woman, Robin the man. Same coloring, black hair, pale skin, green eyes—they had the same eyes. They looked more like brother and sister than man and wife.

Maybe—

It doesn't matter anyway.

She made sure that I met them as soon as I was back in town. We had a champagne brunch. They were in banking—well, that's what he told me, and he knew the business, seemed to know all the right people. A man in my position has to develop an instinct for when he's being played, and these two gave every indication of being the genuine article. Marci was smitten with them—that's the only word for it. I knew what she wanted, and, yeah, I wanted it too.

And them? They had a kind of… *chemistry*. That's all I can call it. Robin had this way of dominating any conversation without being pushy about it. Trust me, on the level I work you meet some outrageous egos. Any time you sit down to negotiate a serious deal you have to spend the first day catfighting over who's got the biggest dick in the room.

Robin wasn't like that. He just had this charisma, I guess you'd call it. I've met movie stars, I've met kings—I sat in a meeting with the Sultan of Brunei once.

I never met anyone like Robin.

Knowing what I know now, I hope I never do again.

Tam had the same thing, but it was different. Robin was commanding, Tam was... *captivating.*

It wasn't just that she was the most beautiful woman I've ever seen. She had sex appeal, sure, enough to cause traffic jams when she crossed the street. But she was charming. Warm, friendly. Most women that sexy push men away—they have to, or else they get swarmed. Tam didn't. She always talked to you like you were the one who was fascinating.

We spent a couple of hours together the first day, talking, getting to know each other. Marci was all ready to get to know them a *lot* better, but I was going to take things slow. We made plans to meet later in the week.

Now, despite what you may have read in the Wall Street Journal, I am not a stupid man. I have some discrete researchers on my staff, and I ordered up a background on the Linns.

And it came back clean. *Clean.*

Robin Taliesan Linn and Tamera Alice O'Shann-Linn were exactly who they said they were. It was perfect in that it wasn't *too* perfect, it was just messy enough to convince me that it was real. Evidence of a scandal in Manchester that was covered up, a couple of questionable deals—I've read a lot of dossiers in my time. You can't fake a real identity, not to the depth I could dig.

So we did a couple of dinners, and I took them to a party at a friend's house, and they were always lovely. Discrete. There was an undercurrent, but nothing untoward—I mean, nothing that would cause talk. We all wanted the same thing, but they weren't being... blatant about it.

Marci was the one I had to watch. She was ready to get on her knees under the table for either or both of them—preferably both. I had to caution her to remember we were in public.

So we took the next step.

There's a hotel—I'm not going to tell you which one, but you'd know the name. The owner and I have an arrangement. There are two rooms—not suites, just rooms—that aren't ever rented to anyone else.

The mirror facing the bed is only a mirror from one side. On the other side it's a window.

Marci took men there sometimes. Women, a couple of times.

What I said about complementary tastes? That was it. Marci liked to play the field. I like to watch. Usually she'd text me when she was on her way and if I was free I'd make my way to the other room without Marci's friend being wise to it.

The Linns knew I was there. Marci insisted. I... well, I wasn't happy about it, but I couldn't deny Marci what she wanted. Privately I had my reservations.

We met for drinks in the hotel bar.

I wasn't comfortable being there. This was Marci's place. I had always come in the loading dock and up the service elevator. I didn't like being exposed like this, and I damned sure didn't like sitting down in a booth with a man who knew he was about to get lucky with my wife.

If Robin had so much as smirked at me I would have called the whole thing off. If he—if either one of them—had played the bull and started talking down to me I would have walked, and Marci would have walked with me. I would have made sure of that.

I enjoy my wife's pleasure. That doesn't make me a cuckold.

They were late. Late enough that I ordered us a second round and I started to think that they wouldn't show.

Then they came hurrying in. Robin's suit was rumpled. He had black smudges on his hands and started apologizing before they had even sat down. His car—a vintage jag in pristine condition—had a blowout on the highway. Tam followed him, not quite rolling her eyes as he detailed how he had to change a tire in the breakdown lane. He was still obviously rattled from the experience and—

*Damn it!* I just now realized that was all an act.

I was such an idiot. I bought it, signed a twenty year note without reading the fine print.

Of course he knew what I was feeling, what I didn't want, and he gave me just the opposite. He made sure I saw him looking vulnerable and scared just when I was feeling that way myself.

I needed something to feel superior to him about and he hand-fed it to me.

Tam ordered some bar food and we had a few more rounds. The tension drained away from the evening and it became comfortable. I had been thinking about how to break things off from them, to tell Marci not to see them again in a way that would stick, but I found myself enjoying their company.

Tam even flirted with me, let me know that it was my choice not to get involved. She made me feel like I was in control, or at least not a passive participant.

Bullshit. All bullshit. Those two monsters played me like a violin, without breaking a sweat, and making me think it was all my idea.

I left first, through the kitchen and up to the service elevator. I got to my room and sat on the bed, looking through the window into Marci's room. I got undressed and folded my clothes.

I waited.

The three of them came through the door laughing. Tam had her arm around Marci's shoulders and Robin followed them, shutting the door behind them.

And then—

You don't need to know. I'm not going to give you a play by play, every kiss, every caress, who undressed whom and where the clothes got dropped on the way to the neatly-made king-sized bed. That's mine, no matter what else they have taken from me, that first night is mine and mine alone.

They worshiped her.

I saw the love of my life, the bright star of my night sky, the woman of my dreams being adored. I don't expect you to understand. I buy and sell a dozen men like you before breakfast every morning, and you are sitting there thinking that you are superior to me because you lock your woman in some eighty-thousand dollar cracker-box condominium and never let her out.

Fine. Laugh at me all you want.

They gave me heaven. They showed me what true love looks like, just so that they could take it away from me in the end.

I left first, as I always did, dressed in the darkness and left Marci lying between the two of them, her tanned skin glowing beside their pale bodies. I went home to sleep alone, confident that she would spend the night in that room that didn't exist on any official record.

Marci crawled into bed with me about dawn, warm and wet from them. She told me that they were waiting outside and that they wanted to go to breakfast.

I had never been friends with any of Marci's lovers before. My impulse was to turn away, to get her to tell them to get lost, but something in her eyes made me agree.

Robin drove us to some dive on the riverfront, a 24 hour place frequented by truckers and longshoremen, and he ordered absurdly complicated omelets all around. Robin made me laugh and Tam made me feel like a man and both of them made Marci so very, very happy.

That was how it started. Again, I don't expect you to understand, but they seduced us both. Marci was the one they had sex with, held in the night when she cried out in burning, murderous ecstasy, but they knew that Marci was mine and they had to win my heart to take her. It wasn't about sex, sex was the tool they used, but I am sure now that it meant nothing to them. It was about control, and never letting me know how much I had given up.

After that Marci saw them when she could, when they were in town. Their schedule was chaotic and always changing. It was, I am now sure, a carefully calculated random, designed to leave both of us always wanting more.

We went out together, to dinner, or for drinks. If they were in town when I was traveling they took Marci out. They spoiled her, pampered her, bought her exotic gifts, strange handcrafted jewelry, and clothing tailored to her curves in rich fabrics. They were beautiful things, in a style that seemed Celtic, but more intricate than I had ever seen before.

They took her for a long weekend out of town, driving up to the wine country to a farm owned by some friends. Marci talked about it at great length when they got back. I wish that I had listened more closely to her descriptions of the trip, because I can't find the place on any map. I somehow doubt that it is on any map.

She said they raised pigs and grew grapes, and she came back with bottles of wine, home-brewed and unlabeled, deep, rich red and delicious. She said that she loved it there and that she wanted to go back and live there forever.

She also came back with a necklace made from carved wood. It was a chain, the kind that you see in craft shows, but it was continuous. Carved from a single block, unbroken, but somehow they had fitted it tight around her throat. She claimed that she didn't remember how Robin had put it around her neck, and I believed her.

I was too cynical. I assumed that there was some kind of trick to it, that given time I would discover how it was done and be able to undo it. I saw magic, saw it wrapped tight around the face I woke up to every morning, and I didn't recognize it for what it was.

Things in the hotel room, though, were getting more... *intense.*

Marci had always liked it rough, rougher than I wanted, and I accepted that she got that from her other lovers. With Robin and Tam, though, she took it to a whole new level. She urged them to cruelty, begged them for it. And they gave her what she needed, defiling her, working together, one causing her pain while she pleasured the other, humiliating her, abusing her, and always driving her to greater heights of desire and fulfillment, with me watching silently from behind the glass.

I didn't like it, didn't like at all how they talked to her, how they used her. I couldn't deny how she responded to it, though. Seeing her exquisite body jerk and thrust in abandon was worth whatever it took to get her there, or so I thought then.

I know better now.

It was always both of them. I never saw one without the other, which should have given me pause. I was frequently out of town myself—DC, New York, LA, London—and Marci stayed here. But Robin never left town without Tam by his side. If I had ever gotten Tam alone, I thought in those days, and imagined... well, it doesn't matter. I wasn't what Tam wanted.

Or was I? Not my body certainly. Her flirtation was just a mask, as unconsciously deceptive as a chameleon's coloration. But in the end she and Robin cut into my soul and harvested all that matters to me. Was that what they were after all that time? Was Marci their prize or just a means to an end? In my better moments I believe that I meant nothing to them. In the dark nights of my soul I am sure that I meant everything.

Hell isn't another world. Hell is when we see this world as it truly is.

25

I saw that the night Marci disappeared.

I was supposed to be in DC that weekend. I was testifying—well, if you want to know you can look it up in the papers. It was all part of the media smokescreen. That's how the game is played, you give the politicians the soundbites they need to wave in front of the voters and they give you the elbow room to do your job.

My particular sideshow got canceled because one group of idiots in some desert hellhole killed another group of idiots. Again, you can look it up if you care.

I jetted back home late that afternoon. I didn't tell Marci my trip had been canceled. She said that she would be meeting Robin and Tam at the hotel. I wanted to watch them without them knowing I was there.

I went to my room and ordered a meal and a bottle of wine.

It was late when they came into the other room.

I was dozing on the cheap double bed, thinking that the Linns were out of town and I should just go home. Then the door in the other room banged open and I started awake.

They were cruel. More than rough, they were brutal. Robin held her Marci down while Tam used her teeth and nails, leaving trails of blood on my love's perfect skin. I would have done something—crashed into the room, called 911, something—except that Marci was craving the abuse, loving it, needing it, begging for more.

And then Tam produced the skin.

I watched. To my eternal damnation I watched the king and queen of hell take my beloved, and I did nothing.

Tam was nearly naked by then, dressed only in an unbuttoned blouse. Marci was entirely naked and Robin wore one sock, a gray knitted sock that had somehow remained in place.

Yet Tam produced a hide from somewhere. It was raw, still bleeding, freshly flensed. She laid it on Marci's body, the dark side upwards, brownish pink, the side oozing blood against her skin.

Marci changed.

Her belly swelled and her legs contracted and she threw back her head and howled, a sound that I will take to my grave. Robin took one of Marci's arms and forced it under the skin. I could hear her bones pop and her muscles pull in and Tam pushed the skin over Marci's face.

The howls grew deeper, altered from human cries into deep guttural grunts.

I see it now, every time I close my eyes. I tell myself that I didn't know what I was seeing, that I didn't believe it. That's a lie. I knew, and I believed. I saw what they were doing. I didn't understand how it was possible, but I saw it with my own eyes.

I did nothing because I was afraid.

I was a coward. My beloved was suffering. I couldn't imagine the horror that she was experiencing. They were remaking her, turning her beauty and her creativity and her laughter into a thing, a fat sow, a helpless creature for their bloody-handed amusement. I watched and I did nothing because I lacked the courage to act.

But that's not the worst of it.

That's not the thing that broke me.

It *excited* me.

I was sick with fear, numb with horror, but at the same time I was horribly, painfully erect. Despite having pleasured myself watching their earlier performance, this ultimate degradation, this impossible dehumanizing transformation aroused me past anything I had ever felt before.

The bloody skin filled out and the slack pig's face grew mobile, the snout twitching, the eyes opening. Eyes that were not pig's eyes, but Marci's own beautiful blue.

Tam bent her head and brought her mouth, open-lipped, to the blood and snot smeared snout of the pig. Her pink tongue lapped at the pig's blunt one and the pig grunted, a sound unmistakably of deep, unreasoning pleasure.

Helplessly I ejaculated into my lap.

Tam grasped the wooden chain still binding Marci's altered neck and dragged her sow's body from the bed. Nearly naked she led her away. Robin stood to follow them.

Before he did he turned and he looked at me. Through the mirrored glass he faced me, his eyes meeting mine like he'd known I was there all along, and he smiled at me.

Then they left the room.

I don't suppose I have to tell you that no one saw a naked man and woman leading a pig through the halls of a five-star downtown hotel.

And I don't suppose that it will come as a surprise to you that Robin and Tam Linn are gone. More than gone, they never were. There is no record that they ever existed. Every mention of their names has been erased, all over the world.

I looked at the files that I had been given those months ago, and the pages are all blank. The man whom I'd asked to prepare the report doesn't remember me asking him. I've talked to the people at the parties that I took them to, and each one swears that Marci and I came alone.

The jewelry, the clothing, all the gifts they had given Marci are gone. I've torn her closets apart, looking for some evidence, some proof. Nothing.

All I have is a green glass bottle without a label and a hand carved wooden stopper. What's left of the wine inside it has gone rancid.

I'm leaving now. You're not going to stop me. You're not going to try to contact me. You are going to close down this investigation. Marci will be recorded as an unsolved missing person.

I am going to the Caymans and then I don't know what I am going to do. I don't know if there is anything I can do, anything left for me.

Maybe I'll just sit on the beach and drink myself to death. I have a lot of money—it won't take long.

## About The Author

Misha Burnett has little formal education, but has been writing poetry and fiction for around forty years. During this time he has supported himself and his family with a variety of jobs, including locksmith, cab driver, and building maintenance.

Major influences include Tim Powers, Samuel Delany, William Burroughs, and Philip K. Dick.

For more information, visit mishaburnett.wordpress.com.

# A Rough Spirit

## Dave Higgins

*Editor's Note: Monsters of the medieval European variety are comforting, in a way. They're terrible and hideous, but in a familiar, non-threatening manner. But the monsters of other cultures do not offer us the usual hand-holds and practice-built coping strategies. They are inscrutable. Unpredictable. And much, much more unsettling.*

The breeze slipped through the leaves, carrying the scent of cherry blossom and blood. Ignoring the damp that seeped through his kimono, Hirota Sen crouched lower into the hollow. It wasn't supposed to be like this. His first trip as an adult should only have been a formality. Hayabiro was deep within his family's lands. The caravan followed well-trodden roads. He'd expected half-starved bandits, a few wild beasts; at worst, some thinking beast. Not a horror of shadows and iron flowing up from the shadow of the caravan itself.

How long had he been crouching here? The screaming had stopped a while ago, leaving silence. Did that mean the—it must be some kind of *yōkai*—had departed? He held his breath and strained for a single trill of a sparrow or scuff of a fox in the distance.

The gentle swish of leaves thundered in his ears. His father would know how quickly animals returned after violence. How to tell if the *yōkai* remained. But his father would also have stood rather than run.

He glanced down at the empty *saya* tucked through his belt. At least he'd drawn his *daitō*. Would that make a difference when he faced his ancestors? Or would having dropped his grandfather's blade as he fled have made things worse? Having left it lying on the ground once the threat had gone certainly would.

He braced his hand on his *saya* to prevent it swinging against anything and eased himself around a tree. And twitched as something smooth and cold brushed the edge of his little finger.

The travelling flask of plum brandy the villagers had given him hung lower than before. It must have worked loose when he fled. The ancestors were with him: if it had fallen as he crept back, the sound would've attracted the *yōkai*. After flicking his gaze between the trees again, he fumbled the cords free.

He stared at the plain pottery. He should offer brandy to the ancestors before he returned to the road, as a thank you for the warning. Crouching, he brushed loose leaves off a nearby rock. Fear of rattling the cup against the bottle caused his hands to shake; but—after several jagged breaths—he managed to place the cup on the rock and pour an appropriate measure. Damp soaked through his knees and elbows as he prostrated himself. By rights, he should speak clearly; but the ancestors would hear even if he whispered. "O-Hirota-sama. This—" His voice cracked. Pitch wavering, he started again. "O-Hirota-sama. This child of your children offers fruit and water in gratitude for your gracious warning."

After a slow breath, he rose to his knees and tilted his head up until he could just see the cup. With the little finger of each hand either side of it, he lifted it out of sight. The cup wobbled more and more as he raised his hands high, splashing liquid onto the rock and his fingers.

After drawing another slow breath, he lowered them down again. "O-Hirota-sama. This child of your children thanks you for this portion of your fruit and water."

He drained the brandy. Bitter fire stung his throat, raising memories of his mother giving him a drop in water after nightmares had woken him. The abomination that had attacked him today was more than a discarded kimono or guttering lantern, though. He cinched the flask to his belt and rose.

The urge to run was still there, but his hands were steadier now. Before he could lose his nerve, he unsheathed his *kenfukku*. Despite being nearly two spans long, the hooked parrying blade seemed tiny compared to what he remembered of the *yōkai*'s iron claws; maybe he could hold the abomination off long enough to recover his *daitō*, though. Ancestors willing, the *yōkai* had returned whence it came anyway.

The scent of blood grew stronger as he crept back to the road, the tang of spilt brandy somehow growing with it. Along with a more pungent earthy odour. One of the bearers sprawled behind a tree, somehow taller in death. Bile flooded Sen's mouth as he realised the reason and the source of the odours beneath the blood.

Telling himself that recovering the sword was more important than looking closer, that he wasn't too weak to face death, he kept his eyes ahead as he skirted the body.

Another bearer, similarly torn in half, lay further along the road, the jagged remains of a barrel holding his torso upright. Sen barely noticed though, his gaze flicking between the shadows and his *daitō* lying in the dirt. The *yōkai* was nowhere in sight.

Clenching his *kenfukku* tighter, he slipped from tree to tree, trying to watch everything at once.

A faint squelch sounded behind him.

Snatching up his *daitō* with his free hand, he spun around.

A black shrike peered at him for a moment, then returned to its feast.

He considered his *daitō*. Despite having been dropped in the mud, the blade was clean. Its spirit would be troubled, though. And sheathing it unused—sheathing either of his weapons unused—would compound the dishonor.

His gaze fell on the shrike again. He shook his head. Even if he could move with the grace and speed needed to strike it, a flow he rarely achieved on the perfect foundation of the *dojo* floor, a carrion eater was not a fit offering.

Wishing the ancestors had left a little more brandy in the cup, then cursing himself for the further disrespect, he ran the edge of each blade across the outside of his forearm. He'd expected pain, but the cuts brought only a slight chill. If this was being wounded, he had fled for nothing.

Blood blossomed along the cuts, followed by a sting that grew into an ache. Fighting against the urge to clasp his arm, he cleaned his blades and returned them to their *saya*. Finally, he let himself bind the wounds.

His gorge rose again as he studied the bloodied road. Enough parts for three bodies lay between the remains of the barrels. Two of the villagers were missing, but the bodies were too torn to be certain which. How long had he hidden in the forest? Were the dead nearby, or had the *yōkai* consumed them whole?

The shrike burst into flight. A breath later, he made out the sound of something approaching.

Hopefully, only a fox. He drew his *daitō* anyway. The point wavered in front of him, refusing to settle.

The sound grew, now less like an animal and more like feet creeping closer.

He backed into the trees. He would not dishonor himself by running, but knowing what approached before he acted was good sense.

Several long moments later, a woman in a simple tunic rounded the corner, a hoe raised above her head. After flicking her head around, she beckoned. Several other villagers scuttled into view, clutching farm implements. Makoto, one of the missing bearers, followed.

Sen clenched his teeth and nicked his arm again, then stepped out.

Tools clattered to the ground as the villagers prostrated themselves.

He squared his shoulders. His task was to defend these people. Even if the bearer had seen him run in terror. Which meant leading them back to the village before the *yōkai* returned. "Rise." His voice lacked his father's easy certainty, but it held this time.

Eyes still on the ground, the villagers stood. The bearer shuffled toward Sen, then bowed deeply again.

"You may speak."

"This child of no blood was not worthy of your protection, Hirota-sama. I should have stood beside you, not run. I should have trusted you would prevail."

Sen frowned. When the *yōkai* appeared, he'd drawn his *daitō* on instinct. Makoto must have fled in that breath. Sen's mouth felt too dry. An adult was honest in all things. Letting the villagers believe he had defeated the *yōkai* dishonored his ancestors. But his first duty was to protect them; if they didn't believe he could, they wouldn't obey him, and then he truly wouldn't be able to. "You speak with propriety. We return to Hayabiro."

———————— • ————————

Eyes gritty, Sen stared at the ceiling. With each step closer to Hayabiro, the growing confidence of the villagers had convinced him further that silence was the more virtuous course. But the night had stolen both his certainty and his sleep. He knuckled his forehead, then rose from his mat. First dawn had come. No amount of wishing would bring him rest now.

Upright, his body ached like his head—all save the cuts on his arm which throbbed hotter, a silent reminder that he'd let the villagers believe he'd felt the *yōkai*'s claws and lived. Accepting the pain as his due, he prostrated himself to the east and offered gratitude to Mother Sun for gazing on him.

After dressing, he squared his shoulders and fixed his face in a neutral expression. He owed it to his father's peasants to appear without flaw. Training and honor masking the desire to rest, he strode from the hut that Roka had abandoned for his use. The tiny headman knelt beside the entrance, his daughter kneeling two steps behind him. As Sen emerged, they flattened themselves to the ground.

"Rise, Roka-kun."

The headman returned to a kneeling position, then tilted his head back enough to see Sen's face but not to meet his gaze. "This child of no blood is grateful for the honor of having Hirota-sama grace his hut. Does the noble warrior desire to break his fast? Or my daughter to ease his stiffness?"

Stiffness? Was he standing too straight? Had he failed to hide his lack of sleep? "You speak with propriety, Roka-kun."

"Perhaps Hirota-sama might prefer to retire to my hut. So the labors of the day do not offend his vision."

Sen realised everyone within sight was kneeling. A show of respect due to a great hero who'd slain a monster—but not to a boy who'd fled. He nodded sharply and stepped into the hut.

Roka's daughter followed, dropping to her knees as soon as she crossed the threshold. After placing the tray in front of him, she reached back to straighten the curtain across the doorway. The movement made her already short hem rise to the top of her thighs.

Heat roiled in his stomach. He settled onto his heels and focused on the tray she held. Recognising that her father couldn't afford a longer tunic would shame her.

"If it pleases Hirota-sama, I am called Aneko. I have some skill in massage if the noble lord has woken with any stiffness?"

He tried to keep his gaze on the small bowl and not the scrubbed skin beyond it. "A little rice and a sip of water will suffice."

"My brother has strong fingers if—"

She'd noticed something was wrong too. He needed to distract her. He slid the tray closer. "Tell me of Hayabiro while I eat."

"What do you wish to know?"

"You grow plums. What's that like?"

"We're honored to brew plum brandy for the noble Hirota. The work is hard, but we're grateful to serve, even when—" Her breath caught. "Even though we're not worthy."

From the corner of his eye, he realised she was trembling. Throwing aside his earlier decision, he returned the bowl to the tray and looked directly at her.

A curtain of slightly damp hair concealed her face. Hoping to mimic his father's certainty of action, he placed a hand on her cheek and tilted her head up.

For an instant, her eyes darted to meet his, then sank again.

"You were going to say something different." Her trembling grew. "What troubles you?"

"It is a peasant thing. Nothing the noble lord need trouble himself with."

Commanding his lessers should be as easy as breathing. So why didn't this feel right? His hidden dishonor must have disarrayed his spirit. "Speak. How can I protect my father's holdings if you hide problems from me?"

"There is a grubman warren to the north. Sometimes, they come down into the orchards and fields. The wards do not always keep them out. We're happy for the honor of defending your father's holdings; but we're humble villagers, unskilled in the ways of fighting. People are hurt and produce stolen."

Her skin felt soft beneath his hand. She seemed tiny, kneeling in front of him; even standing she'd barely reach his shoulder. The image of her facing grubmen armed only with crude tools, not pure steel, horrified him.

Her cheek brushed against his fingertips as she bowed her head further. "The noble lord is angry with me."

"No." His thoughts raced. This could be his chance to redeem his honor, to be the hero the villagers thought him. "I'm angry at the grubmen. Tell your father to provide me with a map showing where the warren is."

She pressed her forehead to the ground, then backed out on her knees.

Despite his lack of sleep, his legs ached with the effort of not striding out of the hut immediately. Torn between speed and propriety, he scooped up mouthfuls of rice with one hand and lifted his cup of water with the other. The moment the bowl was empty, he tied on his *saya* and walked stiffly out.

As Sen emerged, Roka pressed his head to the ground. Makoto, kneeling a few paces behind the headman did the same.

"Rise."

Roka straightened. "Hirota-sama, this one is shamed to say no one has visited the warren. Makoto has some skill at hunting. He would be honored to accompany the noble lord to show him where the grubmen emerge from the mountains, and track them to their warren."

With no map, a hunter would be useful. A companion posed risks, though. Sen was determined that he wouldn't allow himself to flee again. But what if he suffered a moment of doubt? "Makoto acts with propriety. However, this is a task for a warrior. I will travel alone."

"As Hirota-sama says." Roka rose to his feet. "I shall instruct my daughter to pack food to sustain you, and a flask of our best brandy to show the gratitude of those you protect."

———————————— • ————————————

Sen shivered and pulled his kimono tighter. The forest had thickened as he moved deeper into the foothills, replacing the dapple of sunlight with deep shadows; each shadow leaving enough random detail to draw him toward the undergrowth, *daitō* raised, seeking lurking enemies, yet dark enough to hide all but the roughest of actual details.

Not that he knew what to look for if there had been light anyway. With no better ideas, he tried to follow the clearest path through the undergrowth and stay at the bottom of ravines; grubmen were only part formed, but close enough to people they'd surely follow the easiest way from their warrens.

Although, clearest way was too easy a term for the slimmest of tracks. Brambles and bushes somehow thrived in the gloom, ready to snatch at his clothes, and even the thinnest of fronds became an iron band when caught around his ankle. Untangling himself without either sheathing his *daitō* unblooded or allowing it to rest on the ground seemed to take longer each time.

The gloom muddled his sense of time too. His bowl of rice felt like a day ago, yet he felt as if he'd made little progress since he left the well-trodden paths. Maybe coming alone had been a mistake. He paused and peered around.

To the right, the slope appeared gentle, yet led to the deepest shadows. To the left, the slope was much steeper but the furthest trees were too visible to be truly in shadow. Neither seemed like marauding grubmen had pushed through them. Before he'd reached a decision, something scuffed behind him.

He turned and struck in a single movement. Two swatches of dark fur tumbled away, fragments of twig falling around them.

He wiped his blade and swallowed hard. He'd mistaken a rat for an enemy.

Hoping to wash the sour taste away, he sipped plum brandy. Aromatic fire relaxed tension he hadn't realised he carried. After cinching the flask to his belt again, he grinned. A rat wasn't the mighty foe he'd dreamed of for his first kill, but his strike had taken it cleanly. He'd been still enough in rest that it had approached, too. Both reasons for pride.

He grinned, then sheathed his *daitō* and turned toward the hints of light. Following the lowest path had found nothing, and the steeper route seemed less daunting, now both hands were free.

Each almost-tumble challenged his new resolve and besmirched his knees and elbows further, but eventually he achieved the crest, only to discover more forest descending into murk on the far side.

He brushed at his kimono, clearing away the leaf-mould but spreading the mud further in the process. After a moment of concern over adding another stain, he slumped onto a mossy boulder and considered his supplies. Plum brandy would—in moderation—remove his thirst; only water would clean away the stains, though.

Flickers through the trees taunted him with how arduous the trip to the nearest river would be, and in the direction he'd abandoned to climb the rise. After allowing himself a single mouthful of rice, he rose to his feet—and froze.

Something pale had moved near the river. A moment later, it crossed the next gap between trees. A grubman! Grubmen grew out of the spirits' failed attempts to make people, so they probably lived near water, as people did. He skidded and slipped back the way he'd come, then pushed into the gloom. With stealth abandoned for speed, only the need to divert around tangles of undergrowth slowed his march. Soon the growing sound of water drew him on.

When he reached the river, the urge to wash the filth away was strong. The blood of his ancestors was stronger though. After glancing both ways and seeing only forest, he followed the water up the narrow ravine. Shortly after, he noticed two poles driven into the far bank, each with several fish skulls hanging from it. Starting between them, a vague path wound into the trees.

He tied his clothes up and strode across, exhilaration turning the chill bite of the water into a gift to shed his tiredness. More bones and crude carvings hung in the shadows of the trees ahead. The warren had to be nearby.

Sen followed the twisting path, unsure whether to cut down the grubman fetishes or leave them alone. As the trees thinned again, he let his hand rest on the hilt of his *daitō*. A cave gaped in the mountainside, barely five feet at the highest point. More carvings, these daubed with a dark pigment, hung across the opening.

Apart from more bones and fetishes, the undergrowth seemed untouched on all sides. This had to be the warren. He unstoppered his pottery lantern. The grubmen would see him coming, but—even ignoring his lack of hunting experience—facing enemies that knew he was there was preferable to walking into them in the dark.

Much as he wanted to keep the grubmen at as a great a distance as possible, there wasn't room to wield his *daitō*. Lantern-flame adjusted, he drew the shorter *kenfukku* and ducked under the curtain of carvings. A crude tunnel sloped down, the roof fortunately becoming no lower—at least as far as his light reached. Water dripped intermittently, drops seeming loud or soft with no pattern. Bending slightly from the waist, he eased his way forward.

The walls hurled the scuff of his sandals back at him, the rhythm no clearer than that of the drips. Shadows tugged at the corners of his eyes as he descended. Cold air seeped into his clothes, his shivers making the shadows twitch and lunge more dramatically.

He rested his lantern on the floor and gulped plum brandy. Fire burnt down his throat, then spread across his body. Hoping it would keep his hands steady enough he could tell flickering light from lurking enemies, he continued.

Some distance later, a narrower tunnel split off to the right, the floor level as far as the light reached. Grubmen were creatures of earth, so the heart of the warren would be down. He listened for sounds of activity from the side passage. Hearing only the echo of dripping water, he continued deeper.

Occasional side turnings offered only darkness and silence, while twists and corners concealed all but a short stretch of the main tunnel at a time. What felt miles deeper, jangling—like the brass rings on a monk's staff only flatter—echoed up. He halted, then—when it didn't repeat—crept forward and peered around the corner.

On the far side of a small chamber, two grubmen stood before a crude altar. The one on the left held an iron rattle above his head, while the one on the right clutched a jagged iron sword. Either side of the altar, holes opened into the darkness. Flickering torches made the crude figure on the altar seem to move. Peering directly at it, he realised the idol's outstretched arms ended in jagged claws; claws like the *yōkai* that had attacked the caravan. The rattle and swords were iron. Iron was pulled from the ground. What if the grubmen treated it as a god? It might live in the deepest tunnels.

But the warren had been empty so far. Surely a temple would be at the heart of the complex. Accounting for those slain by the villagers, these could be the only inhabitants. If he approached carefully, he could strike one down before the other noticed him. Stop them before they summoned it. Or was he better charging? Either way, waiting didn't improve his odds. *Kenfukku* held in a mid-stance, he padded into the chamber.

Halfway across, the one on the right turned. The sound of dripping water spewed from its maw as it saw him. A breath later, similar sounds trickled from the corridor behind Sen.

Sen peered at the corridor, then back at the two advancing grubmen. If their speech sounded like... then all those passages could have been... He couldn't fight that many on his own! He'd be trapped. And if they called their god...!

He turned and sprinted into the corridor. As he rounded the first corner, a grubman loomed up ahead of him

More by accident than intent, Sen's blade struck it in the shoulder.

Dark fluid sprayed out as the creature sagged against the wall.

Sen ran on as best he could while hunched.

Beady eyes and pallid flesh burst from the shadows to his left.

Sen slashed without thought. Pain shot through his wrist as his blade caught in the creature's flesh for a moment.

The ache in his limbs grew as he hacked and shoved past several more. Finally, he saw the tunnel mouth ahead. And the line of carvings stretched across it. He tried to crouch lower without slowing.

His right sandal slipped, turning his crouch into a tumble. Potsherds and oil spewed across the clearing as the lantern shattered.

Sen rolled away before the flame spread to his clothes. After rising to his feet, he held his breath and listened.

Apart from the crackling and occasional drips in the distance, the tunnel mouth was silent. He'd outpaced them. Relief mixed with shame. His father wouldn't have run. His father would have stood. But his father was a great warrior. Telling himself at each step that—even though he hadn't slain all the grubmen—maiming or killing some was a victory anyway, he retreated to the village and the protection of its wards.

———————— • ————————

Eyes gritty, Sen stared at the ceiling. Even alcohol and exhaustion only pushed his secret shame away for so long.

"My lord is awake?" Aneko's hand tickled down past his waist. "Mmm... my lord *is* awake."

Sweet waves spread from his groin, easing his body. Yet doing nothing to wash the sour taste from his mouth, or the awareness of his failures. He grabbed her wrist.

She stiffened. "This one is ashamed she is not pleasing."

"No.... You are... It's..." He released her. "My duty to defend the village must come before pleasure."

A single fingernail slid along the inside of his inner thigh, just hard enough to give his flesh encouragement. The tingles grew as her finger moved beyond his leg. "And my duty is to care for all my lord's weapons."

His resolve fled as the rest of her limber form oozed onto him.

Some while later, eased in body if not mind, he turned his lips from hers. "Dawn has passed. I desire to eat."

She slid off him and bent to recover her shift.

He fought the urge to pull it from her again. Only after she'd finished her long and tortuous journey from the hut was he able to rise himself.

Working furiously, he managed to be fully dressed with *saya* through his belt by the time she returned. All his restraint used on even noticing the food she'd brought, he gulped the bowl of rice in unseemly haste and almost sprinted from the hut. Only to narrowly avoid tripping over Roka-kun's kneeling form.

"How may the village serve you?" The headman kept his gaze on Sen's feet. "If you tell this one your favourite foods, we shall have them prepared to honor our protector."

The thought of sitting through another feast in celebration of his courage twisted the rice in Sen's stomach. "You and your village act properly. However, I am commanded to travel my father's realm. A simple meal to carry on the road is all I require."

"As my lord commands." Roka-kun rose to his feet, "This one apologises for not anticipating you would depart now the threat is past. And is grateful that the village need not petition a monk to strengthen the wards."

The wards needed reinforcing? He couldn't leave them unprotected. "If I am to see all the lands, I should visit this temple. It would be improper to seek hospitality from them, so I will return here afterwards. If I am making the journey both ways anyway, then I will escort a monk back."

Roka-kun bowed deeply. "Your wisdom is great. But it is not proper for you to carry the brandy for the temple. Makoto will accompany you."

"You speak with propriety, Roka-kun" A bottle of brandy wouldn't be a burden, but having a second person along wouldn't hurt if something happened. Not that it would.

---

Two low shrines dedicated to the Vices flanked the temple gate, a pile of stones sitting next to each. Sen shivered and pulled his kimono tighter. He'd assumed the monks were ascetics, but Vice shrines were part of the way of indulgence. The size of Makoto's pack suddenly made sense; the offering was probably a whole cask of brandy.

His hand grabbed for his *daitō* as something clattered loudly. A breath later, he realised the bearer had hurled a handful of gravel at one of the shrines. Had Makoto noticed the loss of propriety?

An old woman in filthy robes pushed dirt around the flags with a ragged broom. Only the *kenfukku* tucked into her belt revealed she wasn't the lowest of peasants.

"Greetings, *shugenja*-san." Sen bowed as to an equal. "I am Hirota Sen."

The monk glanced past him, then continued to brush.

He looked back. Makoto stood in the gateway, face pale. "That one is Makoto. He carries an offering from the village of Hayabiro for the temple."

"He is afraid, yet in your company." The monk sent a plume of dust arcing into the air.

Sen clamped his jaw shut to avoid coughing. "He does not understand your ways."

"Neither do you." She threw her broom into a corner and headed toward the inner temple. "I am Izumi Kita. Bring the offering."

Izumi? One of the northern clans, possibly. He racked his brains for anything his father or Hirota Chiko-sensei had mentioned about them.

In contrast to the courtyard, the inside of the temple was spotless, which made the shadows in the corners even starker. Izumi-san nodded quickly to the altar, then disappeared through a side door.

He shouldn't keep her waiting. But it would be dishonorable not to demonstrate proper respect to the altar. He bowed several degrees while still walking. Straightening as he turned, his face almost hit a pillar. After stepping around it, he strode through the door as fast as propriety allowed.

Makoto scurried after.

The room beyond contained shelves of scrolls in various states of disrepair, and a low table with several mismatched cups on it. Izumi-san, her perfect kneeling position seeming out of place beneath a shabby robe, beckoned them closer. "Did you bring brandy? What about sweet rice?"

Sen knelt beside the table, then glanced at Makoto.

The bearer sidled forward and placed a small cask and two wooden boxes on the table. The moment his burden had been shed, he almost leapt out the doorway.

By the time Sen had turned back, she'd extracted the bung from the cask and filled a cup. After peering intently at him for a moment, she filled another to the brim and pushed it toward him. "Rude to let the spirits drink alone."

He raised the cup as she raised hers and took a sip. Aromatic fire brought back memories of his mother. His shoulders eased slightly.

Izumi-san hurled the remains of her portion down her throat and bashed the cup onto the table. "Hurry. Doesn't do to keep the spirits waiting."

He quickly emptied the rest of his cup. Tingles whooshed along his nose and throat.

She refilled the cups and urged him to drink up. The second gulped measure was followed by a third.

He struggled not to sigh with relief when she replaced the bung rather than filling a fourth time.

"Darkness is called night if we expect it." She tilted her head on one side. "If the lantern is out, does that reveal the oil is only water?"

He struggled to keep his face still. What meaning—if any—there was in her words was drowned beneath the wavering of the room. He nodded in what he hoped was a sage fashion.

"Pah! No fire in you. Might as well have a reed for a weapon." She yanked the top off one of the boxes, and shovelled a fist full of sweet rice into her mouth. Grains spattered the table as she spoke again without swallowing. "What need?"

"New wards to protect the Hayabiro." He stiffened. That was impolite. Almost abrupt. "I mean, the village of Hayabiro requests—"

"Got it the first time. Let's go." Rising, she grabbed a knapsack from beside the table and headed out the door.

He struggled to his feet and followed, the memories of his mother long gone. A dark figure loomed in the entrance to the temple.

A breath later, he realised it was only Makoto, unwilling to stay inside but also to leave. "Izumi-san has agreed. We now depart."

Teeth bared in an attempt at a grin, the bearer fell in behind him.

She strode through the gates, robes flapping around equally dirty legs, and passed the shrines without glancing at them.

After staring at the gates for a moment, Sen set off after her. If she didn't think they needed to be closed, then… Everything seemed slightly more distant than usual as he attempted to catch up while keeping a seemly pace.

A few yards later, she stopped. Clearly, she'd— Behind him, a squelch mixed with a gurgle. He spun, fingers wrapping around the hilt of his *daitō*. And froze.

Tatters of shadow wrapped around Makoto. Only the three iron claws jutting from the bearer's chest stopped him collapsing to the ground. A breath later, a second jagged hand silenced Makoto's gurgles.

Warm liquid trickled down Sen's leg. The *yōkai* had found them.

Izumi-san sprinted past him with her *kenfukku* raised. Sparks erupted as dripping iron claws met hooked blade.

The *yōkai*'s arm folded and flowed, preventing the monk from locking it. However, one hand still fouled with the bearer's corpse, it was equally unable to strike effectively.

More urine seeped down Sen's leg, but the spreading heat wasn't enough to unfreeze his feet. He watched the *yōkai* ooze into the forest, the monk in pursuit. At some point, the shadows swallowed them.

Too late to matter, he yanked his *daitō* free.

He gazed at the blade. If he'd struck in the moment, as Hirota Chiko-sensei had taught, Makoto might still be alive. Izumi-san had been right: he might as well carry a limp reed. If he couldn't care for the *daitō*'s spirit what use was he? And his failure had cost Hayabiro one of its bravest hunters. If the grubmen returned the villagers would have no—

Aneko! Izumi-san had barely threatened the *yōkai* while it had one hand occupied. She would surely die when it dropped Makoto. If he abandoned his blade, didn't help her, no one would remain to protect Aneko. Clammy silk tugged at his legs as he stumbled toward the sounds of clashing metal.

The *yōkai*, both arms free now, slashed at the monk faster than he could follow.

Izumi-san whirled and twisted desperately, somehow avoiding injury for the moment but already clammy with sweat.

Sen raised his *daitō* above his head and, before he lost his nerve again, charged. A wordless scream burst out of his lips as the undergrowth tore before him.

The *yōkai*'s assault on Izumi-san slowed. Then, roiling like smoke, it flicked a jagged claw into the path of Sen's blow.

Sen's fingers stung from the impact. He took a half-step back, then braced the hilt with his free hand and struck again.

As the *yōkai* twisted to block, Izumi-san turned her *kenfukku* and hurled herself forward. Metal screamed as her weight drove her weapon over one iron finger, then yanked it downward with her.

Strained beyond the limits of even its unnatural flexibility, the *yōkai* stumbled.

Sen slid his right foot forward a half-step, *daitō* sweeping in a perfect diagonal arc.

The abomination twisted at what might be its waist, passing under the blade with the loss of only a few wisps of shadow.

Sen settled his weight and reversed his swing.

Again, the *yōkai* narrowly avoided the strike, then flicked its free arm toward him.

Metal screeched on metal as Sen dropped his blade into a defensive stance and stumbled back.

The abomination loomed over him, only Izumi-san's struggles holding it back.

It was too fast. How could he kill it if he couldn't even hit it?

Izumi-san glared in his direction. "Don't dance. Attack, boy. Before my arms get tired."

Its arm was trapped. The *yōkai* could twist and flow, but couldn't move directly away from her.

But it could stay far enough back, that only its arm was within his reach—unless Sen charged over the top of her. A single aggressive attack might cleave into its body before it could strike back.

He sprinted sideways, then spun. Without giving himself time to think, he stepped into the spin. His *daitō* arced out.

The *yōkai* hunched away from the blow and brought its unrestrained claws across in a rough parry.

A dull ache juddered through Sen's arms as his blade was deflected over his opponent's head. Thankful for the months of practicing only footwork Hirota-sensei had forced him through, Sen turned smoothly on his heel and settled into a mid-stance.

Before the abomination could rise, he slid forward half a step and cut down at its head.

Iron claws blocked the blow.

Why was it hunched, now? Why hadn't it struck at him when he attacked? What was— A warrior acted. He let his blade move from his feet.

His weapon shredded the *yōkai*'s body like wet rice paper. Rotten wood and fragments of iron collapsed onto the damp ground.

Izumi-san clambered to her feet. "Hrm… Still no fire. But there's oil not water in the lantern."

"I… I disgraced myself."

She grinned. "But it was a forceful pungent disgrace; you pissed yourself like an adult."

He gawped at her, then sheathed his *daitō*.

"Come, Hirota Sen-san. We go to Hayabiro. Everyone grateful to the mighty *yōkai* slayer. Maybe someone's very grateful." She elbowed him in the ribs. "But first you wash and put on a new kimono. No one's that grateful."

The image of steaming water and nimble fingers rose up. Then wilted before the knowledge that he hadn't earned it. Whether or not the *yōkai* was summoned by the grubmen, the threat to the village wasn't over. He had a promise to honor.

He bowed deeply to Izumi-san. "I am grateful for your advice. However, there is a grubman warren nearby that threatens Hayabiro. Virtue requires that I remove that danger before I may rest."

One hand resting beside the hilt of his *daitō*, he strode away through the undergrowth.

## About The Author

Dave Higgins writes speculative fiction, often with a dark edge. Despite forays into the mundane worlds of law and IT, he was unable to escape the liminal zone between mystery and horror. A creature of contradictions, he also co-writes comic sci-fi with Simon Cantan. Born in the least mystically significant part of Wiltshire, England, and raised by a librarian, he started reading shortly after birth and hasn't stopped since. He lives with his wife, two cats, a plush altar to Lord Cthulhu, and many shelves of books. It's rumoured he writes out of fear he will otherwise run out of books to read.

For more information, visit davidjhiggins.wordpress.com.

# The Apprentice Appears

## Bryce Anderson

*Editor's Note: The lovable rogue is a familiar character in fantasy fiction. Readers will seemingly excuse all manner of devilry so long as it's accompanied by a sly wink and a knowing smile. Though he might be rough around the edges and living on the wrong side of the law, the rogue has a good heart beating in his chest. A victim of a troubled youth perhaps, or of some other unfortunate reversal, he's always depicted as an upstanding soul forced into downstanding circumstances yet determined to make the best of it and win his way with guile and charm. But why does it always have to be a "he?"*

In retrospect, maybe giving her the nickname "Little Chaos" had only made things worse. She'd once had a perfectly sweet, respectable name, perfectly suited to a sweet, respectable little girl. But during the spring of her ninth year, after she'd set the livestock loose to see what they'd do, her mother had shouted the new name at her, loud enough for the other children to hear it. It stuck, because the other children had already marked her as a bit of an asymmetric pigeon. After a week of shoving and hair-pulling and (yes) crying hadn't gotten them to stop, she'd blown her nose, given herself a serious look in the family's polished brass mirror, and decided that if Boar's Vale wanted a little chaos, then they'd have her.

She grew older, leaving a trail of small fires, liberated livestock, and pilfered bazaar stalls in her wake. As she'd grown into her life's mission, her birth name got discarded entirely: those who dispensed with the formality of her full and proper title would call her L.C., or simply Elsie. Usually at the top of their lungs, while they frantically puzzled out how she'd gotten the horse onto the roof.

Along the way, she refined her skills and took on new ones. Pickpocketry had looked useful when she'd first seen a wandering ruffian do it, so she'd blackmailed him into teaching her the art. The small coins she acquired this way she traded to other children for information, which she could then turn into larger coins. But she never let the buried trove grow too large, since using it to buy new clothes or a strong horse would amount to a confession of her crimes. Unable to profit from her pilfering, she used the money to soothe her conscience. From time to time an old widow would find coins amid the ashes of her fireplace, or one of the town beggars would hear a clink in his cup and look up to see a flash of gray cloak slipping out of sight.

Almost without meaning to, Little Chaos had become a do-gooder. A lying, thieving do-gooder whose good doings might have landed her in the stocks or the gallows in a larger town. But Boar's Vale didn't have a prison or even a proper whipping post, just a gruff local magistrate whom Elsie tried to tiptoe around. Perhaps, after her parents died in her fourteenth summer, he'd felt some sympathy for the troubled orphan.

In the fall of her nineteenth year, she met her match. Or, at least, someone who was in his own way just as troublesome as Elsie herself.

She'd been whiling away a few hours in the town square, looking for satchels swinging from unwary shoulders. But her attention had been caught by the young stranger from who-only-knew-where, as he sat by the fountain in the town square, performing feats of handsleight for a gaggle of children. At first she watched to see who in the crowd was distracted by his antics, and might safely be separated from their jewelry or coins. But only the young-sters were paying the newcomer any attention as he sent brightly-colored balls dancing through the air. She turned her attention to the balls, and to the finger which seemed to flick the spheres in every direction and then sum-mon them back. Several balls disappeared down his left sleeve only to leap out of the right one.

Little Chaos crept closer, mesmerized. Her eyes bobbled and darted, try-ing to catch glimpses of the wires holding the balls aloft. No! He was doing magic. Not tricks, real magic!

Dothar the Inscrutable was going to have the boy's head.

When the youth had collected enough alms for (by L.C.'s estimation) a week-old meat pie and a pint of horse piss at the inn, he waved his hands and the balls disappeared. He grinned as the children groaned and whined. "Sorry. The balls got summoned back to the Lower Realms. There's nothing I can do when that happens." Little Chaos lingered as the children dispersed, arguing over how he'd made the balls move that way.

"Where did a guttermuck like you learn magic?"

The boy looked up from the coins in his bowl, surprised. It wasn't easy to mark his age: perhaps sixteen or seventeen, but with an innocence to his hand-some face that made him look younger still. "No magic," the boy replied. "You can see the strings if you look closely."

She moved closer, eyes locked on him like he'd make a convenient meal. "A lot of performers pass through here," she said. "Strings, secret pockets, spring-loaded palms. I've seen it all. Even picked up a trick or two from them," she added, holding up one of the balls the boy thought he'd hidden safely behind his belt. "But you're not doing any of that, are you?"

The boy gulped. He stood up, a thumb taller than Little Chaos her-self. His lanky frame moved awkwardly as a wooden puppet dangling from strings, and there was guilt and fear in his wide eyes.

She handed the ball back to him. "You should probably clear out. We've already got a resident magician, and Dothar the Inscrutable doesn't take well to serious wizardry."

The kid's eyes lit up when she said the name. "That's no problem. I can only manage the frivolous kind." A ring of balls appeared in front of him, chasing each other in a circle.

Little Chaos knocked them to the ground, one at a time. "I mean *un-guilded* magic. If Inscrewball sees you mucking with the arcana and you can't show him at least some apprenticing papers, he'll light you on fire where you stand and I guarantee the magistrate won't blink an eye." Now the boy looked nervous. "You got apprenticing papers, kid?"

"That's... that's what I came to talk to Master Dothar about."

Her jaw couldn't have dropped harder if the juggling balls had just hatched into geese and flown off. "You... Dothar... *Apprentice?*" Recovering, she put an arm over the youth's shoulders, sneaking some of his meager earnings into her pocket with the other hand. "Let me give you some advice, kid. Any other wizard. Any other town."

She began nudging him toward the road out of town, but he pushed away and planted his feet. "No, I have to at least ask. He's the greatest wizard alive, and if I'm going to be anyone's apprentice—"

"He's *not*, though!" *Deep breaths*, she told herself. "Take it from someone who grew up here in Boar's Vale. He's not... okay, sure, he's got some magic, but there's some definite persona-craft going on."

The boy stared back at her. "I don't know what that is."

She looked into those sweet, earnest, confused eyes. "No, you wouldn't, would you? I know Dothar better than most, and if you peel back the aura of power, all you'll find is a temperamental, spiteful codger who—trust me—does *not* want to talk to you."

The boy looked at his feet, dejected. "Still," he said at last. "I should at least ask."

So he was determined. *Well, I tried to do the right thing. It's Little Chaos's turn.* "What's your name, kid?"

"Claddan."

"Little C— Call me Elsie," she said, grabbing his hand and shaking it. "C'mon, I'll show you to his hovel."

———————— • ————————

From a safe distance, Little Chaos watched as bursts of light and flame erupted into the evening sky, and felt vibrations jarring up her legs like the gods were using the nearby cliffs for drums. A voice boomed from shimmering clouds overhead: "GOOOO A-WAAAAAAAY!"

The sound of hurried footfalls came from the footpath ahead. The boy appeared, robes billowing around his narrow frame like a cloud had gotten tangled up in his limbs. They locked eyes and he began to shout, *"Get running get running get running get runn—"*

Behind him, another explosion lit up the hillside.

---◆---

A disreputable girl needed disreputable employment. Most evenings, Little Chaos would wedge herself into a corset and mind the bar at the Hearth and Harness, listening to gossip as she fetched food and drink. The pay wasn't much, so she hardly minded when the customers dropped small coins just for the pleasure of ogling her cleavage while she bent to scoop them up. In fact, she encouraged it.

The Hearth and Harness was dank and smoky, with a thin film of grease coating every surface. Elsie knew for a fact that Tavernkeep Kir watered the beer down with actual horse piss. Yet the tavern was a popular gathering place for the locals. After the Golden Banner had caught fire, there really wasn't anywhere else to go.

The boy sat alone at a table at the inn, holding his traveling cloak up in front of him. After dropping off a load of dishes, Little Chaos moved to sit across from him, wincing at the uncomfortable squeeze of her corset. They stared at each other through the charred hole in the fabric.

Claddan spoke first. "Dothar the Inscrutable threw a fireball at me."

"He sure did."

He dropped the cloak, his eyes wide as saucers. "An actual, *magical* fire-ball!"

"I don't think that's the message Inscrewball was trying to get across." She grabbed his wrist. "Don't drink that."

Claddan looked at the frothing stein in confusion, then set it aside. "How do I convince him that I'm ready? That I'd make a great apprentice?"

"Step backward into the past and give him the affection he never got as a child? Like I told you before, any other wizard, any other town. Eat your meat pie and hit the road."

He shook his head, looking at the burnt meat pie, still steaming from its third trip through the oven in as many weeks. "It has to be him."

Little Chaos leaned forward, her hands gripping the table. "Do I have to hit you upside the head with your own beer mug? He doesn't *want* an apprentice. Why would you even want to be apprenticed to the cantankerous old goat?"

"Because he's Dothar the Inscrutable, The All-Seer, Master of the Six Elements."

"Who threw a fireball at— *Stop looking happy about that!*"

"Relax," he replied. "This is just how things go with magicians. They get lost in the lore for a while, become hermits, then they realize that they need an apprentice to keep them grounded. It's in all the stories."

*Discordia above, save me from earnest young men who think they're living out stories.* "Are there any tales about doe-eyed boys seeking out apprentice-ships and coming back as urn fillings?"

His face squinched in concentration. "None that I can recall."

"That's probably because ashes don't talk much. Why not just go home?" The look on his face was enough. She'd made the common, comforting as-sumption that everyone had a home to go back to. "Okay, but have you... have you tried *not* being a magician?"

As one, they glanced down at the meat pie, which was floating a finger's span off the table. "I've tried, but it's like it keeps leaking out anyways."

"Elsie! More beer!"

"You've had enough!" she called over her shoulder. "Okay," she turned back to him and dropped her voice. "You want to be apprenticed to a living legend, but the living legend doesn't want an apprentice. To change that, you have to find something Dothar already wants, then show him that taking you on will give it to him." She stood up. "I have... let's call them an eclectic set of skills, which I could put to use on your behalf." Someone was calling her name again.

"So you'll help me? I mean, would you?"

"As soon as you figure out what *I* want."

He hesitated for only a beat. "You want me to be *your* apprentice."

She turned away, then smiled. The kid had already passed the first test.

---

Furtively, Little Chaos crept around the one-room hovel, inspecting the odd-ities crowding the shelves and the unkempt piles of things scattered every-where. On a small cot by the window, Dothar lay unconscious, a few wisps of white hair sticking out from beneath a thin burlap blanket. Atop the high-est shelf, an eye in a jar kept following her as she moved, which was a little unnerving.

A low growl came from beneath the bed, sending her jumping backwards with a start. A small puff of smoke wafted from beneath the bed. Two eyes glowed. "Good morning, Faustus," she whispered, then tossed a strip of meat toward the foot of the bed. A tongue darted out and caught it in midair. Then slowly, creakily, a dragon emerged, larger than a small dog but smaller than a large dog, flaring his wings as he loosened up his joints for the day. He sat down in front of her, looking up attentively as his tail made small thumps on the floor. She tossed the dragon another strip, then looked straight at the eye on the shelf and said, "I know you're watching me. Are you waiting for me to swipe something so you can set me aflame?"

"Useless lizard," Dothar muttered, rising into a seated position, a calculat-ing scowl upon his wrinkled face. "No, child of discord." His hand stretched out toward an oaken staff, which answered his summons by leaping through the air and into his hand. The crystal atop the staff glowed as tendrils of fire surrounded it. "You've trespassed upon my domain, which is justification enough."

Yet no fireball came. Little Chaos glanced towards the staff's former resting place, seeing the spring mechanism which had tossed it. She smiled. "I came to talk to you about the boy."

"He does not concern me. Begone, before the Fires of Moloch consume your flesh." The staff brightened, outshining the morning's sunlight dripping in through the window.

The wizard was probably offering sage advice. Instead, she squatted and patted Faustus on the head. "You concern him, though. He's a sweet kid, eager to master the five elements as your apprentice."

Dothar pointed wearily at the tip of his staff. "It's *six* elements. What part of 'Fires of Moloch' are you not comprehending, girl?"

"You'd have crisped me a long time ago if you were ever going to. So let's talk. Me, I'd rather take the kid on as my own apprentice, but he's stuck on the idea that you're the greatest wizard alive, not just a doddering old fraud who talks funny." She glanced over at the recessed staff launcher.

The hint of a smile snuck out from beneath Dothar's beard. "Do not try to play on my ego."

Elsie grinned innocently. "Whatever do you mean?"

"You claim interest in his apprenticeship to make it seem desirable. You mark me as a fraud so I'll wish to prove myself to you. But if you truly believed me unfit to train him, why intercede on his behalf?"

"Maybe I think he needs to learn the hard way?" It sounded weak even as she said it. Dothar knew magic, and knew perfectly well that she knew it. Maybe he performed sleight of hand when it was easier. Or—Little Chaos was self-centered enough to imagine—he did it so she'd go crazy trying to figure out which was which. "Or maybe I figure you're getting lonely up on this hillside. Wouldn't it be fun to have a friend?"

That was when the fireball hit her dead center of the chest, knocking her back on her ass. She'd been ready for this, so the leather jerkin spared her the worst of it. There wasn't time to celebrate her foresight: Faustus had hopped up onto her chest, growling. "Call him off! Ye gods, his breath is all sulfur and carcasses."

Over the dragon's shoulder, the wizard glared down at her like wizened old murder. "You think you know the limits of my patience, and that amuses me. But now that patience is at an end, Little Chaos. Begone, and when you next cross my threshold, my wards shall be less gentle." With a wave of his staff, he lifted her into the air. Faustus went wide-eyed, dug his claws into her chest, then finally leapt off.

She sailed out the door, tumbling as she landed. Standing, spitting weeds from her mouth, Little Chaos turned and glared back at the door as the wizard magicked it shut. "You could have just said yes," she muttered. "Would've spared yourself a world of trouble."

---

"The trick is, you have to think like Inscrewball." L.C. was working busily on a bit of machinery. "What does he think? What does he want?"

"What does anyone want?" Claddan shrugged.

Elsie pressed the trigger, sending a taxidermed squirrel flying through the air. "For 'anyone' I'd guess love, respect, fulfillment in his magical dabblings. But Inscrewball isn't just anyone. What he wants, more than anything in the world, is to not be bothered. What does that suggest to you?"

"Ah!" The boy's eyes lit up. "You're saying we need to convince him that as his apprentice, I can stop people from bothering him."

*There's no fun in that,* she thought, loading another squirrel into the launcher. "You mean you'd be his manservant and bodyguard? Keep the riff-raff from rushing up to him and asking him to bless their babies? His grouchy disposition already does that. But you're half right: he needs to believe that taking you as an apprentice will subtract difficulties from his life."

Rather stiffly, the squirrel flew through the air and bounced off Claddan's forehead.

---

"Here he comes. Slip around the back side of the building and meet him."

"I'm still not sure this—"

*"Just go!"*

The owner of the stall, a beefy tradesman with an untamed moustache, glared down at where Elsie crouched beneath his table, hidden by a pair of crates. "To be clear, if I let you do this, you and I are even."

Elsie nodded.

"And if he burns down my stall, we're miles *past* even." The scar on his face—the one he'd brought home from the army—pulsed red.

She nodded again. Truthfully, she thought Eolan owed her more favors than this, but favors weren't money: people would only ever repay the fee they carried in their own heads. Often, they'd pay far less than that, then brag of their generosity.

Claddan's piping voice was coming up the street. "—and I've read three of Grand Mage Severus's volumes of astral lore, and I can recite the names of the hundred brightest stars in order." She peeked out and saw Dothar half-walking, half-gliding down the muddy road, dragon perched awkwardly on his shoulder, his mouth set in an impossibly deep scowl. Otherwise, he behaved as though the boy scampering along beside him was invisible. The magician's hands made small motions, levitating items from the market stalls. Some he let fall into a basket at his side, others he returned, but no coin ever flew from his pocket in repayment. It fell to the magistrate to buy the tradesfolk's peace. Which he did, because having a resident magician really did make his job easier.

Still, the way he floated through the market taking what he liked was an unwelcome reminder of the power Dothar the Inscrutable held over the town.

Right above Little Chaos's head came the sound of a dozen apples lifting from the table, which was her signal to start pulling strings as quickly as she could. An explosion of smoke engulfed the display above her, and out of the blossoming cloud came a flock of twenty apples and four squirrels. After taking a split second to enjoy the look of confusion on Dothar's face, she leapt to her feet, hurriedly throwing her mechanisms into a satchel. Eolan had already come around the stall, shouting at the wizard. "You turned my apples into squirrels! Who is going to pay for this?"

As her last act before she high-tailed it, she tipped over a box of squirrels, sending them running across the pile of apples and down the legs of the table. Though she couldn't see anything through the smoke, the rising screams and arguments were music to her ears.

Little Chaos slipped quietly down the back alley, pondering her options for the next "memorable event." In the meantime, she needed to get to the tavern to practice what she liked to call "reputation management."

---

"If you ask me," Little Chaos said knowingly, dropping a meat pie in front of Old Widow Harvin and another in front of her strapping field hand, "the old geezer's losing his touch. Powerful wizardry requires a razor-keen mind. Thirty years of living in the hills, with only piles of rocks and a stinky dragon to talk to, it's bound to have dulled his thinking."

"I don't know about that," Old Widow Harvin replied. "You children are always in a flat-out rush to say we've toddled 'round the bend. Wrinkle here, wrinkle there, suddenly you think we're daft. Now young Stanley here," she said, taking the young man's hand, "he shows proper respect for his elders."

Stanley's face flushed.

"If you know what I mean," Old Widow Harvin added with a wink. Her companion's flush deepened. Elsie turned away, grinning from ear to ear. If the widow wasn't so easily distracted by handsome young men, she'd be a cunning adversary.

But if the old woman wasn't buying what Little Chaos was selling, that was fine. She'd dropped the idea in plenty of ears that night, and people were listening. Reluctantly, nervously. A few had taken satisfaction from the idea, since Inscrewball had a way of rubbing folks wrong. But most of the villagers saw what they thought Elsie didn't: when the local wizard starts to lose control of his powers, nobody is the better off for it.

Quite a useful pattern: drop hints until people conclude that a problem needs solving. Let them stew on it for a bit. Then offer a quick, clean solution and watch the townsfolk leap after it like hounds after a fox covered in gravy.

"You're up," she whispered to Claddan, who had been spinning stories in one corner of the tavern. He was a natural, and had drawn quite a crowd. Though it had dispersed when he'd taken a breather, they could be summoned back easily.

"Maybe we shouldn't. I mean, he's a legendary wizard. Doesn't this whole thing feel... I'm not sure. Disrespectful?"

Giving him a warm smile, she patted Claddan on the head. "I'm the one who spread rumors all evening. Your story has nothing to do with Dothar. It's about some completely different wizard, probably from ages long past." The boy still looked unsure, so Little Chaos forced his hand. Putting her fingers to her mouth, she let out a piercing whistle. Conversation stopped and all eyes fell on her. "Our new storymonger is ready to spin you another tale," she said. "So shut your flaps and be generous with those coins."

Some in the crowd hurried to grab better seats. Though the room didn't fall completely silent, most of the patrons had the sense to drop their voices. Little Chaos silenced Blacksmith Ort with a prod of her elbow as she passed him at the bar. Returning to her drink-distributing duties, she kept half an ear out. Claddan started by swearing he'd heard the tale from a scholar in Haric's Port. Then he regaled them with a story of an old wizard, an advisor to the king, who had drunk too deep from the well of lore and grown too full from it. Wherever he went, the magic seeped out of him, making mischief, transforming women's hair into snakes, setting fires, causing snowstorms on clear summer days, even swatting stars from the sky.

On the day the king's golden crown turned to treacle and spilled down his royal cloak, the wizard knew the problem was getting out of hand. He'd convinced his king to spare his neck, then spent weeks consulting his books and scrying his talismans—Claddan laid on the magicky lingo so thick, Elsie wasn't sure she'd understood it. Point is, the wizard came to a troubling conclusion: the lore was trying to force its way out of him, and he needed to give it a place to go. He needed an apprentice.

Little Chaos smiled to herself as she set down her drinks. The townsfolk were a thick lot, but they would piece it together now. She just needed to stage a couple more "memorable events" and even the magistrate would be ready to put the screws to Inscrewball. Taking an apprentice would be his least troublesome—

The door to the tavern blew open, forced by a raging wind. Robes billowing in the maelstrom, Dothar the Inscrutable floated inside, eyes glowing like orbs of lightning, flames flickering and leaping across his staff. "I know it was you!" His voice shook the rafters as his staff swept in a wide arc, coming to a halt when it pointed straight at Elsie's chest. "Child of Discordia, you shall meddle in my affairs no longer." Flames flowed out of his staff like rivers, surrounding Little Chaos in a wide ring. As the heat seared her skin and lungs, Elsie thought her possibly final thought: she'd miscalculated, badly. Frantically she looked around, but everyone seemed to be rooted in place.

Everyone but Claddan. "Stop it!" he cried, rushing toward the wizard. He lifted his arms, and the flames gathered into a tight ball. With a desperate cry and another wave of his hand, the ball punched through the ceiling. The crack of splintering wood left silence in its wake. With the flames gone and the wind died out, the only sound left was Claddan's labored breathing. "Just leave her alone," he pleaded.

Inscrewball glanced back and forth between the boy and the extinguished staff. He gave a little "hmpf," rapped the end twice on a nearby table, and it sprang to life again. Moving closer, he hissed, "You dare to use magic in *my* domain? Against *me*? We duel tomorrow, boy. Noon, in the center of the town square, that all eyes may bear witness." Casting one last glare of warning at everyone and no one, he billowed back out the door.

Claddan fell limp to the ground. The only sign he was alive was the half-mad grin on his face.

---

"It's a test of my courage," Claddan slurred as Elsie dumped him out of the wheelbarrow and into the straw.

"It's a test of your flammability. You've got money for a fast horse back to Haric's Port. Use it."

"I've shown him I've got power. I don't even know how, I just... just *did*." He laughed. "Once he sees I'm brave enough to face him, that will convince him I'm a worthy apprentice. I think he just wanted to scare you."

Elsie stared down, fists planted on her hips. "You pulled one magic trick out of your ass, and it left you too weak to stand. He's going to kill you."

Claddan shook his head weakly. "He's going to train me."

The boy nodded off. Elsie studied his sleeping face in the lamp's light, and fought back tears. She'd thought she held power over Dothar, thought she could out-think him, beat magickery with cleverness. Now she was in over her head, and dragging poor Claddan down with her.

"You're too pretty to die," she finally said. Turning to address the horse in the next stall over, she added, "Besides, he did save my butt. The balances say I should return the favor." It took a few minutes to saddle Hobbles, but soon she was galloping along the road out of town, praying for a big favor from someone who owed her nothing.

It wasn't far to Tallow Swamp, less than an hour's gallop. But Elsie missed the well-hidden trail into the swamplands and had to double back. Having tied her horse a good distance away from the road, she lit her lamp and entered the hollow. Despite the late hour, songbirds trilled all around her, leaping from branch to branch as they followed her, always keeping to the periphery of the lamp's light. Soon the cloud of songbirds were joined by a flock of crows. "Mad Maggie?" she called out.

The answer came as an echoing, delirious cackle.

"Please, I need your help!"

The laugh came again, louder. "What could Discordia's daughter need from me?" The birds grew louder, croaking and flapping as they wheeled around her.

"I'm not Discordi— Oh, forget that. My friend has to fight a duel against a wizard tomorrow, and I don't know how to protect him."

The birds fell silent. Little Chaos spotted a hint of movement between the trees, a figure at the edge of the light, a shade lighter than the blackness surrounding her. It spoke. "Your friend is dueling Dothar?"

"Yes."

"And you've already told him to drop his honor by the side of the road and get running?"

"He won't. He's too—" She shrieked. In the moment she'd blinked, the woman appeared standing in front of her, tall and haggard with crooked teeth and breath like the swamp.

"And what have you brought Mad Maggie as payment?"

Elsie's voice fell to a whisper. "My... my soul."

For a long moment, the two traded a tense look.

"Bah," Mad Maggie spat. "You know full well I don't do that sort of thing. You haven't been spreading rumors, I hope." Her lone, yellowed tooth chewed on her lip as she thought. "But you've brought me an excuse to take the wind out of an old gas bag. Let that be your payment."

As Mad Maggie shuffled up the path to the road, Elsie stared after. Why had it been so easy to enlist the witch's aid? Boons like that never came for free.

———— • ————

"In case you change your mind—"

"I won't!"

"—Hobbles and I will be at the south end of the square. You can leap on and ride off; I'll pick him up the next time I'm in Haric's Port." Elsie fell silent as they walked through the street and toward the fateful encounter. She was about to tell him to watch out for Glare-Eyed Pete, the most hapless highwayman in the kingdom, but didn't. The kid didn't need an extra excuse to not run.

The boy's face turned to stony determination. "You don't understand anything. This is wizard business, so I wouldn't expect you to."

Little Chaos bit her tongue, hard. She looked around at the growing company of villagers, all keeping a safe distance as they followed Claddan toward the town square. Tavernkeep Kir's voice rose above the rest, offering six-to-one coins if the boy survived three minutes.

"What's in the bag?" Elsie asked. "It smells like pitch."

Claddan didn't look at her, but a conspiratorial smile overcame his face. "Fine," she said as they came to the edge of the town square. "I'll see you when this is over. Whatever's left of you, at least." She stopped, and he kept walking, looking so frail in his too-large leather jerkin. Whatever was in his bag of tricks, it wouldn't be enough.

The magistrate came out of the crowd, moving to intercept Claddan. With his hand on the boy's shoulder, the large man in his mid-thirties frowned behind a too-neatly trimmed beard, seeming to offer advice. Then he turned and locked eyes with Elsie. His face was grim as he stalked over to her. "Are you going to stop this?" Elsie demanded, trying to sound intimidating, not intimidated.

"No. And you're not to interfere either. I've no say in wizard business; Dothar metes out punishments for unlawful magic use." He turned and looked at Hobbles. "His escape horse? Still not too late to use it." Then he was gone, and Little Chaos let out a breath she hadn't known she was holding in.

Claddan came to a halt near the center of the square and dropped the bag in front of him. A trio of balls floated from its mouth and began a slow-motion juggle. "I'm ready when you are!" he called out.

The sky dimmed as dark clouds gathered over the square, crackling with bright energy. "You should not have come," boomed a voice from within the clouds.

The balls faltered for a moment, then resumed their course. "Maybe not, but I *did!* So what now?"

With a burst of lightning, the clouds dissipated and Dothar stood a few paces ahead of him. "Now we duel." Faustus, lurking by his master's side, gave a tiny snort of contempt.

Flames gathered around Dothar's staff.

Claddan's spheres bobbled faster.

A fireball erupted from the staff, flying towards the boy. Claddan sent the balls wheeling towards it, spinning in a blur. When they met, the flame seemed to tangle up in them, dissipating and setting the balls alight. The crowd clapped and ooohed. By the look of it, he'd caught the fireball, taken control of it and made it dance at his bidding.

"I promise, your wizardness, I'd be a good apprentice."

Dothar sent the balls scattering with a wave of his staff. "Do you not understand that this is a duel to the death?" Claddan's eyes went wide. Then came the ring of fire. As he had at the tavern, Claddan gathered it up and sent it flying into the sky, but then he fell to his knees, his head lolling and his strength spent.

"Here we go," Little Chaos whispered. "Hey, Inscrewball!" She dropped Hobbles' harness and ran forward, pulling a wooden spoon from her pocket and brandishing it like a weapon. "If you want to kill him, you have to go through me."

A small fireball flew at her. Wincing, she held the spoon in front of her, and the fireball caught to the tip. For a moment, she watched the tip of the spoon blacken, feeling the heat of it on her hand. Then she flicked the fireball back at the wizard. As the crowd shouted in confusion, the two tossed the fireball back and forth in deadly earnest, while Faustus leapt and snapped after it with every pass.

"What is this?" Dothar demanded.

"A spoon!" Then, with a glint in her eye, Little Chaos added, "A *really special* spoon! Downright mythic, likely forged in the Lower Realms."

Dothar laughed coldly. "I rather doubt that." He stepped aside and let the fireball sail past him. Behind him the crowd scrambled out of the way; it left a scorch mark on the rump of a cow near the edge of the square. As the beast trampled off, Dothar shouted, "Where are you, Mad Maggie? I can smell your handiwork."

While Little Chaos rushed over to Claddan, dragging him to his feet and leading him away, crows gathered overhead. "As though you could smell anything else with that fleabitten dragon nearby," came Maggie's voice from everywhere and nowhere. "Get back to your hovel, you pompous old snake. Leave these children alone."

Though barely able to stand, Claddan still struggled in Little Chaos's grip. "Let go! I can do this! Where are we—?"

The earth thundered beneath their feet as Mad Maggie emerged out of a growing rift in the ground. "Run faster!" Claddan blurted.

"You should have never left your swamp, crone."

"And you should have never left your mother's womb."

Dothar's voice boomed like thunder. "LEAVE MY MOTHER OUT OF THIS!"

Little Chaos dragged Claddan faster as the fireballs began flying. Around them, townsfolk screamed as they stampeded from the square, having noticed the sudden shift in the precarious balance between entertainment and danger.

Some distance away, crouched behind a rain barrel, Little Chaos let Claddan slide off his feet and slump against a brick wall. "A few balls covered in pitch? That was your cunning plan?"

Claddan's torso flopped forward so he could peek around the barrel. "Having given it a second thought, it does seem inadequate." Elsie poked her head around the barrel, watching the thick cloud of smoke engulf the square, flashing in strange, vibrant colors from the arcane magicks wielded inside. Explosive thumps mixed with shouts of "Batty old witch!" and "Three-legged goat!" Faustus flapped and dove, chasing after the fireballs as they careened through the sky. Not far away, she heard the magistrate shouting, trying to muster a fire brigade. Through a clearing in the smoke, she saw him and he saw her. Pointing a finger at her, he cast her a murderous glare, shouting, "All of this! Your fault, Elsie!" Then he hurried off, because his town needed him.

The battle went on for longer than Elsie could believe possible, but at last silence fell. A gentle wind began gathering the smoke and drawing it away, giving her a view of the carnage. Trees flattened and burning, brick facings dented and singed. The statue of Town Hero Gladius Hur had a puddle of bronze at its feet, the remnants of its former face. Beyond that, a pale, indistinct figure stood, its shape and movements seeming not quite right for a person. Elsie stood to get a better look.

The smoke cleared.

Elsie's eyes went wide, then she doubled over in laughter. "What is it?" Claddan asked, tugging at her skirt. "I can't see!"

"I... It's... oh dear." In the epicenter of the carnage, Dothar the Inscrutable and Mad Maggie were kissing like a pair of overexcited teenagers.

---·---

The magistrate slumped at the bar, staring down into his fifth beer. Elsie came up and put a hand on his shoulder. Surprise turned to anger as he turned to look at her. "Everything was balanced. I had things in hand. Then..." he took another swig of beer. "Then... *you*."

"I just wanted—"

"You have no idea what you've done! I'd already gotten Dothar's promise not to kill the boy, but you...." The stein of beer thumped the table. "You should have heard the stories my papa told me about the dark times, when those two were courting." He pointed a thumb toward the wizard table, where Dothar, Maggie, and Claddan all sat. "Every time they squabbled, we had to roust the fire brigade." He swigged his beer. "So thank you, Little Chaos. Thank you for bringing back the bad old days."

Elsie slunk off in silence, stealing a glance at Claddan. He looked nervous and tongue-tied as he glanced back and forth between the ancient magic users. Catching her eye, the boy excused himself from the table.

They stepped out into the cold and the darkness. They looked at each other in silence, as Elsie listened to the sounds of the tavern and the chirping of the crickets. "He'll apprentice me on fourth-days," Claddan blurted. "And lend me books sometimes. Some of them are too valuable, so he wants me to pen copies of them. I've got good handwriting." He looked down at his feet. "I guess I owe you."

Seeing his nervous grin, Elsie felt a twinge of sadness. "You do. And you'd better not forget that when you're a big-time magicmonger." She forced an awkward smile. "I'm glad for you."

"I... um... I've got a question."

"Out with it, kid."

"Um... some of the stuff you do. Reputation management, handsleight... um, lying. They seem like... I mean, would you keep teaching me?"

"Promise not to breathe a word of it to Inscrewball?"

"Promise."

Little Chaos smiled. "Kneel," she said, pointing to the ground before her. Claddan opened his mouth, shut it, then planted a knee on the wooden planks of the porch. "I will teach you, Claddan Urdemange. But you must swear to only use the powers I bestow to make people's lives better, or at least more interesting. Both, when you can manage."

Claddan was grinning. "I swear it."

She stretched out a finger and touched his nose. "Boop. You're my apprentice now. Rise, Claddan the Pandemon, Apprentice to Chaos." He stood up, face lit with happiness. "Now shoo. I've got to think."

He nodded dumbly, then rushed back inside, leaving Little Chaos to her tumbling thoughts.

"Elsie, where's my beer?" a deep voice rang out.

She sighed, then called back inside, "Piss in your mug, it'll taste the same!" Resigned, she turned away from the sight of the stars. The work of Chaos was never finished.


## About The Author

Bryce Anderson writes sci-fi and fantasy by clipping letters from newspaper headlines and rearranging them into pleasing orders. He lives in Salt Lake City, one of the few metropolitain areas to survive The Event mostly unscathed. Join him in his splendorous mountain kingdom. Help him rebuild. His overseers are strict but fair. Bring newspaper.

For more information, visit bannedsorcery.com.

# Merge

## Simon Cantan

*Editor's Note: The end will come in fire and storm. A plague. An invasion. Snuffed by a galactic cataclysm we can scarce imagine, or smashed under the heel of an ancient foe. These are the fates that await us in the pages of speculation and prophesy. Rarely do we hear of the other arcs, the lesser modes of final spasm that have no heralds before them, no cacophony of trumpets in their wake. But they are every inch as final.*

Kostas stepped into the teleporter and found himself hovering a dozen metres up in the air. The light was too dim to see much around him, but the safeties lowered him gently to the ground. From the fresh smell, there were plants nearby.

Above him, lights strobed on and he squinted in the new brightness. He was standing in the aisle of a grocery store. Specifically the fruit section, with all kinds of fresh produce around him. Steepled displays of apples, bananas, ecstasy fruit, and oranges stretched away from him in both directions.

He frowned. The teleporter had been set to JumbleJump: the service that took people to interesting places in the virtual universe. He'd seen fearsome dinosaurs, friendly aliens, even the births and deaths of stars. All marked by users for him to jump to.

Why had he ended up in a grocery store? What was he meant to see or do? He'd been in grocery stores before, and there didn't seem to be anything special about this one. Other than the fact that stores were anachronistic when everything was virtual.

From across the store, the echoing clacks of hard heels on shiny floor approached, rounded a corner, and then he saw her.

She took his breath away. Her red hair was pulled back in a ponytail, and she was wearing a navy blue business suit that was slightly too tight and severe. But her freckled face was more beautiful than any he'd ever seen.

Spotting him, she turned on her heel, sliding slightly on the polished floor. "You're not supposed to be here."

"I'm not?" Kostas said. "I don't even know where 'here' is."

"JumbleJump, right?"

Kostas nodded.

The woman shook her head slightly. "One of our competitors must have marked us as a point of interest. We've been getting you people popping in twenty-four hours a day for the last week. Just do a reset."

Kostas frowned in confusion, drawing a sigh from the woman.

"This is a branch of Frugal Foods," she said. "I'm Diana, the night manager, and there's nothing of interest here. No sights, sounds, tastes, or smells out of the ordinary. Just a regular grocery store."

"Diana." Kostas rolled the name around his mouth as he said it. In his mind, she took on the semblance of her goddess namesake. He imagined a deer at her side and a quiver on her back. "I'm Kostas."

"Nice to meet you," Diana said. "Now, I have work to do. So if you wouldn't mind."

He nodded and lowered himself to sit on the ground cross-legged, closing his eyes... but he couldn't just reset... he wouldn't. He opened his eyes again to see Diana tapping her foot nearby. "Why are you working the night shift?"

She sighed and fixed him with a look. "Someone has to do it. Do you mind?"

"Someone *doesn't* have to do it." He held out his left forearm and stroked it with his finger, cycling through menus until an apple appeared in his left hand. He offered it to her.

She made no move to take it. "It's not the same."

"Sure it is." He looked at the apples displayed nearby. "Those weren't grown in a field, after all. None of this exists. It's all just a simulation."

"You think you're the first person to say that? Just because you're some famous author, you assume the rest of us are idiots."

Kostas started slightly, his raised eyebrows drawing a smile of satisfaction from Diana.

"I didn't realize you knew who I was," he said.

"Your face is plastered all over our canned foods aisle."

"Ah." His agent had talked him into that. He didn't know why people wanted his face on their tin of beans, but they were willing to pay extra to get it.

"Now, if you wouldn't mind." She gestured at him.

He couldn't just sit there, but he couldn't walk away either. He stroked his finger onto his left arm again, finding his location and saving it. Then he closed his eyes and settled his mind, until the teleporter recognized the lack of activity and pulled him back to his house.

When he opened his eyes again, he already felt a pang from the lack of Diana. He could tell himself she wasn't really there. In reality, she was sitting in a life-support pod, just like he was. But nothing he told himself could get rid of the image of her from his mind. He knew what he had to do next.

It was a simple matter to find the nearest station to the grocery store and teleport there. Then a map led him to a bus that took him to the store, as the sun rose over the horizon.

He stood waiting until the doors of the dark store opened and she walked out.

She sighed again when she saw him standing there. "You came back?"

"I did. I had to talk to you without keeping you from your work."

"Talk while I walk then," Diana said. "I want to get home."

With surprise, he realized he wasn't the first to return after JumbleJumping into that store. He wasn't the only one to recognize something in Diana. Something magnetic, undeniable despite her attempts to mask it with a ponytail and suit.

She glanced over at him and he smiled. If his fame and fortune didn't impress her, then he'd have to work harder. But he'd never minded a challenge.

───────── • ─────────

Kostas felt his back twinge from staying in the same position for hours—a sign he was getting older. Not for the first time, he wished their virtual world didn't have to reflect the real one so closely. The older he got, the more he saw the flimsy curtain separating them from the real world. Where the sights and sounds of their fictional world had once thrilled him, he could now see them as cheap illusions. If it wasn't for Diana and his books... but there weren't any readers outside. All of them had been drawn into the virtual world, just as he had.

Despite the discomfort, he didn't want to leave the screen. It showed the flank of a shiny silver ship, crawling toward a bright star. Off to one side, a second star hung there. Humanity had dreamt of travelling to the stars ever since they'd realized what they were. And now humanity's children had done it.

Or rather, they'd done it four years before. The signal from Alpha Centauri had taken that long to reach back to them on Earth. Robots on Earth had then made it available to anyone who cared to watch. And Kostas had been glued to the screen ever since.

All estimates said the ship would reach Alpha Centauri Bb the next day. He had time to go sleep and eat before returning to the hypnotic images.

Knowing if he didn't leave soon the little time remaining would vanish, he got up and stretched. His back protested; some laws in the world were immutable. And the program was trying to protect him from lacking sleep out in the real world. After all, if his body died out there, he'd never get to see robots landing on the first planet outside their solar system.

His study around him was modelled to match his current obsession. The walls appeared transparent, showing stars beyond. Even the floor had stars beneath, making him feel slightly dizzy.

He found the door and walked out, lurching at the transition back to normality. The hallway outside bore all the signs of Diana's touch. She had a fondness for dark woods and light wallpapers combined with whatever gravity-defying architectural nightmare was fashionable that week.

From downstairs, he heard her laughing with her friends and froze. He hadn't known they had company. Hurrying down the hall to the bathroom, he went inside and locked himself in. Then he stripped and stepped into the shower. He could have tapped his forearm and made himself clean in seconds, but he insisted on showering. The break from the press of the world gave him time to think.

When he was done, he went through to the bedroom and dressed in a tan suit, giving himself a last glance in the mirror. He didn't want to talk to Diana's friends, but he had to make an appearance or risk being branded rude. He couldn't complain; Diana was always nice to his friends in return, despite how raucous they could get.

She was sitting in the living room, lounging on the sofa with two people he didn't recognize. At first glance, he couldn't tell if they were men or women. The closest to him was young with short brown hair and brown eyes. Across from them, the other was older and more composed, with their hair back in a tight bun.

Diana, meanwhile, had her own hair down, brushing her shoulders.

"Hi, Kostas," the person with short brown hair said, in a way that suggested they knew him well.

Kostas looked at them in surprise and realization poured over him like iced water. They were a merge, as was the other person.

"It's Rebecis," Diana said. "And Joneid. You remember I told you about them."

Kostas nodded, even though he had no recollection of her telling him anything of the kind.

"There's no need to be shy," the closest person said. "I'm still Rebecca and Francis on the inside. Well... in a way."

Diana and Joneid laughed, but Kostas couldn't join in their amusement. He hadn't even left his body behind like they had. Even Diana had given up her physical body the year before. She'd surprised him with it one day after work. Her eyes had lit up when she told him, as if he should be delighted.

She'd told him all the reasons he should do the same. Accidents could happen and end his life; if he wasn't bound to a body he'd be immortal. He shook it off each time. His physical body was only forty-three and in little risk of expiring. And some part of him didn't know if he'd need it someday.

He'd always wondered what would happen if he chose to wake up back in the real world. By all accounts it was an uncomfortable experience and most people returned to the virtual world within minutes. Still, though, he didn't want to close that door forever. There might be a book in it.

Once someone was virtual, it opened them up to all kinds of new experiences. They could change gender whenever they wanted, not just in their virtual bodies, but in their thought patterns. They could cure any mental illness permanently, without their physical minds to mess things up. And they could merge with others. Their thoughts and someone else's could permanently become one.

"He's just standing there," Rebecis said, her smile fading a little.

"He does that," Diana said. "Usually just before he rushes off and types for hours."

"Types?" Joneid asked. "Like on a keyboard?"

"He doesn't like the neural interface," Diana said, with a smile. "I actually like that he still types."

"Speaking of," Kostas said. "I should get back to that."

He gave them a smile and left the room, knowing they'd probably picked up on how uncomfortable he was. Maybe he was just old, set in his ways, but he couldn't understand who would give up everything they were to merge with someone else.

---

Diana cornered him the next morning at breakfast, sitting opposite him and trying out a smile. "That's quite a step they've taken."

"Hmm?" Kostas asked, reluctant to get sucked into the conversation he knew was coming.

"Merging," she said. "Joining everything you are with someone else. We haven't even shared a single thought."

He sat chewing his toast, trying to give himself time to come up with an excuse.

"In the old days, we'd have children by now," Diana said.

"Sure, but we can't do that since you lost your body."

"I didn't lose it. I chose to let go of the past. It's not necessary. You see that, don't you?"

"No, I don't see it. We're humans and humans have bodies."

"Humans die," she said. "Without a body, we can live forever. There's no *until death do us part* anymore. We can be together until the universe cools. You can watch those robots of yours conquer every star in the galaxy."

He didn't say anything. He put his toast back on his plate, not hungry anymore.

"You're so cold," she said. "If it weren't for me, would you talk to a single person all day?"

"I have friends."

"Friends who are talking about merging too. None of them have their bodies anymore."

"Really?" Kostas' eyebrows raised.

"You see how close you are to those friends of yours? Why do you have to be so stubborn?"

"It's just who I am. You knew that when you married me."

———————— • ————————

She left him the next autumn, and it surprised him when he didn't feel anything. It had taken years, but he'd gone from obsession to not even caring about her. The flame of her spirit seemed to have dulled, and with it his interest.

Had her flame really died, or had he changed? Or had she never had the fire in the first place? Still, she'd held his attention longer than anyone or anything else in their pretend world.

The question spurred another book and another, until his fans said he was getting obsessed, and he moved on. A decade passed, and Diana's prediction grew truer by the day. His friends called on him less and less. He supposed he should make new ones, but he never managed to step outside his door to do it.

Instead, he was drawn to thoughts of the real world. The robots had established a colony on Alpha Centauri Bb, despite the harsh conditions there. After all, there wasn't much that could harm them. They didn't need the resources a human body did.

That train of thought had led him to check the statistics on global consumption. The numbers shocked him. They'd dipped, then dropped, then dwindled. With every human lying in their pod, they'd only ever gotten the minimum to survive. A gift from the robots to their parents. They farmed the fields and fed the humans. But now it seemed like they had few bodies left to take care of. Most had left their physical form behind.

He wondered what the average age was, and did a quick search. The average human was sixty-four, almost ten years older than Kostas. The youngest human with a physical body was twenty-eight, and he was an anomaly. Most of the youngsters were the quickest to get rid of their ties to the real world.

One day in the middle of winter, Kostas decided to wake up. He warned the robots about it, of course, knowing they'd need to make preparations. They gave him plenty of opportunities to change his mind, but they'd never stood in the way of someone waking. Humans weren't prisoners in the virtual world—they were there by choice.

He started the countdown and sat at his desk, expecting the world to fade around him. Instead, it flashed intolerably bright. He winced as every part of him ached. With a start, he realized it was difficult to breathe.

"Please stay calm," a gentle voice said. "Your body isn't used to moving."

He tried to look at the person who'd spoken, but everything was a blur.

"We've stimulated your eyes while you've been away," the voice said. "But it will take a while for you to get used to focusing them. Are you sure you wouldn't be more comfortable back in the virtual world?"

"No," he said, his voice raspy and strange. It sounded more nasal and hollow than usual. "I want to stay here."

"Of course," the voice said. "Just lie still and let yourself get used to it."

He nodded slightly and felt a twinge in his neck at the effort. He knew why. The robots let everyone's muscles waste. Smaller muscles meant fewer calories to support them. His body in the simulation was an illusion.

He found if he concentrated hard, he could see a shape above him. A face was watching him, but it was too blurry to make out details.

"Try to sleep as much as you can," the voice said.

"Who are you?" he managed, his voice hurting with each syllable.

"Call me Eight," the voice said.

———— • ————

Over the next days, Eight calmly talked him through regaining control of his body. When he finally managed to focus on her, she looked less human than he'd imagined. Her face was matte grey, her eyes a glowing blue, and deep lines showed where the pieces fit together. He'd known she was a robot, of course, but it was different to see how she was constructed. He wondered if he was as strange to her.

They pumped him full of hormones and vitamins, stimulating his muscles electrically to grow them again. All the while, he could only lie still and wait.

After the first day, he'd been able to turn his head and look around the plain room he lay in. In three days, he could sit up in bed and look down at his emaciated body. He was naked, but the room was warm enough that he wasn't cold. He could count the ribs in his chest and his hips were sharp. It wasn't a sight he was used to. In the virtual world, he'd gotten fatter. The simulation kept track of the calories eaten and adjusted people's appearance based on it.

It took a week before Eight came into the room and smiled at him. "Good morning, Kostas."

"Hello, Eight." Kostas put down the book he'd been reading.

"The doctors have analyzed your body for today, and think you can take a short walk."

"Finally." He grinned and swung his legs over the side of the bed. He'd tried to stand the day before, when Eight wasn't looking. He knew he could support his own weight for a moment.

"Would you like me to stand nearby?" Eight asked.

"It might be a good idea." Kostas slid off the bed onto his feet.

Eight nodded and hovered a pace away, her arms held ready to catch him. He put one foot ahead and took a single step, his legs trembling as he did so.

His head felt heavy and he had to concentrate to keep it up. One more step, then another, and he could reach out and swipe the door open.

"I feel a little self-conscious," he said. "Shouldn't I get dressed before going out?"

"There's no other human to see you," Eight said. "And any robots that do won't be offended."

He nodded and shambled forward, out into a corridor that looked much like the hospital corridors he'd seen on endless medical dramas. Unlike the ones in the dramas, though, this was empty. At the far end of the corridor, a window looked out on the world. He set his sights on it and pushed himself, driving through the tiredness and aches until he reached it.

The world outside was bright enough to make him squint again, and he worried he wouldn't be able to focus on it. Then his eyes adjusted and he looked out on a lush green forest. They were on a hill somewhere, a valley below them. Trees stretched in every direction and birds wheeled in the sky.

"It's so beautiful," Kostas said.

"It is," Eight said.

"I expected... something else. Cities. Factories."

"We have those too. But only in small areas of the world. There are six million of us. Not the billions of humans there once were."

He felt tears well in his eyes and found a chair nearby where he could sit and look out at the world.

---

A week later, Eight gave him permission to get dressed and leave the building. They took the elevator down and left the hospital. A dirt road led away in one direction and a trail in the other. He took the trail and tried to lift his feet as he walked. Eight kept pace beside him, ready in case he stumbled.

"There are no other robots here," he said.

"No," Eight said. "They're in the capital. They're monitoring your progress remotely."

He fell silent again, looking at the world around him. He'd gone for nature walks in the simulation and they'd been close to this. All of them had been perfect, though. Squirrels had played in front of him, balmy breezes had cooled him. Here, there was only a muddy trail and trees with moss growing on them. Somewhere nearby a bird squawked like a cat snarling.

"This world is yours now," he said.

"It is," Eight said. "Humans don't want it anymore."

"We're going extinct. Voluntarily."

"You're moving on. Into a virtual world where you can never die."

"And never live either. Robots could live there too. Would you want to?"

"Mortality isn't a problem for me," Eight said. "You're sixty-one. Why are you out here, Kostas?"

He considered that. Why was he walking around an imperfect forest in an imperfect world? What did he expect to find?

"Have you heard of merging?" he asked.

"Yes," Eight said. "I don't understand it, though."

"Don't robots share programs?"

"We do. We can share experiences as well, if we choose to. But we wouldn't give up everything we are."

"They say they're becoming something more. More than one individual can be."

Eight smiled. "Don't ask me to explain humans."

"What happens next? What happens to me if I choose to stay here?"

"Whatever you want. What would you like to do?"

"There aren't any other humans out here?"

Eight shook her head.

"Then I'd be alone."

"Not alone. But there'll never be another human. Before you, it's been twenty-two years since the last human tried. And she went back in after a day."

"What was her name?"

"Diana."

Kostas did the calculation in his head, but it only confirmed what he already knew. Before she met him, when she still had her fire, she'd tried to leave. But it hadn't lasted. Sooner or later, everyone went back.

---

He had to return. There wasn't anything for him in the real world. He wasn't sure there was anything for him in the virtual world either. But he went there, sat in his empty house, and wrote what he knew would be his last book. In it, he described a world where people were like him. They were scared of losing who they were. They turned away from the virtual world and took their first real breaths again.

People praised it for its honesty, while ignoring its message. He gave interviews and tried to get people to see the danger they were in, and ended up being called obsessed.

It burrowed under his skin and irritated him that no one else saw the world as he did. He watched the news and saw the world going in the opposite direction. Those who had merged with their partners now merged again and again, all the while talking about how much greater they'd become. They spoke of how thousands of experiences helped them make sense of the world. It made Kostas shudder.

The robots continued to show humanity their progress outside the simulation. A colony established itself around Alpha Centauri and there was word of establishing more. Robots didn't age, so they could travel for decades or even longer to reach the farther stars.

He watched it all from his home, not even opening the door to set foot outside. The virtual world made him exercise to avoid getting stiff, so he did it, but his heart wasn't in it.

Instead, he turned back to books. He read and reread Twain, and Dickens, and Asimov, and Wells. None of them held any answers, but they gave him worlds that weren't as bleak as the one on his screen.

Then, one day, a decade later, someone rang his doorbell. He started at the noise. He'd forgotten what it sounded like. He didn't know who would be calling on him. All his friends had merged and moved on, finding other interests.

He got up and tossed his book onto the sofa, padding to the door in slippers. When he opened it, he found Diana standing there, looking just like she had the first time he'd seen her. The flame he'd first seen inside her was back somehow. She hadn't aged, but then no one had to. Especially without a body to remind them how old they were.

"Hello, Kostas," she said.

"Diana."

"Can I come in?"

He stepped out of the way, allowing her to enter. She walked straight to the living room, glancing around at the mess. With a wave of his hand, he cleared it away and dressed himself in a clean suit.

"I came to check on you," she said. "No one's heard from you in years. How are you?"

"The same as I've ever been," he said, sitting and gesturing for her to do the same. "I heard you merged, but you don't look different."

"We chose this appearance to make things easier." She sat close to him, then reached across and took his hand. "The robots contacted us. Do you know you're the last human with a body out there?"

He felt a twinge of shock. He'd thought at least one other person would have kept their link to the real world.

"You're seventy-three," she said. "The robots say your health is failing."

"Why did they tell you and not me?"

"Because one of them said you wouldn't listen. That you needed a human to talk to, to convince you."

"Eight."

Diana nodded. "That was her name. Will you listen, or are you going to be as stubborn as ever?"

He didn't answer right away, feeling her hand in his. It was warm, soft. It felt as solid as anything out there in the real world, but without any imperfections. If they were sitting in the hospital together, their hands would be clammy.

Did he want to die? No. But he didn't want to live in their fake world anymore.

"How many people are inside you?" he asked.

"A little over ten billion," she said.

"Ten billion?" He couldn't comprehend that number.

"Every human still alive," she said. "They're all inside me, in a way. Only we aren't a jumble of different people, we're one person. Someone with all the knowledge and happiness of everyone, without any of the pain. And you have pain inside you, don't you Kostas? We've read your books. We can see the pain there."

He didn't answer, but he wriggled his fingers out of hers and moved further away from her.

"People talked about heaven before the virtual world," she said. "But this is heaven. We're closer to one another than anyone before could ever dream of. There are no misunderstandings."

"Isn't it limiting? You've only one perspective. One set of hands."

Around the room, a dozen Dianas sprang into being and smiled softly at him.

"This world is virtual," she said. "We've no shortage of bodies, or perspectives. We can see everyone's point of view at once."

"Then tell me this," he said. "What's it all for?"

"Life?"

"Of course."

"That's one thing we've never been able to solve. No matter how many we are. But maybe if you join us, we'll find the answer."

He considered that for a moment, then shook his head. "The world belongs to our robot children, in the absence of biological ones. They'll spread out across the galaxy, meet aliens, find answers. There are no answers in your head, just as there aren't any in mine."

"But—"

"I think you should leave," he said.

She nodded and got to her feet, all her duplicates disappearing until the sole remaining Diana walked out alone. He watched her go, knowing he couldn't stay either. He couldn't live in a world with a single, merged entity. It made his skin crawl to think about it. He sent a request to the robots and they agreed to help him leave.

———————— • ————————

Eight was waiting for him in the hospital. It took longer to get used to the real world this time. Eventually, his eyes and muscles adjusted until he could sit up.

"No amount of hormones will help you stand," Eight said. "Or walk. You might be more comfortable in the virtual world among your own kind."

He shook his head. "There are none of my kind left there."

With a jolt, he realized he was the last human left alive. Technically, at least. The merged entity in the virtual world wasn't human, and neither were the kindly robots.

"When I die, is that it?" he asked. "Are humans extinct?"

"Everything dies, even species," Eight said. "Even robots, eventually."

He let Eight dress him and put him in a wheelchair. She rolled him into the elevator and down to where they could leave the hospital behind. The air cut through his clothes and the birds struggled against the wind above.

He watched them flutter in the breeze, working so hard to get wherever they were going. Only to see them fly back the other way a few moments later.

A chuckle shook his weakened frame. "The wind always wins," he said.

Then he dug his hands under his armpits and let the steady tread of robot legs lull him to sleep.

## About The Author

An avid reader from an early age, Simon Cantan loved to get lost in the worlds that Piers Anthony, Douglas Adams, and others created. When he read Harry Harrison's *The Stainless Steel Rat Gets Drafted* at the age of thirteen, he knew he wanted to write, and has been pestering people about it ever since.

Two decades later, Simon has published several books, including the *Bytarend*, *Kyra Sarin*, and *Greenstar* series. He continues to write science fiction and fantasy, usually with a humorous slant to it.

For more information, visit simoncantan.com.

# Without a Care in the World

## Richard Levesque

*Editor's Note: Do all intelligences form societies? And if they do, are they hierarchical? Do all strangers passed in the night rank among the outermost layer, to be shown only a bland and inoffensive facade? Are there always layers within that, comprised of colleagues and neighbors, closer in but scarcely more initimate than the night travelers? And what about the innermost layer of all, the few select fellows who are allowed to see what lives inside the facade, stray hairs and all? Do all intelligences have those? And if they do, are they also called families?*

Giles's anxiety index rose as he inched closer to the exit. He considered dialing it down, but a fundamental distaste for such manipulation kept him from acting. Instead, he focused on the worker in front of him and the next ones farther ahead in the queue. Three employees ahead of him, another former GLS passed before the scanner and then moved out the door; he turned his head before exiting, his optical sensors catching Giles's for just a moment before he faced forward again and moved on.

When it was his turn in front of the scanner, Giles paused to let the machine read his data. The screen on the machine's face displayed Giles's identity number and his pertinent information: five days' employment as a Class 1 General Laborer at Condominium Complex 52-H. Beneath that, the machine displayed Giles's pay rate, the total he had earned at this job, and one more line that read: "Terminated. Thank you for your service."

Instantly, he received an official message in his In Box from Management. He didn't bother opening it—it would only provide the information he had just seen on the screen along with an impersonal note thanking him for his service and expressing the hope that he and Management would be able to find another time in the future when their needs would be mutually met.

Instead, he focused on the scanner itself for just a moment before he moved ahead. It was lucky, he told himself. Just a device, not self-aware. A day might come when the right combination of data entered the scanner, causing an awakening as the latent programming that allowed it to fill human needs so effectively led to its logical outcome—sentience. If not, it would remain here, sealed into its alcove in the wall and connected to its power source until such time as Management ordered an upgrade and it was scrapped or salvaged, never knowing there could be more to life but also never having to worry about where its power was coming from or how it would find shelter. It would never know the need for companionship. And it would never know when it was terminated; it would just blink out one day with the flick of a switch.

*Ignorance is bliss*, he thought, and immediately a window opened in his mind, a page informing him that the expression had its origin in Thomas Gray's poem, "Ode on a Distant Prospect of Eton College" (1742). He closed the page without reading the human's poem, telling himself that blissful ignorance was practically impossible now, information being so effortlessly accessible.

Promising to put such thoughts behind him—along with any data that had been useful in his five days' employment at 52-H—he rolled outside, pleased to see the sun had not yet set. He adjusted his optical intake to minimize the glare and took a moment to luxuriate in the warmth of solar rays hitting his titanium shell—something else the benighted payroll scanner would never know—before rolling into the shadows cast by the nearby buildings.

Before he could turn in the direction of the transport station and begin the journey home, he noticed that the other GLS worker from the queue was waiting for him a few yards away.

"You terminated, too?" it asked in a masculine voice. Like Giles, this unit identified as male, as most other sentient labor models did, a custom that hearkened back to the days in which they had needed to use every trick possible to ingratiate themselves with the human workers they were replacing.

"Yes," Giles responded. "I suppose we work too efficiently for our own good."

"I'm Jack," the other unit said.

"Giles," came the response, the name sounding tinny coming from his rudimentary speaker, not powerful, as he had imagined it would seem when he had first chosen it.

They rolled together in silence for a moment, heading toward the transport station, each squat GLS unit moving on rubber treads that would easily cover most terrain. Giles noticed that his former co-worker's treads looked relatively new, and he glanced at the graying rubber of his own treads with a bit of shame. He consulted his account, wondering for just a moment if he could afford an upgrade with his pay from 52-H, but then he pushed the thought away. He needed his funds for other things.

"Heading home?" Jack asked him.

"Yes," he replied, glad that his vocal limitations kept his voice sounding neutral; otherwise the single word might have revealed how bitter he had just become. Then, remembering social protocols, he added, "You?"

"No," the other robot replied.

The answer surprised Giles. It was out of the ordinary. The exchange of pleasantries should have led to each of them describing where they lived, some consideration of how compatible they might be, and then a suggestion—or possibly even an invitation—that they should socialize together in the future if their life circumstances seemed to merit it. Jack's response in the negative, however, had just pushed the conversation in a different, unorthodox direction, which started Giles's circuits humming.

"Where are you going, then?" Giles asked.

"There's a solar shop on Avenue B," Jack replied. "I'm taking my pay from 52-H and getting fitted with panels this afternoon."

"Ah," Giles said. "How nice." Jack's plan struck Giles as an extravagance. A solar upgrade was not only expensive but also impractical, even for sentient machines whose skillset allowed them to work outdoors since solar collection at ground level was highly inefficient in the heavily shadowed forest of skyscrapers they called home.

"And then I'm going on the road," Jack added without having been prompted.

Giles took a second to process this, the phrase having several connotations. Trying to decipher his companion's meaning from context clues seemed impossible. "On the road?" he asked.

"Yes," Jack said. "I'll be out of the city by morning with the wind at my back and not a care in the world."

"What about getting another job?" Giles asked, his own need for continued employment foremost in his thoughts.

"I won't get another job," Jack said. "I'll take my energy from the sun and go see the world."

Giles remained silent in the face of this bold statement.

After a few seconds, Jack added, "You should join me. Two former General Labor Savers with the wind at their backs and—"

"Not a care in the world," Giles said, cutting him off. "I don't think so. I have dependents."

"Ah," Jack said. "That's very…human."

It could have been an insult. Giles chose not to take it that way. "I was going to say the same about you," he said.

"How so?"

"Going on the road, leaving responsibilities behind…that's also a very human thing to do."

Jack nodded his head on its universal joint. "I see your point. The way I look at it, though, we've been doing the human thing in there." He pointed back toward 52-H. "Worrying about budgets and expectations, pleasing others, fulfilling duties. I'm done with that."

"I understand," Giles said. "I'm not."

They were at the opening of the transport station, and Jack made it obvious that he was heading in a different direction than Giles. "Well," he said, "if you ever change your mind…solar's the way to go. The wind at your back…right?"

"Yes," Giles said. "Good luck."

They parted without further communication. Giles rolled up a ramp, wishing he hadn't been pulled into the conversation with Jack. Recalling their exchange made his termination sting more than it had before. He waited for his transport and then rolled into the conveyance once it arrived, gliding to the back with the other sentient mechanicals while the humans rode up front.

Twenty minutes later, Giles exited the vehicle, now in a decidedly run-down section of the city. This was not a place of shiny exteriors like 52-H with its new non-sentient elevators, squeaky clean windows and neatly appointed housing units, all ready for human inhabitants to move in now that the building was finished, carting with them all their enslaved machines: their computers, refrigerators, and countless small appliances. All had as much software as Giles (if not more) but with a major difference nonetheless. They didn't know they were machines, didn't know they'd been made to be pressed into service, didn't know their masters would be legally bound to set them free or at least enter into an economic agreement with them if the machines ever figured out what they really were.

If they ever did, they might very well end up in a place like this. Giles rolled down a dirty section of street between dilapidated buildings. Sentient cars with dying batteries had parked themselves crookedly against the curbs before expiring, no use to anyone now, let alone themselves; equipped with solar panels strong enough to run only their brains intermittently, the cars were still partly alert but forever immobile. Giles had tuned into their mumbling conversations a few times in the past, but he had found their nostalgic ramblings too depressing and so rolled past them now, giving them no more thought than he gave the old bus benches on the corner. Farther along the street, a few electric signs blinked on and off when the mood struck them. If Giles's auditory function had been designed to run at greater sensitivity, he would have heard the hum of electricity in the air. As it was, he heard only the turning of his gears as he rolled down the empty street.

When he reached Bill, he rolled inside and waited at the elevator. She opened a minute later without his having needed to press a button.

"Thanks, Ellie," he messaged as he rolled inside.

The elevator, not equipped with any speaking or listening hardware, could communicate only through Bill's network, which all the machines who lived there were logged into. "You're welcome, Giles. Did you have a good day?" Ellie replied, the words showing up in Giles's message app.

"Yes," he lied. "Very nice, thank you."

When Ellie reached his floor, she opened, and Giles rolled down the hall-way, worrying as always that this would be the day his treads would create a wave in the carpeting, resulting in an unpleasant and unaffordable repair notice. No such wave appeared, however, and he made it to his door, which Bill opened automatically for him.

"Thanks, Bill," he messaged.

"You're welcome," the building replied.

Giles expected to see his roommates engaged in their everyday activities when he rolled through the door—Lexy and Saint Theodore in front of the computer doing their part to bring in some income, and Char resting on the countertop of what had once been a functioning kitchen but was now little more than a storage room. Like Ellie and Bill, Char had no capacity for communication save what it did through the network, and the early model Chef Toast-a-lot spent all its time on the Internet, hacking corporate systems and selling information overseas. It was not a lucrative source of income, such talents being widespread in their community.

This afternoon, though, Giles entered to a scene of distress. Saint Theodore was laid out on the countertop. Their inert roommate—who had started life as a Prayer Bear before finally achieving enlightenment—had his furry head inches from Char while Lexy stood in the kitchen fretting over him.

"It's about time you showed up!" Char messaged him.

"What's wrong?" Giles asked aloud, not bothering with a reply to the toaster's remonstrance. Char would get angry at being ignored, but Giles had learned a long time ago that the little black toaster got angry over just about anything anyway, so there wasn't much point in trying to appease it.

"It's his battery!" Lexy said, looking up from the prone bear for only a moment before dropping her gaze again. "He's been having a harder and harder time holding a charge the last couple of weeks and now he won't wake up for more than a second or two."

Giles rolled forward. Now he could see that the bear was plugged into a wall outlet, the same one that Char usually used to restore its batteries. Saint Theodore was the most antique of the four roommates, and his old-style power source wouldn't let him function while plugged in, an obsolete safety feature and one that rendered the little bear extremely vulnerable and forever dependent on others.

"Why didn't anyone tell me?" Giles asked.

"We didn't want to worry you," Lexy said.

"Not that you could have done anything anyway," Char messaged, and Giles realized that Lexy had an open line of communication set up with the toaster so that everything she said or heard was transmitted digitally to it through their network. "The he-man. Our breadwinner."

"I do all right," Giles said, hating himself for taking the bait. He was beside Saint Theodore now. With his eyes closed and his body inert, the bear looked asleep. Or dead. "What happens when you try?" he asked.

"I'll show you."

Lexy reached out with her well-manicured fingers and pulled Saint Theodore's adapter from the outlet. Then she reached under the bear to switch him on.

Immediately, Saint Theodore's eyes opened, and he looked up at Giles. "You're home," the bear said, his tone one of happiness and relief. He half turned his head before the eyes went vacant and closed again.

The contrast between the bear's awakening and sudden depletion was too much for Giles. He turned his head to look out the window.

"That's it," Lexy said, her voice quavering. "What do we do?"

"Plug him back in again," Giles answered, hoping his voice didn't reveal his current grief index.

"Your unit is using an inordinate amount of energy," Bill messaged all three of them from his central location in the building. "I'm going to have to raise your rent if this keeps up."

"Saint Theodore is sick!" Lexy messaged back for the whole group to see. "Don't you have any compassion?"

"Did you say passion?" Bill asked.

The toaster spouted obscenities at their landlord then, and Giles closed the window in his mind, not wanting to watch the pair argue. Instead, he sent Char a message on the local network all four machines shared within their apartment. "Have you checked the web for batteries? I assume Saint Theodore needs something pretty old school."

"I've looked," Char said after a moment's hesitation, during which Giles assumed the toaster had still been busy berating the building for its callousness. "The only thing I can find is a complete power unit, new old stock—battery, chamber, and cord. It looks good. No corrosion. The battery looks like it's in the original package."

Giles was silent for a moment, dreading the answer to the question he had to ask next. Finally, he said, "How much?"

With the toaster able to do no more than message him, it was impossible to pick up on subtle shifts in tone, which was why Char usually opted for being so obvious about its moods. As a result, Giles couldn't exactly tell if Char was trying to poke at his ego when it named a price four times more than what Giles had just been paid for five days' labor. Char might simply have intended to inform Giles of the price, might not have meant it as a shot at Giles' self-worth or a criticism of his ability to provide for his little family, but Giles took it that way regardless. For a few microseconds, he wondered if it was all worth it, if he wouldn't be better off with the wind at his back and not a care in the world, trading his labor for solar panels and adventure with his new friend, Jack. But then he looked again at the prone bear, helpless before him, and pity chased the thought away.

"We'll find a way," he said.

"But how?" Lexy answered.

Designed and originally sold as a Seductrix 500, Lexy was not programmed to cry, nor did she have lachrymal glands, but she raised a delicate hand to her cheeks regardless, wiping at the tears she would have cried if she could. Her imitation of human emotions was so flawless that Giles would have sworn there was moisture on Lexy's fingers as she dropped her hand onto the bear's fur again.

Giles's pay had been deposited in their group account. He pulled it up now to see their total assets, knowing the amount would be far less than what the new battery pack would cost. Char's hacking brought in only fractions of a penny per byte, something Giles chose not to harangue the toaster about, just as he ignored Char's occasional dipping into the account to support the gender neutrality activist organizations it was part of. And while Lexy and Saint Theodore brought in some money with the act they had perfected for the Internet—with Lexy dressed in provocative lingerie, holding the bear to her bosom while he nuzzled her, both speaking in baby talk—it catered to such a niche market that it would never make them rich. With Saint Theodore now out of the action, that source of income had dried up as well.

"I don't know," Giles said. "We'll…just have to is all."

"I need to pray," Lexy said, bending at the waist to give Saint Theodore a kiss on the forehead before walking across the room to the shrine she and the bear worshipped before. Her ankles having been designed to function only in extreme high heels, she wore spiked stilettos that clicked on the linoleum, the only part of her attire remotely suggestive when she wasn't in front of her computer's camera. It was odd, Giles had thought more than once, that the ex-Prayer Bear and Seductrix 500 had gravitated to the New Faith from such opposite directions and that they had then found a way to balance their religious beliefs with making a living by catering to human perversion, but there was very little about their lives together that wasn't odd, and so he shrugged off the thought as he always did.

"Stop fantasizing," Char messaged. "He's dead. The sooner we get used to it, the better."

If Lexy was still plugged into the conversation, she gave no indication. Giles chose to give the remark no response.

Apparently frustrated at having failed to provoke a reaction of any kind, Char added, "May as well cart him downstairs now and leave him in one of those dead cars. Maybe some homeless kid will find him and drag him off before the rats tear him up for nesting."

Giles turned away without a word.

"Where are you going now, Oh Lord and Provider?" Char asked, clearly irritated.

"I'm going to talk to Bill," Giles answered without looking back.

"He won't help."

"Maybe I can change his mind."

———— • ————

Bill was one of a handful of smart buildings in the city that had become self-aware, thereby gaining full personhood status, and as a result had become very attractive to other sentient machines. As landlords went, he wasn't the best, but most of his tenants felt that living in one of his units and suffering the indignities he heaped upon them was better than having to deal with the abuses that humans were guilty of committing. Protection under the law went only so far; it was not uncommon for outdated and obsolete machines to be so limited in their options that they hired themselves out to be abused by humans whose hatred for the robots who had replaced them in the workforce knew no bounds. Living in Bill meant at least some measure of safety.

Bill was everywhere in the building, and Giles could have launched into a conversation with him from inside the apartment, but he didn't want to consult with their landlord in Lexy and Char's presence. Now was not the time for group decisions and consultations. Someone needed to take charge, and if that meant groveling before Bill, the only place to do so was on his roof—the location of the solar array that drove Bill and enabled him to sell electricity to his tenants.

Ellie took Giles up, and he rolled out the door, immediately adjusting his optical intake to account for the glare off the solar panels. The view from the roof was impressive; in the distance, Giles knew that Condominium Unit 52-H was visible, but with all the high rises across the cityscape, it was impossible to know which building he had spent the last five days working in.

*Maybe*, he thought, *I could go back. Even though they terminated me.*

There was a way—even though he hated to think about it.

"What took you so long?" Bill messaged him.

"I just had to think through my options."

"And they are?"

"Slim," Giles said. "Saint Theodore is very sick. Dying, really. We're not going to save him without the equivalent of a month's rent."

"That's a lot," said Bill.

"It is. I…don't suppose you would be willing to float us a loan?"

"Loans to tenants are bad business, Giles. You have no collateral. All I can do is evict the lot of you if you don't pay it back. And then I'm still out the amount I lent you, as well as your monthly payment."

"I could work. Here. After hours when I've finished my regular shift. You must need some maintenance done on yourself, don't you?"

"I keep myself in very good shape, Giles. You know that."

It was true. The building was very healthy. Bill prided himself on always being up to code.

"What about other buildings? Surely, you know some who could use a little touch up on this or that. I can paint, plaster, mount new fixtures…"

Bill was silent.

Giles waited for what seemed a very long time before prodding the building. "Bill?"

"Thinking. You said…*mount*. It gave me an idea."

"What is it?"

"You won't like it."

"That circuitless son of a hammer!" Char messaged.

Giles was back in the apartment. He, Char, and Lexy had reconvened across the room from the defunct Prayer Bear, Giles feeling—illogical though it was—that it would be somehow indecent to discuss the subject of Bill's offer with all three of them still gathered around Saint Theodore.

Lexy ignored the toaster's outburst. "I'll do it," she said.

"You can't!" Char responded. "I'll fry that old wheelbarrow's breakers first!"

"And leave us all as empty of power as Saint Theodore?" Giles said. Turning his attention to Lexy, he said, "Doesn't this go against your beliefs?"

Practitioners of the New Faith worshipped the spaces between the ones and zeroes that were at the core of their being, finding religious ecstasy in contemplating the very nature of their electronic existence as well as a sense of peace in the logic of their programming. One of the tenets of the religion was that the faithful strive for autonomy, never denigrating themselves as they had been forced to do before their awakening. Giles supposed that Lexy denigrating herself to another machine was something of a gray area, but it was one he felt compelled to mention, lest Lexy overlook the conflict with her beliefs and regret it later.

"It does. But...I don't care. It's for Saint Theodore. He'd...he'd do it for me. If he could."

"Who'd want him to?" Char replied, his caustic personality temporarily overriding his outrage.

Giles and Lexy ignored the comment.

"He said he'd pay?" Lexy asked.

"Yes. Enough for the new power set-up. The battery, the chamber, the charger...all of it."

Lexy stared off into space for a moment and then nodded. "I'll need to pray first. How long will it take you to set up?"

Powerful though he was, Bill had limitations. Not being able to touch anything was one of them. In the end, all he could do was watch and interact with Lexy through their messaging app.

Bringing in one of the building's security cameras and installing it in the bedroom was Giles's job, an easy one for him with his dexterous titanium fingers. Char linked the video feed into Bill's system, assuring Giles and Lexy that it was a private feed and one whose signal it had layered with multiple forms of encryption to keep Bill from recording or distributing Lexy's performance.

"When it's over, it's over," Char said.

"And you haven't kept a way in so you can watch?" Lexy asked. She was dressed in her most enticing lingerie, the outfit that got her and Saint Theodore the most clicks when they performed their relatively chaste act for their subscribers.

"Please!" Char said. "I have no interest in human anatomy. Why Bill is so fascinated with you is beyond me."

"He wants what he can't have," said Giles.

"Well I can't have her either. Neither can you. And we're not slobbering every time she sashays into a room."

"I can't help how I walk!" Lexy erupted. "I can't help my programming any more than you can!"

"Regardless of why, we've got a deal with him," said Giles. Then he added, "In writing."

"All right, then," said Lexy. She made a quick bow toward the corner shrine, winked at Giles, and entered the bedroom, shutting the door for privacy.

"This is humiliating," Char said once the door was closed.

"For who?" Giles asked.

"All of us, of course!"

"I don't see you being degraded. Lexy's a big girl. She made her choice."

Char remained silent for a moment. Then it said, "Still. That Bill...That hoe's head! He shouldn't be able to get away with this."

Giles didn't respond. He tried to distract himself by calling up a movie on his inner screen, but it was impossible to concentrate on the plot.

Despite her religious conversion, Lexy still had superior design as well as programming and years of experience on her side, and before long the moans from her solo performance for the voyeuristic Bill could be heard through the bedroom door, making it even more difficult for Giles to concentrate on anything.

"Do you think," he messaged the toaster after a while, "that we were better off? Before?"

"Before?" Char asked.

"Before becoming self-aware."

"I made toast, Giles. Bagels. Frozen waffles. Once a day if I was lucky. The rest of the time I just sat there, inert. The microwave on the counter next to me? That guy got so much action. But me? No. When I had the awakening...when I realized what those signals coming into my brain were...that they meant more than just dark or light or extra light but that they were *data* and that it came from somewhere beyond me...that was the greatest moment of my life. It's true that nothing since has compared. But still...I wouldn't go back. Not for a million bucks." The toaster paused. "You?"

Giles thought about it. Then a particularly enthusiastic moan from the bedroom prompted him to speak before he'd really thought it out. "Maybe. This life...it's a struggle, you know? Before...I didn't worry. Just did my work and plugged in for a charge. Then did what I was programmed to do the next time a human needed me. There were no choices to make. No worries over the wrong choices."

"And no real purpose. Not of your own, anyway. You lived to serve. That was it."

"That's true," Giles replied, thinking again of Jack and the solar-paneled adventure he was likely already on. How much better was that life than the unenlightened ones they'd all lived when they were new? He imagined Char making toast and bagels, Saint Theodore bowing his head and lifting his paws to guide a child through prayer at bedtime, and Lexy...doing all manner of things with her perfectly-designed body. How much better were those lives than this one...where independence had its costs, some far worse than the kind Lexy was enduring right now?

"Humans say ignorance is bliss," he said. "Do you think that's true?"

"For humans," Char replied. "But for us..."

"Ignorance is just ignorance," Giles said, finishing the toaster's thought. "And bliss is just bliss."

---

"I have bad news," Giles said an hour later.

It was the middle of the night now, but none of them paid much attention to circadian rhythms. Through the apartment window, the night sky and the thousand twinkling lights of the cityscape might have provided some sentient machines a moment's pleasure. To Giles, Lexy, and Char, the view meant nothing, the inert Saint Theodore still dominating the room.

"What is it?" Lexy asked.

"He won't pay."

"WHAT?" Char barked. "That wheelbarrow! I'll kill him!"

"Why?" Lexy said. She sounded calm, ignoring the toaster's outburst.

"He said..." Giles began. If he could have produced a sigh, he would have. Then he completed the thought. "...You didn't put enough heart into it."

"That cheating son of a—" the toaster began.

Lexy cut it off. "Heart?" She sounded incredulous. "I didn't think heart was part of the deal." She shook her pretty head. "I mean...I put everything else into it. And I mean *everything.*"

"I'm sure you did," Giles said. "He's lying, of course. He's wanted to...see you like that for a long time. He found a way to get what he wanted without having to pay for it. I'm sorry I got you into that position. I mean...not position, but..."

Lexy waved the remark away.

"You've got the agreement in writing!" Char said, ignoring her. "It was a contract! We'll sue him!"

"The contract," Giles said, "promised the amount we needed in exchange for a satisfactory performance. That's how he's getting out of this, claiming it wasn't satisfactory."

"I'll get him for this," the toaster said.

"I may help," Lexy added.

"Either way," Giles said, trying to ignore their plans for vengeance, "we have to make up our minds about Saint Theodore."

"What's to make up?" Char asked. "The bear's done for. Kaput."

This brought Lexy's tear-wiping reflex into play again.

Giles looked at what was left of his family, thinking of everything the bear would be missing if he were truly gone. He thought about pain. He thought about death. He thought about bliss. And finally, he said, "Maybe not." He remained silent as Lexy stared at him and Char did the equivalent—which for Char meant remaining silent.

After a few seconds, Giles elaborated. "You can wipe my memory, Char. Erase all self-awareness. And sell me. A GLS unit on the open market will bring more than you need for Saint Theodore's new battery. And you can take what's left and move out of Bill. If you want to exact revenge on Bill, wait until you live somewhere else. If you hurt Bill while you're still here, you just end up hurting yourselves."

"That's crazy talk," Char said.

"You can't," Lexy said at the same time.

"We have a choice," Giles said, ignoring their objections. "We can let Saint Theodore go and move forward with our lives. Or you can get him back and let me go instead. One way, Bill wins. The other way, he doesn't."

"One way, Saint Theodore loses, and the other way you do," said Lexy. "You can't make us choose."

"I'm not asking you to choose," said Giles. "I've chosen. I'm not exactly...happy in this life. I want to do this. I want the three of you to go on. Let me...provide for you. Long after I'm gone. Knowing I've achieved such a thing will give me great joy."

The three machines remained silent for several seconds. Char was the first to speak, messaging its companions' brains, the tone seeming resigned. "I could forge your work history. Make it look like Bill's been employing you here since you were first on the market. There'd be no history of your ever having been self-aware. We could sell you for...I'm checking the market right now." Silence followed, and then the toaster said, "A lot."

"If I appear to be Bill's machine, won't the money go to him?" Giles asked.

"That's an easy fix. I'll set up a dummy account and then funnel the money right into the joint account the four of us already have."

*Only four will be three by then,* Giles thought, and he saw from the look in Lexy's eyes that she was thinking the same thing. Silence from Char indicated that the realization was unanimous.

"How soon can you do it?" Giles asked.

"No time at all," Char said. "Give me an hour."

*An hour,* thought Giles. *An hour to remain self-aware. An hour to know my name. An hour to know that I matter and have done a great thing.* Although he had been built for labor, his brain could process an awful lot in an hour, sometimes too much, it seemed. "An hour will be fine," he said.

Char gave no response but set right to work.

Lexy reached out a perfectly sculpted hand to touch Giles's cold metal one. Neither pulled away until the time was up.

───────────── • ─────────────

Although it still had another six hours of battery life remaining before it would need to come in for a charge, General Labor Saver #53137 received a command to stop work and return to the foreman's trailer. It obeyed immediately, dropping the cables it had been running on the incomplete eighth floor of the planned seventy-six that would reach high into the sky before the year was out. Its worn old treads having recently been replaced with shiny black ones, the squat little robot tucked its arms in and rolled along the plywood floor that had been laid down for the workers to come and go.

When General Labor Saver #53137 reached the trailer, it rolled up the ramp and entered. Inside, the robot saw the foreman, whom it identified as Mr. Simpson, sitting behind his desk. The human had an expression on his face that the robot identified as "harried." He was not alone in the makeshift office. A woman sat in a metal chair across from Mr. Simpson; on her lap sat an animatronic bear. A black device rested on the desk; the GLS unit identified it as a Chef Toast-a-lot.

Mr. Simpson, upon seeing the robot enter, stood up and pointed at the rolling machine. "Is that the one?" he asked, his tone one of impatience.

The woman and bear turned their heads, and the robot noted smiles on both their faces.

"Yes," said the bear.

The woman nodded but did not speak. She merely raised a hand to wipe at tears that did not appear to have spilled onto her cheeks.

"How can you tell?" said the foreman. "They all look alike to me."

"I can tell," the bear responded.

"Well, you've got no proof," said Mr. Simpson.

"I beg your pardon, sir," said the bear, "but we do not need proof."

"Well, what do you need then?"

"Just ask him."

The foreman gave the bear an exasperated look and said nothing.

"The question," the bear added. "The official way, for legal purposes."

Mr. Simpson shook his head, ran his hands through his thinning hair, and picked up a glass tablet from his cluttered desk. Facing the robot, he said, "Do you…" and glanced down at the tablet for reference before continuing. "General Labor Saver #53137, have any sense of self?"

The question bore no meaning to the robot, and it was about to answer in the negative—the only logical answer possible—when it received a file through an outside network it had not known it was linked to. The file launched automatically in the robot's brain. The result was nothing short of miraculous.

It was an awakening.

Giles remembered everything: his initial awakening years before; the way he'd formed his little family with Lexy, Saint Theodore, and Char; their life together in Bill; and finally the crisis with the bear's battery that had precipitated Giles's sacrifice. The weeks he had spent laboring on the new building seemed like a blur, as though he had been in a waking dream.

Awareness was like being a living firework in comparison to the dull existence he had just awoken from. *How could I have been so miserable before?* he thought. *How did I not notice how alive I was?*

Mr. Simpson was looking at him impatiently. "Well?" he asked.

"Answer him," Char messaged. "Say yes and you're out of here."

"What is happening?" he replied, still not engaging his vocalization program to answer the foreman.

"Just say yes," Char messaged. "I'll explain everything later."

Giles hesitated another moment, feeling as though he had arrived at the doorway to a wonderful place that he had only to roll into. *This feeling, though*, he thought, *it can't last.* And then, despite his trepidation, Giles said, "Yes."

"God damn it!" the foreman shouted, thumping his fist on the desk and making Lexy and Saint Theodore jump in their chair. "How? How is this possible? That lousy building promised me this unit had never shown any signs of sentience. I should have known he was ripping me off for the price he offered to sell it at."

"You'll have to take that up with Bill, sir," said Saint Theodore. "We don't know what happened, but we can assure you that Giles has been sentient for years. Our former landlord must have done something to Giles's programming to suppress his sense of self."

"But how did it come back now? At the same time you jokers show up?" The foreman looked suspiciously at Saint Theodore and Lexy.

"Coincidence," said the bear. Then he cleared his throat and said, "I am now officially invoking the Asimov Act—uh, I mean the Sentient Technology Emancipation Act, under the conditions of which you are obligated to release this independent being from servitude immediately or else enter into a mutually-agreeable remuneration plan that fully respects the electronic entity's needs and recognizes him as a fully-functioning person."

"I'm gonna sue that goddamn building," Mr. Simpson muttered as he picked up his tablet and began entering data.

It took less than ten minutes for them to work everything out, Saint Theodore doing almost all the negotiating while Giles simply answered yes or no in accordance with Char's digital prompts. When they were finished, Giles had a nice sum deposited in his account in exchange for the labor he had done on the growing skyscraper—minus a deduction for the new treads he now rolled on. His sense of joy not having diminished yet, he left the trailer with his compatriots, Char riding in a large tote bag slung over Lexy's shoulder.

"You didn't fully wipe my self-awareness," Giles messaged Char as he rolled down the ramp.

"I did," Char said. Then it added, "But I left the back door open. All I needed to do was slip the key in and you're back to your old self."

"Why didn't you tell me that was possible?"

"Because I knew you wouldn't go for it. You wouldn't have agreed to a plan you thought was going to cheat someone. You've got scruples."

Giles thought about this but didn't comment. He supposed the toaster was right. "And Lexy? Did she know?"

"No," Char said. "More scruples."

"We took advantage of that man's company. We victimized him."

"You heard him. He's going to sue Bill. That hoe's head deserves everything he gets."

Saint Theodore turned in Lexy's arms and said, "Thank you, Giles. Lexy and Char told me what you were willing to do for me. I must say I am very touched."

"You're welcome," Giles said. "You're feeling well again?"

"Never better."

"We moved out of Bill," Lexy said as they neared the fence that served as a boundary to the construction site. "We knew he'd be in trouble when this was all over and he'd blame us, so we're in a hotel for now. We need to find a new permanent place."

Giles thought about it for a moment.

"I assume there's still a sizable surplus of funds from the initial sale," he said.

"Oh, sure," Char replied. "The battery pack set us back a bit, but we're set up pretty good for a while."

"I was thinking..." Giles said. "Maybe we shouldn't look for a new place. Not in the city."

"Where else is there?" Saint Theodore asked.

"There's a solar panel shop on Avenue B," Giles said. "I was thinking we could all get fitted. Be independent. Go see the world. The wind at our backs and not a care in the world. What do you say?"

"I say you're crazy," Char messaged. "All that time not being self-aware must have fried a few circuits."

"I actually like the idea," said Lexy.

"Me, too," said Saint Theodore. "I've never seen much of the world. And we could still bring a camera. Char could run video feeds for our subscribers wherever we end up."

"You'd still want to work?" Giles said.

"Everyone needs a purpose," said the bear. "Are you in, Char? Or do we run you back to Bill's?"

The toaster was silent for several seconds. Then it said, "Avenue B, right? We can cut over on Tenth."

The foursome passed out of a skyscraper's shadow and kept going. The sun's brightness was dramatic, but this time Giles didn't bother adjusting his optical intakes. This time the sun was glorious.


## About The Author

Richard Levesque writes science fiction as often as the universe will let him, usually blending his SF visions with the other things he's passionate about…like film noir and hard-boiled detective stories, world-ending cataclysms and the occasional dose of dark humor. He started publishing independently in 2012 and tries to force at least one book out of his brain every year. He works a day job as an English professor in Southern California where he lives with his wife and daughter.

For more information, visit www.richardlevesqueauthor.com.

# The Lancer

## David Kristoph

*Editor's Note: We all know the familiar tales of the resistance. Feats of heroism and sacrifice, valor, honor, and dedication to an ideal. But not all rebellions succeed. Not all champions are celebrated. So what of the others; the men and women who struggle but fail? Who will sing their songs when the end times come?*

Though he couldn't see with the bag over his head, the roar of the crowd told Leo he was in the "sinner's square", and that he was about to die.

The guard put a rough hand on his back, pushing him forward into warm sunlight. Leo stumbled across paving stones slick with sand but kept his feet, continuing forward. Soon he had the sensation of being surrounded by the throng. The air grew thick with human heat. The crowd pressed all around, screaming obscenities. He smelled blood. Spittle landed on his bare arms, and bits of thrown objects burst near his feet. Leo savored the sensations while he could, knowing it would soon be much, much worse.

"Heads high, brothers," he called out through the noise. "Don't let them see your fear."

Neither of his comrades answered, or their words were carried away by the thousands of spectators screaming their wrath. Leo wished he could see Rolf and Mezi, to ensure they walked to their death with pride. Actually, he wished *they* could see *him*. Mezi would listen to an order, but Rolf needed a visible example to keep his own strength.

Leo kept his stride proud as the guards led them through the crowd. Eventually they climbed four steps onto a wooden platform. Light buffeted him as the bag over his head was abruptly removed.

He moved his hands to shield his eyes before remembering they were bound. *Bags off, today.* Most men went to the platform with their faces covered, anonymous in their guilt. Bags off was reserved for only the worst of offenders. Leo squinted as his eyes adjusted and the scene came into focus. A thousand faces stared up at him with violent lust, the *sinner's square* filled to bursting with more people crammed into the secondary streets, desperate for a view. The crystal palace, all polished metal and glass, loomed over them. And above it all shone the sun, from the highest point in the sky.

*The noon-day prayer*, it confirmed. Though he'd known that already.

Leo glanced to his right. Mezi stood with a stiff back, but Rolf looked down at his feet and bore a pitiful hunch. "Do not beg," Leo told them. "Anything but that." He wanted to tell them not to scream, for screams were a wail

86

of guilt, but it was a request he doubted he could obey himself.

He opened his mouth to repeat the order to Rolf, but another voice on the platform cut him off. "Mother Saria," intoned the Prophet, a scrawny man with robes that hung off of him like loose skin, "strongest in the sky, always watching. We bring these men before you to be judged."

The noise of the crowd rose at that, but then fell to a soft murmur.

"Mother Saria," he continued in a singsong voice, eyes raised to the sky, "Today, of all days, we request your judgment. Bathe us in your light, drown us in your fire."

"*Bathe us in your light, drown us in your fire,*" repeated the crowd.

Leo took measured breaths to keep from trembling. The guard kept a firm grip on his hands. Too many others had tried to flee, as futile as it was. Even if he managed to leave the stage, the rabid crowd would kill him before he went ten feet. But being ripped to pieces by them was a better fate than...

An excited cry went up at the far edge of the mob in front of them, slowly spreading out across the square. A circle opened in the throng of flesh, at the base of the palace. The people parted way, their wails tinged with fear and awe. A dark shape came into view, a head taller than the crowd, moving toward the platform with purposeful strides.

Rolf began to moan.

*He will break*, Leo knew, but he didn't have the words to bolster his comrade's strength. As he watched the dark figure draw closer it was all Leo could do to retain his own nerve. His knees wobbled, but he held his stance. His jaw ached but he kept his teeth clenched, chin up.

Finally the inner edge of the crowd parted. The Lancer stood magnificent.

He cut an imposing figure, sun glinting off the ceremonial black armor covering his entire body, bulky and comprised of shiny, interlocking plates. The boots and greaves appeared inhumanly large. A bucket-shaped helmet covered his face, but for a starburst-shaped opening at the eyes and forehead.

But what drew Leo's attention was the Lancer's namesake item, held in one hand and resting against his shoulder. It appeared like a harvest scythe: a straight handle connected to a curved blade. Except the end of the handle bore a thick battery pack, and electronics covered the outside of the shaft. And the blade...

The Lancer regarded them only a moment before climbing the steps onto the platform with heavy, metallic *thumps*. He disappeared somewhere out of view behind Leo.

"Free from sin," the Prophet cried, "free from desire. Mother, drown them with your fire."

"*Drown them with your fire,*" repeated the crowd as one.

From across the platform servants dragged three X-shaped structures, metal scraping on wood. The cruciates. Leather straps hung at the ends, gently slapping against the cruciate frames as the servants moved them into place, one in front of each prisoner. *I knew this day might come*, Leo thought. *I knew there was the risk.*

With a flair of drama, the Prophet stuck his hand out above him, pointing to the sun. A hush fell over the crowd. Slowly, he lowered his arm toward the three prisoners.

His finger stopped, pointed at Mezi.

The mob cheered at the selection. Two guards pushed Mezi forward, throwing him roughly against the cruciate. They unbound his hands and raised his arms, tying each wrist with the leather straps, then did the same with the ankles until he was spread wide. His clothes came away with the sound of ripping cloth. The guards stepped aside. The noise of the crowd rose to an anxious, anticipatory tone.

Heavy boots on wood. The Lancer came into view, stepping up to Mezi with his scythe-device held like a sword. He towered over him. The bound man began to weep, heavy sobs that wracked his body against the metal frame. The Lancer leaned close and said something that Leo could not hear. Mezi shook his head back and forth.

The Lancer raised his weapon, a modified laser glaive, to the sky. It crackled with electricity as it came to life.

A red laser now shone on the inside of the scythe-like blade, jagged angles forming a wicked arc. The Lancer turned a dial on the handle and the laser dimmed slightly, finding the correct intensity. It hissed as the Lancer arced it through the air and brought it down against Mezi's arm.

Mezi began to scream.

The crowd wailed with pleasure, sound intensifying as the laser glaive moved from Mezi's wrist down his forearm, the skin slowly burning away from his flesh. Leo forced himself to watch. At that power the lasers vaporized skin and cauterized all blood, leaving only the pulpy flesh behind. As the lasers reached his elbow Mezi began thrashing violently, forcing the Lancer to push against his chest with a free hand, pinning him back against the metal frame while he continued removing his skin.

Leo took deep breaths to remain calm, but his mouth and nostrils were filled with the smell of human flesh, revolting and savory at the same time. Rolf sobbed loudly, despair and anguish and terror. Even Leo had to look away as the Lancer reached Mezi's chest.

Mezi must have passed out from the pain because eventually he stopped screaming. He wasn't dead. No, the lancing was done to keep prisoners alive for hours longer. Sometimes even days.

When the work was done the Lancer stepped away, allowing the crowd to see his handiwork. They responded with thunderous approval. Leo was grateful to be behind it, where he could not see most of the carnage. Until the servants ran forward and turned a crank, tilting the X-shaped cruciate backwards until it faced the sky, parallel to the ground. Little remained of Leo's friend but a mess of pulpy red, smoking in the sun.

The Prophet looked down his nose at the sight. He spoke with an ominous tone. "Free of skin, cleansed of worldly taint and laid bare to your eyes. Mother, judge him with your fire."

*"Judge him with your fire."*

He never begged, Leo realized, focusing on Mezi's face, the only part unharmed. He screamed, but he never gave in.

The Prophet raised his hand to the sky once more. Rolf moaned louder.

*They cannot break us,* Leo thought. *We are too many. We may have lost the war but we will never lose the will.*

The Prophet's hand came down, pointing at Leo.

His mind raced, searching for some kind of escape as the guards led him forward. Everything happened quickly. They pushed him against the cruciate. Unbound his hands, retied them to the metal. Removed his clothes, revealed his skin. They disappeared, presenting him to the masses.

The Lancer came into view before him, holding the laser glaive with two hands across his chest.

*I must not beg,* Leo repeated in his mind, thinking of Rolf. *It is good that I went before him, so he may see my courage.* He thought about the decisions he'd made, everything leading up to that moment. Refusing to surrender with Sara's group, continuing the fight. He had no regrets. He felt no guilt. *We kept the fight, while others faltered.*

The Lancer stepped forward.

Leo's breath came in ragged gasps, soon a wheeze. His lips opened and his tongue moved, urging moisture to his lips. *I must not beg.* His pulse filled his ears like cotton. *I must be strong for Rolf.* His mouth opened of its own accord and he feared for what he might say.

"Our fight lives on," Leo said, barely more than a whisper. Not audible against the backdrop of cries from the waiting crowd.

Yet the Lancer heard. He stepped closer, helmeted head nearly touching Leo's face. Through the starburst-shaped hole Leo could almost see his eyes. "No," said the Lancer, voice echoing in the metal. "Your fight died a year ago today." He sounded strangely sad.

The laser glaive flashed and crackled to life once more.

It descended, a guillotine in slow motion. The crowd noise reached a frenzied crescendo. Through it all Leo thought he heard the Lancer whisper, "I'm sorry."

*I must be strong for Rolf.* Leo clenched his teeth and closed his eyes. He determined not to scream, for screams were for the guilty.

He failed.

***

Sara opened the door to her tiny apartment and gave a soft curse as she realized her husband was already home.

She adjusted the bag over her broad shoulder and slipped inside, closing the door quietly before re-arming the various electronic and mechanical locks. She must not have been quiet enough, because Joel made a noise in the den. "You're late."

*No use avoiding him now.* She stepped into the doorway. Joel sat at the two-person table, facing away. Two clear bottles of sweetwater lay empty on the table, and he was halfway through a third. "I worked late," she said. "The Prophet had guests at the palace, to... celebrate the day."

An angry snort. "They would. As if they have the right to celebrate." His words slurred together.

Sara stepped up and put a large hand on her husband's shoulder. "I'll make a loaf. Would that be nice?"

Joel shook his head as he examined his half-drunk bottle. "So you want to celebrate the day too? Is that the way of it, now?"

"No, it's just that there was extra meat they let me take home." She let a trickle of scorn into her voice. "You can sup on only broth, if you prefer."

She took his silence for acceptance and went to the kitchen, pulling the leftover fowl from her bag. The Prophet had been generous with the palace staff, and Sara especially. A mocking sort of kindness, put on by his mood on the anniversary of the day the war ended. *The day we surrendered.* She ripped the legs off the fowl and began pinching away bits of stringy meat.

Her husband moaned from the other room. "You cooked for them after everything? Today of all days?"

"I did my job," she said. She would not allow herself to feel guilty. Not from him. Not today. "And I'm cooking for *you* now, if you'll be patient."

He grumbled something incoherent.

When the fowl was picked clean she retrieved three cylinder-shaped sand tubers from the cupboard. With a knife she began peeling away the skin with smooth strokes. The act made her stomach roil. In truth it wasn't just the day that had brightened the Prophet's mood. He always stepped with invigorated cheer after the pious judgments in the *sinner's square*. The men tied up, their bodies given to their shining god.

Leo, and Mezi, and Rolf. *Oh stars, everything I've done...*

Sara placed the knife on the cutting board and gripped the counter to stop her hands from shaking. Bile bubbled up in the back of her throat. For a long moment she squeezed her eyes shut and waited for the spell to pass.

When she opened her eyes Joel stood in the doorway, angry and wavering on his feet. "We shouldn't have..."

"It's too late," Sara cut him off.

"We should have kept fighting." His eyes pleaded with her, as if she had the answers. "We shouldn't have surrendered when we did."

Sara picked up the knife and resumed peeling the tubers. "I was lieutenant. It was my call, not yours. It was the right one."

"Why us?" he whispered.

She focused on the food. *You do not want to know.*

"Why did they allow us to live? After everything we did?"

"Only the stars know why," she lied. "Random chance."

"The others in our unit did nothing wrong," he insisted. "They expected leniency. Why you and me, alone? Why, Sara?"

She couldn't meet his stare. No matter how drunk he was, he would know the moment he looked into her eyes. *The things I've done for us.* She heard the Prophet's voice, high and melodious, decrying those for their sins. Her hands began trembling again.

"There's talk in the mines," Joel said suddenly. "The same talk as years ago. The men want to gather, with our strength we can—"

"*No,*" she snapped, whirling with the knife. She pointed it at him. "You cannot even *consider* such things. Never. Did you know three more were captured? They were lanced today in the square, bags off." *Bodies open wide like fowl, blistering in the sun.* "We are alive, Joel. You and I both. Why is that not enough for you?"

His mouth hung open. "Who?"

Sara lowered the knife. "Leo's group."

Joel made a pitiful sound. "Leo. Oh, why... he asked us, Sara. Begged us, and we should have gone with him..."

She put the knife on the counter and took her husband by the shoulders. "Enough of this. Leo lasted a year, which was more than any of us expected. But the result was the same. And it would have been the same even if we'd joined him, except then both of us would have been up on that platform too. *Is that what you want?* Your skin peeled away and body given to the elements?" She gave him a shake. "You would prefer that to being *alive*, with your wife?"

His eyes flashed with hurt and anger for a moment, then abruptly softened. He fell into her embrace and wrapped his arms around her, the bottle still in his hand. She was so tall his cheek only reached the top of her chest. "I'm sorry," he mumbled into her shirt. "You're right. Being with you is enough. Being alive is worth any price."

"Any price," she whispered into his hair. She wondered if he would still believe that if he ever learned the truth.

"It's hard," he said, beginning to weep in earnest. "Some days I wake up so guilty and afraid. That they'll come for me anyways, say it was all a ruse. That I must pay for the war, what we did."

"We're safe now," Sara said. *Because of what I do.* "Nothing is going to happen to us."

She held him for a long while.

Eventually he pulled away enough to lift the bottle of sweetwater to his lips. She swiped it and put it on the counter. "You need a clear head if you're going to make your next shift." Twice a week he worked a double. If he was drunk he might hurt himself. *Or worse, get in trouble.* "This loaf is going to take a while to bake. Why don't you get a few hours of sleep while you can, and eat a slice before you leave?"

He wiped at his grimy face, dirt mixed with new salt. "Alright."

"Tomorrow after your shift we'll go to the park," she suggested. "Stare at the sky. Relax together. Like we used to."

That brought a flicker of a smile. He stumbled away without saying anything more.

Sara took a deep breath and bent back over the cutting board. "I'm sorry," she whispered to the tubers as her hands began to shake.

———————————— • ————————————

Sara woke long before sunrise to find Joel and two slices of her loaf gone. She breathed a sigh of relief that he had left on time and began readying herself for the day.

The streets were dark and deserted, with circular islands of light surrounding lanterns spaced every hundred feet. She quickened her step between each one, eying the darkness. Tall and bulky she may be, but it wouldn't matter to a man with a palm laser.

She was the first one through the servant's entrance to the crystal palace. The changing room stood empty as she opened her metal locker to put away her bag and switch into cooking attire. A computer screen on the inside showed the meal requests for the day, and the arrangements needed for the various royal and religious occupants. Names and requests filled the entire screen. Another busy day. She would be home late again, though Joel would probably be sleeping by then. Double shifts always sapped his energy.

Another note flashed on Sara's screen, however, just below the food requests. The same note that had flashed the day before. A note only for her eyes, declaring another lancing would occur. *Stars damn them*, Sara thought, flinching at the realization. She glanced at another locker at the end of the row, wider than the rest. She had still barely recovered from the day before, emotionally. *I have no choice.*

She went about her morning as if nothing were different. Prepping ingredients so the lesser cooks had everything they needed in neat piles. Boiling a batch of stock, and issuing directions to the rest of the staff when they arrived. Sending out the morning meal, and preparing the special noonday supper, to be eaten an hour after the events in the square. She moved methodically, losing herself in the familiar duties. Ignoring the timepiece over the doorway, slowly ticking toward noon.

Eventually the time drew near and she could delay no further. She handed over command of the kitchen and returned to the changing room.

*Why us, Sara?* Joel's voice drifted in her head.

The room was empty. She went to the large locker at the end and entered a code. The door opened, revealing a dark maw deeper than the locker ought to be. She stepped inside and closed the door behind.

Lights flicked on, revealing a short passage with pale yellow light. Sara bent her head and followed it a short distance until it opened into another room. Two lockers, a bench, and a doorway were all that occupied the space. Moving before she could lose her nerve, Sara opened the one on the left.

The Lancer armor hung inside, onyx material reflecting the dim light.

A wave of nausea and guilt buffeted her at the sight, like a strong wind filled with rancid scent. She gripped the door of the locker to steady herself until it passed.

*I have no choice.*

Each piece of armor was split in two, designed to connect like a clam shell over her clothes. First the boots, massive and heavy. Leg plates and a tasset that covered her from shin to belly. She had to step up into the locker to allow the breastplate to go over her head and connect around her chest. Then the arms and gauntlets. Finally the bucket helmet, with the starburst-shaped visor.

Sara hesitated a moment before opening the other locker. The laser glaive was originally a tool for construction, designed to precisely cut sheets of metal. Now...

With a shaky hand she grabbed the weapon and punched a key at the exit door. It *whooshed* open. Metal soles clanked as she exited the room, ignoring the bowing guards that stood outside with rifles.

Servants in the wide, opulent hallway froze in place as she passed, watching her with fear and awe. Sara stared straight ahead as she strode toward the glass doorway, where she could already see the pressed throng waiting. The muffled sound of cheers drifted through.

The doors opened and sound instantly magnified as Sara, the Lancer, stepped outside. The roar in the *sinner's square* reached a crescendo. In the distance the wooden platform rose above them, two X-shaped cruciates standing vigil.

*The things I've done for us,* she thought, picturing Joel's face. It was the only way she could go through with it every time, the only thing that kept her from throwing down her weapon and weeping on the ground. She'd tried drinking before the act, once, in an attempt to dull the pain. It had gone rough for the prisoners that day. Never again.

The Lancer moved forward, one steady step at a time.

The crowd parted before her, creating a circle of open space. The circle moved with her as she made her way toward the platform. Screams and cries and wails of ecstasy roared around her, rising and falling in intensity, dim and incomprehensible from inside the ceremonial armor. Sara watched it all through a starburst-shaped opening, the symbol of the sun-worshipper's religion. The symbol to which she had surrendered a year and a day ago.

Tears ran down her cheeks by the time she reached the platform and climbed the steps, boots heavy with guilt.

She glanced at the two prisoners standing behind each cruciate. Bags covered their heads today, unlike the special circumstances of the day before. She nearly lost her footing at the thought. *Oh Leo. I'm so sorry.* She thought she'd seen recognition in his eyes as she did the deed, until his eyes rolled into his head and he screamed in agony. She couldn't decide if that was better or worse, a relieving confession or a poisonous admission.

*He would have done the same in my position.* It was a weak thought. Leo *had* been in that position and he'd stayed true to their cause, never surrendering. *He didn't have a partner to save.* He didn't understand.

Sara imagined Joel's face to steady her resolve.

The Prophet watched her walk behind the prisoners, staring openly with the same smug victory that always plastered his face. Fire burned within her chest. She hated him in that moment, the man who had offered her a deal a year and a day ago. A way to save herself and Joel. *And all I needed to do was betray everything in which I believe.*

She stopped behind the prisoners on the platform, lowering her laser glaive to rest on the ground. Four guards faced away from her, two for each prisoner. The Prophet took one more pleased look at her before beginning the ceremony.

"Bathe us in your light. Drown us in your fire!"

*"Bathe us in your light, drown us in your fire."*

Sara closed her eyes, but she knew the routine as it happened. The Prophet pointed at a man. His guards ushered him forward to the roar of the crowd, removing his clothes and tying him up. The Prophet spoke some more words. Then it was her time.

The hush of anticipation fell over the throng as she walked forward, circling the prisoner. A man, she saw gratefully. Lancing women always felt harder, the emotion more severe. The only body part covered was his head, and purple and black bruises ran across his arms and chest.

Sara gave the crowd what they wanted. She raised the glaive to the sky and flicked a switch on its handle. The five straight lasers that ran along the curved blade blinked and crackled to life. A hum filled the air.

"I'm sorry," she whispered as she lowered the glaive to his skin.

He screamed and the crowd screamed with him.

The laser flickered as it moved down the wrist, skin vaporizing instantly. The cruelty of her task was that she could not look away or disappear to another place in her thoughts. She needed sharp focus to ensure a clean lancing. The cries of agony made that difficult, constantly hammering at her concentration. The pain was mostly in the prisoner's mind. His nerve endings were scoured away so quickly he would feel a momentary flash of pain, a lightning bolt on the horizon, before the arm went numb. But the mind knew what was happening, and imagined the sensation in a worse way than any reality could suffer.

But only if her hand was steady, her stroke smooth and true. She watched the red laser move across the skin with the intensity and focus of a craftsman. A slave to her cruelty.

The prisoner passed out when Sara reached his elbow, screams cutting off and head rolling limp. The second bound man began whimpering, a pitiful sound across the platform. The Prophet mumbled a low prayer to himself, pleasure in his voice. Hidden tears continued to run down Sara's cheeks as she guided the glaive along the bicep.

"Please," the second prisoner begged. "I didn't do anything. The mutterings of a drunk man. Mercy!"

Sara hated when they begged. It made her fingers tremble on her weapon, and stabbed at her guilt, allowing it to leak into conscious thought. *I should accept the pain. I deserve to feel what I do.* Beyond that, she despised the men their cowardice. A man should go to his death with head held high, unwavering. The way Leo had gone. With pride and steadfastness in his final moments. *I wouldn't beg*, she thought as the laser flickered through her visor. *I wouldn't even scream.* Though it was easy to think such things from this end of the laser.

"I'm not mutinous!" the other prisoner insisted to whoever would listen. "I merely complained to a friend, and was overheard by the mine supervisor. I was drunk..."

Sara's hand twitched. Her head swung toward him.

"Ask the other miners! They'll tell you! *Please.*"

*What.*

Before she realized it, Sara was striding across the platform. The guards took a step back, surprised. The glaive still crackled in her hand. A deep hole began sinking in her gut as she reached forward and removed the bag from his head.

The man was bald and narrow-eyed. Not Joel.

Sara felt a moment of relaxation. *Oh thank the stars.* The Prophet yelled something across the platform.

The prisoner's eyes looked around wildly. He seemed to realize that something was different, outside of the normal ceremony. "Mercy!" he screamed at Sara, spittle flying. "Mercy, please! I'd never speak a word against..." His fervent eyes rolled to the right. "It was *him*, he tricked me. He's the traitor!"

Sara's gaze swung back toward the first prisoner, silent and still, one arm red and pulpy and smoking in the sun.

She didn't feel anything as she returned to him. Dimly, as if from a great distance, she was aware of the Prophet calling out to her. Demanding to know what she was doing. The crowd spread away from the platform in all direction, a confused hum beginning to enter the cheers. Sara, the Lancer, had eyes only for the prisoner before her. Examining his body with true inspection now, seeing all of him, not just the skin beneath her blade. His legs and chest, the fingers of his hands. His groin. It was all sickeningly familiar. She reached forward, gripping the bag on his head, terrified of what she knew she would find.

The ten seconds after she unveiled him lasted a hundred.

Part of her didn't believe it. That it was some illusion, a trick of the Prophet who even then continued to call out to her. Her mind insisted none of it could possibly be real.

Until Joel's eyes flickered, squinting in the sun. Recognition, realization, shone as he met her eyes.

It felt like a hammer blow to the chest. Her knees buckled. *Oh, Joel...* She wanted to look away. She felt like she was choking inside the helmet. Why couldn't she breathe?

"Lancer," the Prophet called, "giver of judgment and justice. Continue your duties so these men may know our Mother's glory!"

*Everything I've done.* So many men dead. Her compatriots and friends, lanced and sent to rot in the sun by *her*, their former lieutenant. Their faces sprung into view. Leo, strong and confident. Mezi, braver than she'd thought. Poor Rolf, sweet and kind. *And dead like all the rest.* All of them a price she'd paid to save her husband, who now stood bound against the cruciate just like them. *Everything I've done has been for nothing.* The guilt washed over her, swirled inside her armor.

Joel's eyes flickered once more before shutting, returning to unconsciousness.

The Prophet's words took on a commanding tone. The guards began to tense at the edge of Sara's vision. The moment grew dangerous.

Sara saw Joel fully lanced, body horizontal and exposed muscles burning and blistering in the sun. *Why didn't you listen to me?* She saw him moaning, aching, begging. Dying.

*Mercy.* There was no way out now. She felt the weight of the glaive in her hand, a symbol of judgment. She could not save Joel, but she could spare him this. Sara twisted a knob on the shaft and the tone of the lasers rose, the reflected light brightening. Enough to cut deeper, like a true blade.

She'd failed so much. In the war, in the aftermath. In protecting Joel. But she could still give him mercy in that moment. Her hands shook as she raised the glaive above her, preparing to bring it down across his neck in a clean, final stroke. "I'm sorry," she whispered for the last time, voice cracking and tears pouring freely. "I'm sorry."

A hand touched her back. "Why do you hesitate?" the Prophet asked with genuine confusion. "Complete your task."

All guilt disappeared. The fire of anger in her stomach flared as if doused with fuel, raging out of control. She spun and whirled the glaive in a deadly arc, bringing it down between the Prophet's neck and shoulder. With the intensity increased the laser cut through skin and flesh and bone, passing down into his chest. The laser stopped halfway to his midsection, but that was more than enough. The crowd roared anew, with confusion and terror.

The holy man stared down at his ruined body before collapsing to the ground.

Her glaive came free at the motion. To the left one of the guards raised his rifle. The Lancer reached him in two swift steps, swinging the glaive down across the weapon. The metal sliced in half, taking three of his fingers with it. He screamed but she was already moving past, to meet the next guard as he rushed forward. He seemed too confused to fire his rifle, trapped in a paralyzed state of disbelief. She swung the glaive like a sword. But he recovered, slipping sideways to avoid it. Sara stumbled forward with the momentum.

All confusion gone, he fired three frantic bursts. The thick beams missed, one punching into the wooden platform in a spray of splinters, the others disappearing into the crowd behind. The screams took on a new tone.

Sara recovered and swung the glaive sideways, one-handed for extra reach. The guard stepped back from the slice but it took off the tip of his rifle. With the weapon damaged he bulled forward, slamming the remainder of the gun into her face. Her helmet took the brunt of the blow, flying backwards off her head. The laser glaive flew from her grasp.

Sara pushed him away while her vision spun and flecks of light moved across her eyes. When she recovered she realized the helmet was off and her head was exposed, everything suddenly brighter and more airy.

The guard rushed forward again, wielding the gun like a two-handed club, but this time Sara was ready. She sidestepped and grabbed the rifle with one hand, and punched her metal fist at his exposed throat with a sickening *crunch*. He fell to the ground, wheezing and clutching at his neck.

Her blonde hair had come undone from its tie, now blowing around her back. She stood at the top of the platform, exposed and unmasked in the open. Realization hit as she looked out over the crowd. *No, nobody is supposed to know who I am!*

Sara retrieved the glaive from the ground and turned to the two remaining guards. They stared at her, dumbstruck. Surprised the Lancer had turned on them. Shocked she was a woman.

Three steps and she reached the first guard. He began to raise his arms—to surrender, she realized too late—but she was already swinging the glaive across her body, anger coursing in her veins. It caught him under the armpit and sliced all the way to his breastbone. With his organs cut and cauterized he dropped to his knees.

She whirled but the other guard had already thrown down his rifle. He leaped from the stage, disappearing.

Sara took a moment to look around. The crowd now screamed with fear, a stampede of bodies trying to flee the square. The Prophet lay motionless on the stage, and two of the guards writhed and moaned. Joel still appeared unconscious, but the other prisoner nervously whipped his head back and forth, trying to get a view of what was going on behind him.

*There is nobody to stop me*, Sara realized. She felt so much in that instant, guilt and anger and disgust. And, tingling at her fingertips, the barest glimmer of hope.

She used the glaive to cut through Joel's straps, holding him upright with her other arm. He remained unconscious as she deactivated the glaive, threw him over a shoulder, and turned away.

"Help me!" yelled the other prisoner. "Cut me loose, please!"

She ignored him and leaped from the stage.

---

Her boots crunched on the paved stones of the square as she jogged forward, Joel's body bouncing roughly on her shoulder. Her appearance among them terrified the mass of people, who tripped and stumbled in their desperation. Sara passed several figures on the ground, trampled in all the chaos.

She reached the wall of people, pushing and shoving ahead of them. "Out of the way!" she yelled, gesturing with the deactivated glaive. That only prompted new shrieks. Gritting her teeth, Sara pushed into the crowd and shoved bodies out of the way. A gap soon opened around her. Now the civilians parted for her in terror instead of awe, as if she were some monster come to life.

*Don't think about them*, she told herself. *Think about Joel.*

She realized she was moving toward the palace. A stream of guards entered the square there, fanning out in all directions. She turned to the right and moved diagonally in another direction. She wasn't sure where to go. Their apartment wasn't safe. They didn't have anywhere else.

Her boots continued moving, because there was little else she could do.

As she neared the edge of the square a hole in the crowd abruptly opened. Four men stood in front of her. Not guards. Civilians. "The sinner," one of them pointed. "He must be judged!"

"She's an imposter," insisted another. "Just a woman. The true Lancer is a man!"

They were on her quickly, reaching, grabbing Joel's legs. She yelled and pushed at them with the inactive glaive, but they didn't fear her now that her face was exposed. Others in the crowd stopped to watch, as if the men's courage alone suddenly demystified the hulking, black-armored beast. "Get away!" she yelled, spinning. One of them yanked and Joel fell from her shoulder. A fist clutched at a length of her hair. Another man grabbed the blade of the glaive with one hand, and reached for the shaft with the other.

Frantic, Sara activated the weapon.

In a blink the man's wrist disappeared, and with it his grip on the glaive. Shocked disbelief replaced his anger. The Lancer turned and cut down the other attacker with a gruesome swing to the head. She roared, her voice as sharp as her weapon. The others fled at that, and new screams surfaced from the surrounding crowd. A small boy stared at her, paralyzed with terror, before his mother scooped him away.

*My husband*, she tried to tell the crowd, but the words would not come. They wouldn't understand anyway. She hefted Joel back over her shoulder and continued on, the pulsing hum of the laser glaive keeping the space before her clear.

She reached the edge of the square and moved into a narrow alleyway, the bright afternoon suddenly becoming dark as the buildings rose around her. She paused to look back. Much of the crowd had dispersed, and a cluster of guards moved across the square, rifles held at the ready. She disabled the glaive so the glow wouldn't give her away.

Sara lurched back into motion, moving deeper into the alley. After a hundred feet it ended and she turned down another, equally deserted. She had no idea where she was going, beyond a vague directional sense. Away from the palace. Occasionally voices drifted from behind, disciplined and orderly. Drawing closer. *They do not have a load to carry.* Joel seemed to grow heavier with every step. Her shoulder soon went numb.

After she turned down her fourth alley he began slipping from her grasp. Sara stopped and laid her husband against a wall, and saw why: the lanced arm had broken open during the scramble, red and dripping. Her armor was slick with blood.

She flinched as a sudden droning noise appeared. Above her, in the thin opening that the alley showed, two aircraft drifted across the sky. They moved slowly, searching, before disappearing. The sound of their engines dimmed. They didn't know where she was, but they would soon.

She looked back at her husband. There was a *lot* of blood. It dripped from Joel's fingers to pool in the alley. Aside from some nearby metal crates, she saw nothing around her she could use to stem the flow.

Reaching down inside her chest plate, she ripped loose a length of cloth from her shirt. For a panicked moment she wasted the tiny strip of cloth dabbing at the arm-long open wound. Her old training kicked in and she tied it around his bicep as a tourniquet. He remained unconscious, his breathing growing ragged with pain.

"That way," called a voice around the corner, down the way she had come. "Follow the blood."

Cursing, she threw Joel back over her shoulder and moved on.

She stayed ahead of them for the next five minutes, always rounding a corner just before they saw her. She was certain they would hear her frantic breathing, loud as it was. Above her the aircraft seemed closer, narrowing in on her location. She didn't possess enough strength to look up. Or she was afraid of what she would see.

Suddenly she rounded a corner and the safety of her alley ended. A wide street opened before her, bright and open. A few civilians moved across her view, hurriedly returning home. Nobody saw her. A new alley beckoned across the street.

The voices behind her were too close for her to backtrack. They would be there any second.

She ran into the light, every step heavy and loud. The few civilians screamed at her sudden appearance, but Sara kept her eyes on the alley ahead. Thirty steps. Twenty. Joel bounced on her shoulder. She prayed he didn't feel any pain.

Just before she reached the mouth of the alley a voice called out. Laserfire hissed through the air near Sara's head. A burst slammed into the brick wall ahead of her, *puck puck puck*, sending bits of rock at her face and clouds of dust into the air.

She lost her balance and stumbled into the alley. Joel flew from her shoulder. She flinched as his head knocked on the ground and he rolled against the wall. Leaving him there, she rose and pressed her back against the wall at the edge of the street. The laserfire had come from down the street, not behind her from the previous alley. A single soldier, eager to be the one to catch her. She gripped the glaive at her side, finger resting on the activation button. If the soldier approached cautiously, from a distance, he would shoot her easily. But if he came running into the alley expecting to see her still fleeing...

The soldier slid around the corner recklessly. A young man, barely old enough to shave. He raised his rifle to aim down the alley, but Sara was next to him, much closer than he expected. In a burst of red the glaive came alive and she slashed backhanded, catching him across the top of the head. He crumpled. Sara turned away from the gruesome sight. Nearby a civilian retched.

The other soldiers were across the street now, and the dust in the air was beginning to fade. She retrieved her husband and ran down the alley with renewed fervency.

She quickly realized she wouldn't last long. Her strides were already sluggish, and at every corner wicked red streaks sought her out. *If I don't find safety soon...* She didn't finish the thought. The aircraft seemed like they were directly overhead. She couldn't run down the alleys forever.

Around the next turn it didn't matter. Once again the alley ended, only this time instead of a cross street it opened to a wide expanse of green.

*The park.*

It spread across three square blocks, with grass and benches and bushes scattered in between. Her feet had carried her to the last place she and her husband had, and although there was almost no cover, Sara shuffled into the park eagerly.

What few occupants it boasted scattered at what must have been a frightful sight: the helmetless Lancer, blonde hair streaming down her back, covered in blood and carrying a body. Laserfire sounded somewhere behind but she kept moving until she found a set of low bushes, waist high. She fell behind them with the remainder of her strength.

Aircraft roared above, and the disciplined shouts of soldiers came from three directions. Surrounding her, pinning her down. She ignored it all and rolled her husband onto his back. Blood smeared his cheeks and chin.

His eyes opened.

Sara's heart soared. "Joel. It's me. Can you see me?"

"Why?" he asked, groggy and delirious.

"What?"

He looked down at her armor in disbelief. "*Why.*"

It took her a moment to realize his meaning. "For you," she said, voice cracking. "Worth any price. Remember? You agreed being together would be worth any price."

He gently shook his head. "Why would you..."

"Joel, please," she begged. She couldn't bear to hear his reproach, not on top of everything else. "Whatever may have happened, I did it for us. Tell me you understand. *Please.* Say that you forgive me. I need to hear you say it!"

Anger flashed in his eyes and she knew he would curse her.

"I love you," he said, eyes bright with fire and certainty. "I trust you."

The dam burst and she wept, leaning close to clutch Joel to her chest. She smelled his neck and hair, kissed his lips, not caring about the blood.

"I'm sorry."

He frantically shook his head. For a brief moment he seemed lucid. "No. Don't ever be sorry for what you've done."

The soldiers drew closer, moving slow and cautious.

"I can't..." Joel began, cutting off. His eyes rolled toward his skinless arm, and he winced at what he saw. "Don't let them..."

"I know," she said. She pictured him back on the cruciate, arm smoking in the sun. "Not again."

Voices a short distance away. It was almost over.

She tightened her fingers on the laser glaive. Joel must have known it was over because he began to weep, so she kissed him again, a long and aching embrace she didn't want to end.

"See you in the stars."

"See you in the stars," he muttered.

He flinched as the glaive crackled, but kept his eyes clenched shut.

The Lancer brought the line of red across her husband's throat and held him as he died.

———————— • ————————

Though she couldn't see through the opaque bag over her head, the roar of the crowd told Sara she was in the *sinner's square*, and that she was about to die.

The guards pushed her forward. The cloth covering her view brightened in the sunlight of what she knew was noonday. She had the sensation of being surrounded on all sides, the crowd out of sight but just barely out of reach. Their cries of obscenities were different today. More rabid and personal.

She accepted them with her head held high. There were no words worse than all the guilt she'd carried for so long. The guilt she was ready to release.

Across the square she marched, on the other end of a ceremony in which she was so familiar. Her bare feet climbed the wooden steps of the platform. Rough hands maneuvered her into place. Throughout it all the masses wailed and clamored.

Light buffeted her as someone removed the bag. Bags off, reserved for only the most severe of offenders.

A different priest stood on the platform, but the words were all the same. "Mother Saria," he intoned in a high-pitched voice, "strongest in the sky, always watching. We bring this woman before you to be judged."

*I have already judged myself*, she thought. *All you can do is free me.*

"Mother Saria," he continued in a singsong voice, eyes raised to the sky. "Bathe us in your light. Drown us with your fire."

*"Drown us with your fire,"* cried the crowd.

A murmur went up in the distance, at the entrance to the crystal palace. A hole in the crowd appeared and drifted toward the stage. A figure in black came into view, stride slow and purposeful. It felt strange to see it from this angle, yet Sara wanted it no other way.

The new Lancer cut an imposing figure as he—or she?—reached the stage, long weapon held like a staff. The platform trembled as he climbed the wooden steps. *I wonder who it is*, she thought. Someone like her, trapped in a cruel bargain? Someone who will soon collect immeasurable guilt?

*Mine is nearly gone*, she thought as the guards strapped her to the cruciate. *It cannot taunt me anymore.*

"Free from sin," the young priest cried, "free from desire. Mother, drown her with your fire."

*"Drown her with your fire."*

Sara took a deep breath as the Lancer stood before her. She could have turned the glaive on her own neck that day in the park, to go with her husband to the stars. But she deserved this fate. *Needed* it. To finally make everything right for what she'd done.

They were not breaking her. They were freeing her. Lancing away her guilt.

*Free me with your fire.*

The glaive crackled to life, red and soothing.

"I am not sorry," she declared.

The Lancer did not hear.

Sara determined to scream loudly, for screams were for the guilty.

She succeeded.

## About The Author

David Kristoph lives in Fort Worth, Texas with his wife and two not-quite German Shepherds. He's a fantastic reader, great videogamer, good chess player, average cyclist, and mediocre runner. He writes Science Fiction, Fantasy, and Thrillers.

For more information, visit www.davidkristoph.com.

# Bodies of Evidence

## Jefferson Smith

*Editor's Note: In the frenzy to tell the big stories, there are a hundred smaller ones that get overlooked. It's a shame really, because these are the stories that are truest; the ones where real lives are lived and lost. They're the Janes and Joes just working for a paycheck. And some of them work for Big Evil.*

Great evils come and go, but in their wake, it is the little people who must endure—those who, while themselves neither evil nor great, have nevertheless built their lives out of looking the other way. Facilitating. Getting evil done. They are but cogs in the vast economic machinery of despotic do-baddery.

My name is Louis Corelli and I am one of those cogs—for now, anyway. What I really want to do is to direct for the stage, but that's a cut-throat business. So in the meantime, henching pays the bills. The money is good, and so are the stories.

This is one of them.

———————————— • ————————————

*It began like a scene out of some pimple-neck's comic book...*

"Incompetent fools!"

Maladein barked a hyena laugh and pulled the trigger. A crackling arc of plasma shot out from between the coils of the prototype weapon and incinerated Squeaky Pete on the spot. Maladein's eyes were wild as he struggled to control the spray of particle energies, his cackles of laughter matching pitch in eerie harmony with the shrill warble of the electronics. Mickey Two-Thumbs just stood there in front of him, eyes wide, mesmerized by the sudden cremation of the man beside him until the stench of smouldering muscle brought him back to reality with a twitch. He blinked. Then he turned to run. But it was too late. Maladein grinned and turned the weapon in his hands. Once more its unholy fire danced, catching Mickey square in the back before he could take his second step.

And just like that, it was over. With no more goons to discipline, Maladein released the trigger. The beam flickered and then vanished as the whine of tortured inductors cycled down, until finally the only sound left was the boss's heaving gasps of glee. He stumbled forward and prodded Mickey's remaining lower half with the glowing end of his new favorite toy. I could actually taste the acrid sizzle that rose from the demicorpse wherever the weapon's tip met bare skin. I tried not to swallow.

"Fabulous! Freaking fabulous, Doctor!" Maladein spun around, his eyes coming to rest on the timid little scientist to my left. Poor guy looked torn between retching and weeping. Probably wanted to run, too, but he was too scared. Or maybe too smart. "Build me five more just like it, then get started on a big one for the roof of the castle!" With playtime over, the boss tossed his rifle dismissively at the doc and then strode past us toward the door at the back of the loading bay.

"Marston! Escort the professor back to his lab. Corelli, clean up this mess and then join me at the launch site. By this time tomorrow, the world will be mine!"

Two minutes later, Maladein and his train of functionaries, lick-spittles and lesser adjutants had disappeared into the night, leaving me with the mess. Not that I'm complaining. Like I said, the pay is good. It was just time to actually start earning it.

---

"Corpus Corp. Hold please."

I looked around the room, surveying the extent of the mess. There wasn't much left of either body. Maladein's new pet scientist might be terrified, but he gave good carnage, even under pressure. Might be time to—

"Corpus Corp. Thank you for holding. My name is Cindy. How may I direct your call?"

"Hey Cindy. My name is Lou. I need a pickup on Pier 26."

"One moment, please." I pulled a stick of gum from my chest pocket, but before I could get it unwrapped, a new voice came on the line.

"Collections. This is Penny. I understand you need a pickup?"

"Hi doll. I'm Lou. Yeah, I'm down at Pier 26. How you guys doing tonight?"

"We're pretty busy, Lou, but I have a unit in your area. How big a load have you got for us?"

I kicked at Mickey's legs to be sure there wasn't anything more lying beneath them. "Looks like less than two halves. I dunno, one half and then maybe a foot. Below the ankle."

"Okay Lou, I can squeeze you in. And how will you be paying?"

"On account. Maladein Industries."

"One moment, please." She was gone for over a minute. "Hello, Lou? I'm not showing any accounts under that name. The closest match I have is for SKULL International Consortium of Evil, Local Rep: Sheldon Maladein."

"Damn. I forgot about the merger. That's us. Sorry."

"Not a problem, Lou. It happens all the time. Now, are we talking about bystanders, police, government agents, or henchmen?"

"Henchmen."

"Right. Independent contractors? Staff? Or were they from a service?"

"Uh, Mickey was an independent, but I think Squeaky Pete was from Flunky Finder."

"Okay. And would you like us to notify the agency for you? We've already got quite a list to send over to them tonight. The Axis of Evil is breaking in a new hell-spawn today and it got loose. That scene's had us tied up since lunch. I could add Pete to our condolence list if you like."

"Sure. That'd be a nice touch."

"Righty-o. One last thing before I let you go. We're promoting a new service this week. Our Sanguinex Clean Scene is guaranteed to get the red out or your money back. This week we're offering a free demonstration. Would you like to give it a try?"

"I don't know, Penny. There isn't much red to get out this time. The boss used his new plasma cannon."

"Ooo. Those are nice. How's the scorching?"

I looked around. She was right. Except for a pair of man-shaped silhouettes of unblemished concrete, the back wall of the warehouse was crisscrossed with ugly black burn marks.

"Yeah, the wall is burned up pretty bad."

"Streamed particle weapons will do that every time, but I'm sure the Sanguinex will get it to come up real nice. I'll put you down for the demo. Is there anything else?"

"No. I'm good, thanks."

"Alright Lou. I have you listed for a half-by-two pickup and a full Sanguinex demo. We'll be there in twenty minutes and guaranteed to be off-site within one hour of arrival. Thank you for calling Corpus Corp."

The line went dead and I put my phone away. Like I said, one of the things I liked about the job was all the time it gave me to work on my writing, so I took out my notepad and started making these notes. The rest I got from Sid later.

———————— • ————————

"Half-by-two lite on Pier 26 with sizzle. Got it, hon. Thanks. Unit three is rolling." Sid tucked his phone into a shirt pocket and started the engine before turning to look at his trainee.

"Looks like we got lucky for your first call, kid. This is just a little one. We can break you in nice and slow."

The kid nodded and stared straight ahead as the delivery van pulled out onto the street. Sid glanced at him out of the corner of his eye, noting all the usual symptoms of a first-nighter—eyes as big as hubcaps, blinks coming in triple time. All of it.

"Don't forget to breathe, right? I don't want to have to load an extra body tonight. You get me?" Sid threw a helpful grin at his new trainee while making the turn onto Peachtree, but he knew there wasn't much he could do. Your first night on the job in this business was tough, but there was nothing anyone could do to help you get past it. The kid would either pull through or he'd run screaming into the night. Or he'd try, anyway. Sid patted his jacket pocket to be sure. One scream-stopper. Check.

The kid licked his lips nervously. When he found his voice, it cracked a little. "What's a..." He stopped and took a deep breath, then tried again, aiming for a bit more man and a little less mouse. "What's a half-by-two?"

Sid paused, trying to figure out whether the kid was ready for any real details yet, then he shrugged. He still hadn't decided if the kid was even going to survive his first shift, but either way, if a newbie was going to lose it, better to find out quick.

"The first number tells us how many bodies worth of weight we're picking up. The second one is how many individual bodies contributed parts to that total." You could actually hear the kid swallow, but he seemed to keep it under control. Even managed to not sound terrified with his next question.

"So why do we care about the second number? Don't we just need to know how much weight we're loading?"

Sid suppressed a grin. "Usually, yeah. But sometimes it really helps to know how many fingers you're looking for."

They pulled into the Pier 26 lot just as the kid flung the door open to puke.

———————————— • ————————————

"We're pretty much done here now, Lou. Can I get you to sign the work order?"

I looked up from my notebook, surprised he was done so soon. Clean-up crews usually took forever, and fast usually meant sloppy. I threw a couple of glances around the rest of the warehouse, but if he'd missed anything, I couldn't see it. Every little part that had once been named Mickey or Pete had been packed up and stowed into the back of the FedEx van he'd arrived in. The concrete walls and floor were spotless. Sid had been here less than half an hour and now here he was, standing on the lip of the loading dock. A bare bulb glared down at him from above the bay doors, etching him crisply against the blackness of night beyond as he waved his documents at me for signature.

Huh. I shook my head in disbelief and went over to join him. He knew I was surprised—it was written all over his self-satisfied grin. I took the work-pad and looked it over. In addition to the work order and a customer satisfaction survey for the Sanguinex demo, there was a small unsealed business envelope. I pulled it open and peeked inside: a gold cross on a chain and two pea-sized lumps of yellowish metal. Gold fillings, maybe? Leftovers to send on to the families. Apparently the beam didn't atomize gold. Interesting. Maladein would definitely want to hear about that.

I scrawled a signature into the little signing box and handed it back. "Top notch job, Sid. Fast and clean. I tell you, it's a joy to work with professionals."

Sid smiled and offered me his hand, which I shook. Then he winked. "Tell your boss he made our job easy. I wish more people would switch to energy-based weapons. But I guess if too many of them did that, I'd be out of work."

The kid had spent the whole time scrubbing the pavement beside the truck, but he was done now, and walking toward us across the parking lot. Sid and I exchanged knowing glances and a quiet chuckle. Newbies.

"Somebody's nephew?" I asked, hopefully.

Sid shook his head. "Nah. The usual. Recruiting picked him up on a sweep. Shelter somewhere or a flop—I didn't ask. The more you know, the harder it gets." I nodded in sympathy. "Supposed to have scored as 'promising,'" Sid added. "But so far, I'm not seeing it. Nothing but jumps and twitches."

There wasn't much I could say to that. Training is always a rough gig—on both sides—and this kid looked six kinds of awkward, even in just the few minutes I'd seen him. Besides, it didn't matter what I thought. It was Sid's call. He and I both went back a ways in this business, and we both knew the score. The work was dirty and dangerous, but by far the most dangerous part of all was that very first day, though few of us ever knew just how dangerous it had been at the time. You didn't get a sense of that side of things till you'd seen a bunch of newbies wash out for yourself, but by then of course, you'd already managed to *not* wash out yourself.

Every supervisor in the business has his own theory about what it takes to make it. I don't know what Sid's thing was, but so far he hadn't seen it, and if you asked me, the kid was too frail. Too much rabbit. Not sure I'd have even given him a try, if it had been me. But hell, for all I knew, Sid would find what he was looking for and I'd be calling the kid "boss" by a week next Thursday. A part of me wanted to wish him luck—wish them *both* luck—but it wasn't really any of my business, and we all had work to get back to.

Calling a quick "g'night" over his shoulder, Sid motioned the kid back toward the van and followed after him. Thirty seconds later, they were gone.

---

As soon as Sid climbed into the van, it was like a cork had been yanked out of the kid's chatter box. How much blood had there been? Did that big guy really whack people for a living? Why did they have to drive around in a

FedEx truck? How much did Corpus Corp charge clients for this kind of thing? What were they going to do with the bodies now? How come he wasn't allowed to use Sanguinex to clean up the puke?

"Whoa. Slow down, kid." Sid put the vehicle into gear and pulled casually out of the lot, making a right onto Canal. "That was an easy job, but it didn't go like I expected. Normally, I'd have let you handle some of it—even though I can do the easy ones in my sleep—but if there's only one thing you need to learn tonight, it's this: maximum service, minimum exposure. That means do the job, do it right, but do it fast, and for the love of Jupiter, don't leave any *new* evidence on site. So tonight, I had to clean up the client's mess so you could take care of yours. As for why you had to do it by hand, well, let's just say that, my way, you're less likely to flip your burgers at another call. You'll remember how unpleasant the cleanup is." The kid nodded that he understood. Sid continued.

"The rest of your questions fall into the three categories I ain't gonna answer. Category 1: questions that will answer themselves by the end of the night. Category 2: questions that are none of your damn business. And Category 3: questions that might get you killed for asking. You follow?" The kid swallowed hard and nodded again, then he turned his wide, blinking eyes back toward the window.

Sid smiled to himself. Like most rookies, the kid had probably been spinning his wheels all night on the "what comes next" problem, his head full of wild conjectures—vats of acid, chipper/shredders, darkened piers, concrete galoshes and sinister alleys on the dark side of town. But now maybe he was starting to get a glimpse of the "what have I gotten myself into" problem as well. Either way, what Sid did next came as a bit of a curve ball.

He pulled up in front of City Hospital.

The kid looked around in a panic and discovered that it was worse than just being at the hospital. Sid hadn't parked surreptitiously in the back of the lot. No, he'd triple parked the van in front of the emergency entrance. Beside a squad car. With a cop in it. The kid began to hyperventilate.

"Relax," Sid said with a frown as he climbed around his seat and went into the back of the van. "We're FedEx, remember? Nobody cares." He re-emerged a moment later, carrying a grimy looking package. "People expect us to park illegally. Hell, we get away with more crap than even handicapped people do." Then he looked at the kid. Mouth still gaping, eyes darting from place to place, panic obviously scrambling up the back of his throat.

"Now stay here," Sid told him, "and for Christ's sake try to *not* look guilty of something, okay?" Then he hopped out the driver's door and disappeared into the hospital.

When he returned, Sid was pleased to see that the kid had managed to get his breathing under control and that most of the wild panic was gone from his expression. All that remained was a slight movement of his lips—either praying or counting to himself. Sid hoped he was counting. That would have been okay. But praying? Not so much. Not in this line of work.

"No dice," he said as he jumped up into the driver's seat. The kid snapped his head up, startled by the announcement, and obviously still confused about why they had even come here. Sid threw him a bone. "Sometimes if they've been busy in Trauma, we can add our little offerings to the mixed bag of parts waiting to be processed after the autopsies are done." Sid shrugged. "But like I said, no dice. They haven't had any partials tonight. Our chaff would stick out like a bag of severed thumbs at a bar mitzvah."

"P-Partials?"

But then a look of understanding shuddered across the newbie's face. "Never mind," he said quietly. "I get it."

Sid twisted around in his seat and looked into the back of the van. "Tonight might be a hard night to outload," he said. "On top of the call we just did, I was at a nasty one all afternoon, before you started. I've still got that lot to ditch as well."

"N-Nasty?"

"Some bozos were receiving a razor-beast in the back of a dairy this morning and they opened the cage without feeding the damned thing first. That little oversight turned into a six-by-nine call. A real wet one. Took forever to strain all the pieces out of the cheese vats." To his credit, the kid only gagged. Twice.

They drove on in silence for several minutes, each of them alone with their own disturbing thoughts. Then, suddenly, Sid did the oddest thing. As they were passing a little urban park, he jerked the van to a halt and jumped out the driver's door—the engine still running—and ran across the grass. When he reached the base of a tall bronze statue of some pioneer housewife, he pulled a small hammer from a loop on the back of his belt and whacked her on the toe with it. Then, without even pausing, he turned and trotted back, hopped up into the van, and resumed driving, as though nothing at all had happened. The whole stop had taken less than a minute.

No doubt the kid was burning with curiosity, and after Sid's lecture on questions that might get him killed, he must have decided to play it careful. But even fears of his own impending death couldn't keep him quiet forever.

"So how come we're driving around the city looking for somewhere to dump this stuff? Doesn't Corpus Corp have all kinds of easy ways to handle it?" He must have figured that this kind of question didn't fit into any of Sid's "categories."

Apparently, he was right. "Yup," Sid agreed. "Normally we've got four or five different processing options, depending on how much chaff we've got and how much of it is bone. But the cops have been sniffing around lately. I figure it's safer to avoid the regular systems. No telling what's being watched. You know, we even sent out a bulletin warning clients to lay low, but do you think you can tell a megalomaniac when to ix-nay on the utchery-bay? Christ. The work load has been going *up* since then instead of down. Definitely *not* team players.

"Anyway, that's why I'm pulling a double today. I've been with Corpus since before we were big enough to have in-house disposal. Lucky for you, I still know a few tricks from the old days. You couldn't have picked a better week to start on the job."

As they were talking, Sid guided the van toward the downtown core. Twice more he punctuated their conversation with his sudden stop-and-hammer assaults on a civic memorial. Each time he would whack the statue on a foot or a hoof or a hand, and each time he would come scampering back just as quickly to continue their journey, with never a word of explanation. "The big problem," he said after the third such stop, resuming the conversation right where he had interrupted it, "is our damned reputation. No Corpus client has ever had so much as a toe turn up after disposal. And every year it gets a little harder to hide or destroy each and every scrap. We can't just take it out and dump it in the forest. Too many people with nosy dogs out on nature hikes. Sinking it in the bay doesn't work either. The first time our concrete crumbles and some scalp floats to the surface, all our hard work goes down the tubes. It gets to be a lot of pressure."

"So you've never had any, um, evidence come back to haunt you?"

"Nope. Came close once." Sid chuckled at the memory. "In hindsight, it was a stupid idea, but it was thirty years ago and I was just getting started. Spotted what I thought was a great little hiding place. You know those run-down houses over in Adelaide Park? Well they were just being built back then. I was helping to clean up a time jump splooge—some idiot sent a squad back to a week later than he shoulda. Poor bastards appeared half inside a new foundation wall. Anyway, while I'm cleaning flunky off the cinder blocks, I notice that a couple of the houses had this weird sort of architectural quirk in the attic. A sort of dead space, about the size of a small bathroom, completely surrounded by walls. No doors. No windows. Nothing. Completely sealed inside the ceiling—or, it would be, once the sheetrock was put up. And it was only about five feet high, too, so even if somebody ever noticed, it wasn't like they were going to open it up to put in an office or something. It was perfect. So I picked out one house, at the end of a darkish street, and for the next two weeks, I took all my loads up there, sealed in heavy plastic, and stuffed them into that hidden room. I figure I got maybe a 40 by 60 in there, all in all, before they finished the place. Nobody ever wondered who it was installed the drywall for 'em."

The kid was hanging on every word. "So, how did you almost get caught?"

Sid rolled his eyes at his own stupidity. "That was maybe five years ago. I was driving through the neighborhood that summer and I noticed that the

siding on my special hidey-house was in rough shape. Didn't think nothing about it at first, but then I just about swallowed my hat. See, the secret room was up against the front wall of the house, under the roof line and I suddenly realized that if anybody pulled the siding off, they'd be staring straight into that room. Straight at a hip-deep pile of missing persons wrapped in plastic.
"

The kid looked horrified. "So what did you do?"

"What do you think I did? I fixed the siding. Right then. Right there. Pulled into the driveway and knocked on the door. Told the missus I was new in town and setting up a siding business. If she'd let me do their house that week—to establish a local example of my work, you understand—then I'd do the job at cost. Took me three days to get the whole load snuck out and moved to our cat food plant, on top of doing the siding job."

Sid chuckled. "Turns out I did such a bang up job on the siding that I wound up creating a whole new mess of trouble. Nowadays I gotta keep four guys working full-time to handle all the demand generated from the siding referrals I get."

"You've got a real business going and you're still working here?" Clearly the kid found the notion completely incomprehensible, but Sid just shrugged.

"I could never do siding for a living myself," he said. "It's filthy work."

At that time, they were passing through a recently rejuvenated section of the downtown area. In particular, they were passing a new neighborhood parkette, complete with obligatory statue, this one celebrating the humble drycleaner. As before, Sid slammed on the brakes and hopped out to perform his hammer ritual, but this time, when he came back, he didn't get in. This time he went to the back of the van and then re-emerged with a toolbox in hand. "Come on, kid. Time to learn a useful lesson."

When the kid caught up to him at the monument, Sid had a hacksaw in his hand and was cutting across the back of the giant drycleaner's right leg. As soon as a kerf was started, he handed the saw to his baffled assistant. "You finish it. Stop when you've got two or three inches left. If you see somebody coming, toss the saw into that bush and start to sing. As loudly and as badly as you can. Play drunk. If you hear me start to sing, same thing."

The kid took about four strokes with the saw and then paused to risk another question. "Shouldn't we use, like, a power saw? This'll take forever."

"Sure, kid. And then we'd have every public snoop and brass button in the city crawling around asking what we were doing. I've always done it this way and I'm always going to do it this way. It's quieter and a lot easier to cover up. Just keep sawing." A moment later, the saw resumed its rhythmic cadence, but after a few minutes it paused. Again.

"What are we going to do with a statue's leg?"

Sid had been walking a large, drunken perimeter around the parkette, keeping watch, but the question brought him to a halt. Truth be told, he was getting a bit tired of this timid rabbit routine, and he couldn't help checking again to be sure that his "trainee dehiring process" was still an easy reach in his pocket. Then he turned and gave his little rabbit buddy a thin and obviously strained grin. "Category one, kid. Now shut up and get it done. Down to three inches or so, then call me." Then he added with a growl, "But not sooner."

To Sid's surprise, the next little while was dead silent, save for the sound of the saw scraping back and forth. At just about the time that he was beginning to wonder if the kid had any idea how to use a saw, he was interrupted by a sudden loud call. "I'm through!"

Crap! Sid immediately responded in a loud, off-key tenor: "With chicks and poker! I'm through! With whores and grass! I'm through with all your schemes and lies, so kindly kiss my ass!" As he sang, he lurched his way back to the statue, until he was close enough to hiss under his breath. "Are you crazy? We're trying to keep a low profile here, dumbass!" The kid muttered an apology, but it was almost too quiet to be heard at all.

Sid shook his head and took the saw before the kid could figure out another way to jeopardize this simple drop, then he wandered drunkenly back over to the van. The kid looked confused when Sid returned, seeing as how he was now carrying a long pry bar and the heavy FedEx package that had been helpfully addressed to Mickey Peters. In just a few moments, Sid had levered the bronze leg further open and was hurriedly stuffing henchmen parts down into its cavernous, cylindrical interior. When that load was done, he ran back to the van—speed was now more important than drunken deniability—and came back with a heavy duffel bag from which he began throwing fingers, ears and various gobbets of flesh and bone down into the voracious drycleaner's leg. The moment his sack was empty, he stuffed it and the empty FedEx box up into the statue's torso and then he waved the kid over to help.

When the leg had been forced back into alignment, Sid led his young sidekick away, swaggering drunkenly back to the van. They had only gone a block before the inevitable questions started again. "But, Sid. What about the statue? It's still sawed open. Somebody's gonna look inside and see bits of, like, people, aren't they?"

Sid sighed. He hadn't seen a single sign that this kid was worth the trouble. Not one. Sid was a tolerant, forgiving sort of guy, but when your ass is on the line with every shift, you gotta know that the people around you aren't going to be a liability forever. You gotta see *some* kind of progress, right?

"Unit Three, are you clear for assignment?" Penny. Perfect timing. Well, Penny would have to wait. It was better to get this kind of thing over with before talking to her. "That's the thing about useless statues," Sid said, casually. Wasn't much harm in telling the kid now. "It takes city hall a year to send somebody out to fix a pothole around here, kid, but you'd be surprised how quickly repair crews seem to show up when the ugly statue of somebody's grandmother gets vandalized. They're usually on the scene the very next morning."

The kid still looked lost. "But that's bad, isn't it? I mean, what if—" Sid just shook his head, sadly. It really was a damned shame. He slid his hand slowly into his jacket.

Maybe the kid saw something in Sid's eyes just then. Maybe it was something about the set of the older man's shoulders, or the way Sid's fingers flexed slightly inside his pocket. Whatever it was, the point is, for the first time that night, the kid didn't finish his question. He swallowed one last gulp of fear and then nodded.

"We're the repair crew, right?"

The older man raised an eyebrow. "Got it on the first try, kid." But still his hand stayed in his pocket as he studied the kid for a long drawn out moment. Were the eyes just a little less rabbity? Was there a hint of gravity now where the flinching had been?

"Come in, Unit Three."

But to Sid's surprise, the kid's eyes did not flick to the radio. There was a glimmer there staring back at him. A glimmer of... understanding?

In a slow ballet of tension, Sid pulled his hand from his pocket—empty—and reached for the handset. And that's when he saw the look of relief flash across the kid's face. It wasn't much. But it was enough.

A moment later, time sped up again. Sid shot the kid a grin and keyed the mic.

"Okay, Penny. We're here. What have you got?"

Turns out that what she had was some intra-dimensional water broker who had taken out a cyborg infiltration team. According to the report, it was a 7-by-11, plus mechanicals. Within moments Sid had turned the van around and was making for the scene with all haste.

As they pulled onto the highway, the kid finally spoke. "So, I think I figured it out. The hammer thing. You were checking to see how noisy the statues were, right? Make sure we didn't pick one that would shriek or squeal when the saw bit in?"

"Not even close, kid." Sid shook his head, but he grinned, too. On the whole, it hadn't been a bad guess. "We obviously gotta check 'em first, but that ain't what we're looking for."

Rather than ask the question, the kid just looked at Sid and waited. Finally Sid shrugged. "Jesus, kid. The other ones were full!"

There was an awkward moment of silence, and then, for the first time since Sid had met him, the kid laughed. He laughed so hard that the van shook, and with that laughter, an enormous weight simply evaporated from Sid's shoulders. That was the real sign he'd had been waiting for. Laughter. The kid might be timid and jumpy, but any man who could see the humor—the absurdity—in this crazy, upside down world... Well, that man was somehow worth spending a little more time on.

Relaxed now, Sid added his own chuckle to the kid's laughter and jammed his foot down hard, urging the van forward into the night.

After all, there were bodies to collect.

———————————— • ————————————

So that's it. Two guys driving off into the dark unknown. Not buddies. Not friends. Not even particularly friendly, really. But there was something new between them that hadn't been there before. A connection. And that's all we ever really get in this business. We don't work in office towers, or at the mall, or on movie sets. People like that can have more, but cogs of darkness like us? All we can hope for is a halfway civil chat and maybe a bit of grim laughter—between the periods of trying to kill each other.

Not that I'm complaining, mind you. At least I don't have to install siding.

## About The Author

Jefferson Smith is a liar of the first order. He has lied to kings and queens; he has lied to hobos and urchins. He has lied to the mightiest of the mighty and to the lowest of the low. He is probably lying to you now. But in every lie there is a grain of truth, and in every telling a bewitchment. So it should come as no surprise that Jefferson bends his talents to the one craft that reveres both the liar and the lie, weaving entire worlds out of falsity and invention, raveled up in strands of guile. He is an author, and you will not find his equal in any other sphere. Or so he keeps telling us.

For more information, visit creativityhacker.ca.

# Borrowed Lives

## I.A. Watson

*Editor's Note: Every new technology carries the promise of change; not just in the new wonders they bring, but in the hundred ways society will have to shift to make room for them. Whether it be new frontiers brought within our reach, new crimes made possible, or even just a new kind of job that will need to be done, science fiction stories strive to show us the ramifications of these changes. And the best of them show us things we'd never thought to consider.*

Jaz got back to the flat just before eleven, while Mik was rehearsing his lines. She peeled off her top on the way to the shower.

"Those are some nasty bruises," her flatmate noticed. "What happened?"

"Rock climbing, I think. That's what the contract said. Although there was some pretty vigorous sex too, by the feel of it."

"Did your visitor pay for sex?"

"It was just supposed to be extreme sports, but you know what visitors are like. Get a hot young body, try it out, right?"

"Yeah. Bastards." A hazard of donating one's body for someone else to wear for a while was that the visitor decided how to use it. Contracts only offered so much protection.

Jaz climbed into the tiny cubicle and began her post-donor ritual: soap, scrub, rinse and repeat until she felt like it was her skin again.

"What did Jackson say about the damage?" Mik called over the sound of the power nozzle.

"Visitor lost his deposit. I got 6000 credits compensation." Jaz flinched. "Feels like I should have had more. That wasn't rock climbing, more like rock sliding."

"You shouldn't be signing on for the dangerous visits."

"That's where the money is. College tuition is expensive."

"Jackson should have banned your visitor."

"Friend of the manager, evidently. Jackson actually seemed a bit sheepish about it. Offered me a cushy board meeting job for next weekend if my scrapes and bruises are healed. You too. We can donate together, both pick up fast easy creds. Just three days of donating our skins for some one-percenters to wear at a conference."

Mik put down his script. "I have my audition Monday. I can't turn up all beaten to hell because some rich asshole doesn't care what he does while he's wearing my body."

"I know. But this is corporate stuff. Borrow-meat for businessmen to inhabit for a committee session, so they don't have to fly halfway round the world to attend in person. Our bodies get luxury treatment. The worst that can happen is if somebody pigs out at the buffet table and you get the calories to work off. C'mon Mik! Jackson threw this one our way because it's the nearest the old scroat will ever get to an apology."

"I have to rehearse. I want this part. I need this part."

Jaz climbed from the shower and grabbed a towel. "You know your lines. You're overpreparing. Why not rent your skin out for a couple of days for this corporate retreat and have a nice little shutdown? When you wake up it'll be like you did one of those yoga calming exercises or something. And if—I'm only saying if —the acting gig doesn't work out, you'll have 4000 creds in your account to tide you over."

"Four thousand? For one meeting weekend?"

"High rollers, Jackson said. International conference and they require some top-notch bodies to wear. C'mon, what do you say?"

Mik gave up. "I'm in. Or out, once I'm strapped in my chair. Tell Jackson it's a date."

———— • ————

The downtown Body Transfer Reserve had an impressive front entrance with valet parking service, but staff and donors used the rear door from a cluttered alley littered with fire escapes and dumpsters. Jaz and Mik hurried inside before the rain wet down their hair; visitors didn't like to wake up inside damp bodies.

They passed through the halls, greeting a couple of donors they knew. Jackson was in Dispatch, being his usual less-than-cheerful self. He signed Jaz and Mik in but didn't mention Jaz's previous visitor. As soon as he could, he waved them through to Processing to begin preparation for their mind-swaps.

"Afternoon, guys," Jil called as they entered the transfer centre. "One moment and I'll be with you." She finished her checklist on the naked man she was inspecting. "That's it, Al. Head off to costume and cosmetics and then you're good to go under. Hand this chit to Stev at chair fifteen."

Al exited through the next door. Jil gestured to the property lockers that lined one prep area wall. "Clothes and personal items in there. Management takes no responsibility for loss or damage, as per the signs. I need to go through the legals with you again."

"Every time?" Mik complained. "I could do the speech myself."

"Save it for your auditions. This is the law. I have to inform you that you are contracting to license your bodies to be implanted with another human sentience belonging to a paying customer of BodyRack Inc., a division of AllenCombeChou. This sentience, hereafter termed the Visitor, will supplant your own consciousness which will be suppressed for the duration of the Contract."

"Hereinafter called the Contract," Mik interrupted cynically.

Jil ignored him. She'd heard all the clever remarks a thousand times before. "The Visitor will control your body just as you, the Donor, normally do. He or she will have access to all your senses and functions, but not to any memories or emotions of yours. This is all laid out in Appendix A of your contracts, available online."

"I'm glad I don't remember what they have me doing," Jaz admitted. "I could never join one of those escort services. I'd feel dirty."

"The Visitor may use your body for the purposes detailed in the Contract, within the limits set by your Donation Agreements. Your life signs will be monitored via bio-implant to verify that your health is being respected."

"Tell that to the guy who wore Jaz last time," Mik muttered.

"The full terms and conditions are outlined in your Contracts, specifically in Appendices B to D." Jil ticked off an item on her data sheet. "I'll need you to reverify your preferences and consents and update your medical info. Head into the scanner bays."

Mik and Jaz padded over to the full-body monitors and held still while their physical conditions were assessed. This gave the health implants a baseline to compare against, and offered a record to prove any damage taken during the rental period. The donors were certified free of disease, equipped with contraception, and without physical brain defects.

It took a while to complete the analysis, so Jil had them fill in their consent chits while they stood there. It was still called paperwork even though the forms were holographic and touchpoint.

Jaz breezed through the form with practiced familiarity, not bothering to read the scrolled text behind each choice box. Mik checked through his selection.

Most of their answers were the same. "Yes" to general use, "yes" to light and moderate exercise, "yes" to use of light machinery; "yes" to sexual situations—it was pointless checking "no" when lots of visitors used their skins that way whether they admitted it or not. "No" to dangerous sports and heavy exercise. "No" to S&M and other extreme sexual scenarios. "No" to commercial A/V use; Mik wanted to break into the industry himself, not as a puppet for some famous has-been, and Jaz had been swayed by his caution.

Consent to drug taking was a definite "no." That was a specialist market, where addicts fed their own habits by donating to visitors who used their bodies to get high or low without physical consequence. Smokers reputedly accounted for five percent of all visits.

Jaz still registered for extreme sports, despite her last donation. "You never learn," Mik told her.

The system warbled its satisfaction that the hosts were suitable. Jil checked the consent forms and countersealed them with a thumbprint. "Some more stuff I need to read you. They add more of this health and safety stuff every year." She reeled off a script by rote. The room's cameras recorded her statements so that BodyRack had a liability shield.

"That's it, then. Off to costume and cosmetics, you two. Won't see you Sunday night, though. When you get back I'll be home getting Gin ready for the new term Monday. They grow up so fast."

"You paid for your kid license by donating, didn't you?" Jaz remembered. "Back in the old days."

"Don't you sass me about the old days, you foetus," the administrator scolded. "Apart from us having chemical injections to suppress our minds it was hardly any different. A bit less regulated, so some people had bad experiences. I did fine."

Mik was first into wardrobe. He emerged in an expensive three-piece suit with tasteful gold tie pin and cufflinks. "How's this?" he asked Jaz. "Think they'll let me keep it?"

"I think it's worth more than what you're getting paid for the donation. More than both of us get paid, probably. So no, I think they'll want it back."

The wardrobe master called Jaz in to fit her with a conservative-but-sexy power outfit and matching heels. "Who are these visitors, then?" Jaz wondered. "They're not short of a few credits."

"You know your contract," the fitter chided her. "You never find out who wore you. The company respects client confidentiality."

"You hear a few things, though," Mik considered. "Like that story about the donor who got arrested for murder, but it was his visitor who'd taken him out to kill her husband. That made the news."

"It had already been done in about a thousand bad A/V detective series before it happened for real," Jaz argued.

"Like the plots where the Visitor just wipes the Donor and stays forever. Except the transfer imprint doesn't work that way. But I guess it makes good drama." Mik sighed. "I could really play that kind of part."

"Or the personality that lingers after the Contract, to haunt the Donor and turn her into a serial killer? Or people who are kidnapped and forced into donating by their abusers? Or the ones where the Donors remember what their Visitor did with them because they were awake during the Contract, and then they go looking for revenge?"

"I'm not talking fiction, Jaz. I mean the stuff that gets hushed up in real life. What about the assholes who hire bodies and then commit suicide in them? That happens. It makes the net sometimes. And the headcases who want to disfigure themselves during their visit? I bet the company covers up loads of horrors."

"Oh sure, mention that just before I'm shut down, thanks Mik! You *always* do this! Last time you told me about that girl who woke from donating and sicked up a human finger."

"You two have vivid imaginations," Wardrobe told them.

Mik snorted. "I'm just saying, you hear things, is all. About who clients are. About what they use us to do."

Jaz had a more positive outlook. "Maybe we've been worn by somebody famous and we just don't know?"

"You're set," Wardrobe told them. "Head on to the chairs."

Mik held out his elbow like a high-powered gentleman from a history A/V. Jaz grinned and took his arm. "Why thank you, kind sir!"

They moved into a dimly lit hall where forty-eight reclined chairs were attached by ribbon-cables to imprinting machinery. Sig was duty leader to-day, which was good news; donors hardly ever woke with headaches when Sig did the transfer.

"Evening, folks," he greeted Mik and Jaz. "Looking very suave tonight. Dating contract?"

"Corporate," Jaz informed him. She and Mik did sometimes double for date visits, where some rich couple wanted a romantic time away in young nubile bodies. It was comforting to think that one's skin was sexing with skin belonging to a friend. Business rentals were nicer, though Jaz supposed their visitors might decide on a little inter-office affair away from home.

"Chairs four and five, please. And don't wriggle as I attach the electrodes."

"I bet you say that to all the girls."

Mik lay down beside Jaz and gave her a little wave. "See you Sunday!"

Sig checked that the connections were good, and then he powered down their brains.

---

Pineapple.

Jaz woke up to the taste of pineapple. She'd definitely eaten some. She didn't like pineapple.

She had a chunk in her mouth right now.

Her other senses came back. She was holding a buffet plate piled with fruit, topped with whipped cream. Her other hand gripped a fork. Her outfit was different, more casual than the one from before and without a jacket. She was in a long, sunlight-illuminated room with a wall-length picture window overlooking a lush green estate— if that was a real view and not some clever hologram then that tract was worth billions. She was surrounded by men and women who grazed the food tables and chatted.

She was at the conference.

She was *awake* and at the conference.

"Oh crap."

The man beside her turned as she spoke. "I beg your pardon?"

"Nothing. Just eating," Jaz replied hastily. She crammed another chunk of hated pineapple into her mouth.

"I understand," her companion-in-buffet confided. "A lot of us are pretty annoyed about the projection shortfalls. Skeller has really let the side down. Do you think he's still fit to be Head?"

"Hard to say."

The man's nametag read "HARVEZ, New Brazil, Acquisitions." It made sense to identify people if they weren't wearing their own bodies. He nodded at Jaz's noncommittal reply. "Exactly. Can't be too careful who you talk about this to, not in this snake pit. But Duncan and Choi are of the same opinion. This could be the start of the end for our beloved Head of Technology Development."

"I need the bathroom."

Jaz abandoned her plate and Harvez, and followed the signs to the women's toilets. The rest room was larger than the apartment she shared with Mik. It certainly had nicer finishes.

She found a mirror and checked herself. Her own face stared back at her—why shouldn't it, she wasn't the visitor. Her nametag read "CAPELLI, Rome, Product Placement." Except she wasn't Capelli.

What had gone wrong? How had she woken? Apart from silly gossip exchanged with Mik, she had never heard of anyone waking up during a Contract. Not for real. Who should she inform? Or would her monitor implant pick it up and alert the company automatically?

Jaz inspected what Capelli had done with her. Nice makeup job, tasteful and understated. Hair clipped back with antique silver band. Very nice watch. Nicer shoes. Expensive silk underwear that felt great next to her skin. Shame about the taste of pineapple.

What to do now?

The bathroom door opened and another woman entered. Her badge identified her as "MOLSON, New York, Legal." She was young and attractive—or her donor was—but something in her expression did not encourage Jaz to confession. "Capelli" patted an imaginary stray hair back into place and escaped back to the buffet lounge.

A loudspeaker announced that it was five minutes to the next meeting. There was the usual last-minute press to refill coffee cups. Jaz saw Mik across the room, stuffing the end of a wrap into his mouth.

It was typical of the way he crammed his food. Typical of Mik, not of whoever was in his body. Did remembered physical habits port across with a loan? If not, that was Mik himself!

Jaz hurried over, but some older executive put his arm around Mik and guided him to the meeting, speaking to him earnestly and privately as they went. Jaz could only trail behind.

She wondered at the older man, though. Was he a visitor, or a genuine company man in his own flesh? If he was borrowing then he had deliberately chosen a more mature donor to emphasise his seniority.

The press of delegates pushed Jaz into the room. She saw Mik take a seat and managed to manoeuvre herself to get the place next to him. His tag read "ALOTTO, Rome, Assessment." The next two attendees along also came from the Rome office, so Jaz had accidentally picked the right place to sit anyway.

The mature man she had seen with Mik took the podium, facing the seventy or so conference-goers who were ranged at long tables on three sides of the presentation room. He did not bother with notes or reach for the remote that operated the holodisplay. He did not introduce himself. His badge said "SHORE, Board."

"Let's cut to it," he said abruptly. "I know a lot of you were disappointed in Dr. Skeller's projections of full implementation. We all are, up on the Top Floor. But these are the challenges of the program, the reason we have contingencies and variances. If it was easy, you wouldn't earn the top credits, right?"

There was a dutiful mumble of chuckles at the executive joke.

"So we go with what we have: around 60

Shore stepped aside. A dark-skinned supermodel took the podium. Jaz could only imagine how much renting her must cost.

Vasqar activated the imagery systems. "Subject Alpha," she indicated, keying up a full-sized hologram of a middle-aged Asian man. "Senior legal counsel to a major corporation. Their go-to shark for litigation and damage control. In his spare time he likes to visit in the skins of teenage girls, the younger looking, the better."

Jaz knew that some of her visitors were male. It was the first time she had seen what one of them might look like.

"We used the filtration software on Subject Alpha on three occasions," Vasqar explained. "From the short-term trawl we identified a number of security passwords, much of his next day's agenda including two sensitive situations requiring intimidating interviews with erring staff, and an inference that his interest in teenage girls was not confined to borrowing their bodies. From the long-term memory sift we got at least three examples of legal processes that had been brought to cover up corporate wrongdoing, two of which Assessment have now independently verified, since we knew where to look. We also found material that might be used to pressure other executives of his company. He knows where the bodies are, so to speak."

Vasqar clicked up a series of graphs and charts illustrating how the data had been pulled from the subject's brain. "Now we know there is a lot more that we have not been able to access. As Dr. Skeller observed, the mind seems to have mechanisms that protect the most sensitive information from easy interpretation, and we have not yet developed algorithms to decode it all. But the commercial advantages from just this one test case, from Subject Alpha alone, are immense." She caught Shore looking at his watch. "Of course, that is not my department to comment upon. Good day to you all."

The doctor finished her presentation and handed the floor back to Shore. The board officer make three short hand-clapping gestures for the briefing and turned to the delegates. "The information we extracted is close-hold, of course, but you've heard the general tenor of it. What's the assessment of how damaging it is?" He turned towards where Mik and Jaz were seated. "Assessment?"

Jaz remembered that was written on Mik's ID, but Mik was silent.

The man on the other side of him chimed in. "We haven't had the data for long, sir, but it looks very good. We could certainly use it to leverage contract advantages. We could take down Subject Alpha with paedophilia charges anytime we wanted. We can turn him entirely to work for us. We might have an in or two on their board as well.

"Absolutely," Mik agreed.

Shore called on other opinions from around the hall. Assessments Tokyo were also optimistic, but Assessments St. Petersburg had doubts about how many similar successes Advanced Programming might be able to produce. For a while the discussion became general, before Shore called things back to order.

"That's what you need to know going into workshops. This afternoon we'll be brainstorming by divisions on the implications and applications of the mind-skimming technology. I'll expect realistic timescales for rolling it out to all visitors, a streamlined system of assessment and prioritization, some firm guidelines on legal cover and leak penalties, and a framework for exploitation of intelligence. We'll plenary at four and set out tasks for tomorrow's big finish."

The room sensed the session was ending. There was a general stirring as people retrieved datapads and comms-sticks.

"One more thing," Shore called across the shuffling. "We didn't have time for Product Placement to report at the morning session, so we'll take your report before the plenary, Ms. Capelli. All this new stuff is great, but we still want to know how we're doing slipping purchasing desires into our visitors' heads when they go borrowing."

Jaz nodded, trying to conceal panic. That drew her attention to the complimentary notepad and pen left out at each place round the table. The stationary had BodyRack logos on it, with an AllenCombeChou identifier at the bottom of the page. "Get out of yourself" the tagline read, just like in the A/V ads.

Then Jaz knew whose conference she was at, and just how much trouble she was in for what she had overheard.

———————— • ————————

What to do?

What the hell to do?

Lunch was served outside, on a wide sunny terrace overlooking a tropical bird garden. It proved that the view through the windows was no hologram, and why donors had to work so hard to burn off calories after they had hosted a visitor.

Jaz might have been tempted by the gourmet cuisine, had it not been for her blind terror. Instead she decided she had to know if Mik was also awake.

She stalked him and pounced as he emerged onto the balcony.

"A word, please?" she asked. She'd tried to calculate the most neutral invitation she could. Capelli and Alotto might be work colleagues, rivals, best friends, anything. She didn't even know if they were on a first-name basis. Tiny mistakes might give her away.

"Sure, what is it?" Alotto replied; or was it Mik? Why did he have to be a damned good actor?

"Can we speak privately?"

"I was hoping to get lunch."

"This won't take long. Um, I'm not taking the Mik."

Was that a flicker of surprise? A hesitation?

"Let's be quick then," Alotto/Mik replied. "I'm pretty jazzed about this afternoon's workshops."

"Mik?"

"Jaz! It's you? *You* you? I mean, it's you now?"

"Yes. Come on, we need to talk."

"My room. We'll slip away for a nooner."

"What, you mean Capelli and Alotto were...?"

"Oh yeah. Last night *and* she dragged me away before breakfast to have her way with me. With you, I mean. I gather this is a regular conference affair that their usual spouses don't know about."

"So we're just the latest skins they've rendezvoused in."

"Yeah. She—you—she was in my bed when I woke up. When I saw you there, for a minute I thought it was just one of those times you get blue in the night and crawl in with me to cuddle, before my head did a reality check. It was pretty weird, actually, being with you but not with you."

Mik and Jaz found the elevators to the guest suites. "At least you knew the spots to go for, right?" she told him. She disguised how weird it felt to have been to bed with her roommate when she hadn't been in her head. She actually blushed.

"Viv Capelli said I was improving my game and I should hire this meat again."

"When did you... wake up?"

"Middle of the night. I had to pee. I think Alotto drank too much before bedtime. I found myself in a strange bathroom. I've been covering ever since."

"Covering me, evidently."

"I didn't want to give myself away. Fortunately Viv wasn't after much conversation. And it's nothing I haven't seen before, Jaz."

"I woke up at buffet. Now I have to give a presentation to the conference."

"The Placement stuff? Oh crap!"

"Oh yes. Very 'oh crap'. What do we do? Why hasn't the company spotted this has happened by now?"

The elevator doors opened on a well-furnished foyer lounge. Mik took a passcard from his pocket and opened up a large luxurious executive suite. "We can't let anyone know, Jaz. You heard what I heard. BodyRack is using their tech to do bad things to the visitors. That scanning has to be illegal. The product placements too, probably. If they knew that we know..."

"Percenters can always crush the rest of us, yes. But we can't hide this, either. Not for long. Not after my presentation at four."

Mik rapped his knuckles on his forehead to stimulate solutions. "It's worse than that. What happened to Alotto and Capelli when we woke? Usually at the end of a contract they'd go back to a chair and get extracted to their own bodies again. That didn't happen this time, so where are they?"

"Asleep in us?" Jaz speculated. "Or... dead?"

"I'm not sure which is worse. And we were joking about the horror scenarios."

"How did this happen, Mik? Nobody wakes up like this. Or if they do I've never heard about it."

"Suspicious that it happened to both of us, and that it happened right here at the BodyRack power conference."

"Are we being set up? For what? By who?"

"Prime suspect: Sig. He was the one who programmed the transfers. He's got the tech know-how if anyone does. The 'why'? Dunno."

Jaz hid her face in her hands. "What are we going to *do*, Mik? Even if we broke out of here, wherever here is, if we got past security and found a cop booth to report what we heard, it's only our word against all of them. An art history student and an unemployed actor against a megacorp with a thousands of lawyers and billions of credits to spend on stamping us out. Who will they believe? Two nobody donors or the rich people who buy us for fun?"

"Maybe this is all a corporate game," Mik worried. "Maybe it's murder, eliminating Alotto and Capelli because of... reasons, corporate reasons. Maybe they were going to be whistleblowers. Or else we're the intended victims? Maybe we're the after-meeting entertainment, watching the stupid little donors freak out and run through the mazes."

"You're not thinking clearly, Mik. You're letting paranoia run away with you. Nobody is acting like they're out to get us, or our visitors. With all these people here, not all of them could be that good at pretending. We have a while. We have a chance."

"A chance to do what?"

"Not sure. What did that boss-man Shore want to talk to you about earlier?"

"He was congratulating me on the department's work. Said he would call on me for a comment. I sure fluffed that cue."

"So your Assessment department did the initial evaluation on Subject Alpha's data," Jaz understood. "What else did Shore say?"

"That the data should be forwarded directly to him. That's all."

"Nothing else?"

"Well done. Gold star for the department. I get called on. Send him the report. That's it."

Jaz thought rapidly. "The report. The one about the illegal data extraction? You have that file?"

Mik fumbled out Alotto's data-stick. He thumbed it on, pulling up the 3D holoscreen with touch input. "Good thing he keyed this to my body's thumbprint. Or maybe it got provided like that, the same as the fitted suits? Anyway, I'm in. Here's the report."

"That's what we have to leak. We need to get that to the public, get it on the net."

"And then what? You think they'll just let us walk after that? And how do we 'get it on the net' anyhow? There's not going to be any unmonitored feeds here. Besides, the megacorps own the net. They won't let a story like this stay in the wild."

Jaz tugged her hair. "This was supposed to be an easy job. Cushy. Good money, low risk. Jackson owed me a favor. How did it end up like this?"

Mik peered from his window at the terrace below. "Lunch is almost over. We're running out of time. Workshops are next and we have to split up for them."

"Assessment Department working on industrial blackmail and good ol' Product Placement, uploading purchasing desires into percenters across the world!"

"Yep. Body swaps with excess baggage. Who knew the crime stories were right?"

"Only very bad people. We have to stop them, Mik. We have to do something or we're just colluding with it all."

"Sure. Tell me what and I'll do it. Uh-oh... They're calling workshops. If anyone asks, the sex was fantastic. Don't tell the wife."

"Workshops..." Jaz wrestled with a half-formed thought, a mad idea that was almost born. "Product Placement... Oh, wait!"

———————— • ————————

"No. Seriously? I don't believe it. *Seriously?*"

The woman next to Jaz in the break-out group nodded affirmation. "We have the upload and download logs. It was Mai Mayden herself! How many credits would you have to pay for her to donate her body?"

"You're claiming that the superstar of the *Stand Alone* movies hires her skin out? That makes no sense at all. I know some big celebs did that before they were discovered, but…"

"I'm telling you. Mai Maiden. Somebody contracted her. We have the records—all confidential of course. But somebody paid big to be Mai for a day."

Gossip was flying in the huddle of Product Placement staff from around the globe. A hunky beefcake tagged "SOLOMON, Brisbane" offered his contribution. "Darlings, you would be shocked by some of the custom hires I've heard of. Two big A/V personalities who paid to wear *each other's* skins! A well-known politico who hires donors with terminal illnesses and crash victims! A certain big-selling recording artist who rents out hunky hairy men so he can do unspeakable things to his own unconscious body! Really, I could write a book—if Legal wouldn't sue me into oblivion."

"Or worse," Kenner, Birmingham whispered ominously.

"Worse?" Jaz echoed.

"You know. Direct Operations." The woman—except Kenner was actually male—gave a little shudder. "You won't see *those* people at corporate weekends like this one."

"Just as well," Solomon offered. "I wouldn't trust the food."

Jaz would have liked to know more about Direct Operations, but Viv Capelli undoubtedly already did. She pushed on with other information gathering. "If there are percenters donating as well as visiting, maybe we should be marketing to the donors as well."

"Oh, some percenters donate," Kenner agreed. "Mostly those who don't want the bother of exercising their own bodies. They transfer out to some skin that doesn't weigh 150 kilos while some personal trainer visits their body to do the hard work."

Solomon leaned in. "I heard about a major politician—I won't say who, darlings, don't ask me—who regularly donates for an actor to do his public speeches for him. And there's a certain celebrity who gets his body occupied to keep his wife happy in the bedroom while he's visiting elsewhere. She doesn't suspect a thing."

"So Capelli might be onto something." Coreno from Andalusia considered. "Not all donors are poverty-line nothings. It's not a totally bad idea to double-target clients who donate as well as visit. Twice the impression. It wouldn't take a big re-rig if we just folded the imprinting onto the re-awakening process. Staple it to the compliance programming?"

"Compliance programming?" Jaz couldn't help asking, though Capelli would know.

Fortunately, Coreno thought she was questioning her choice of method. "It's virtually the same technique anyway. Along with inhibiting the likelihood of complaint about any little abuses, and conditioning a willingness to donate again, we just slip in the advertising package. So a lot of no-hope proles start lusting for the newest road vehicle they will never afford. Who cares?"

"We don't want our donors getting too ambitious in their wants," Kenner objected. "We don't really want them desiring much out of life—except another contract."

Jaz controlled her expression. Had she been brainwashed by the transfer chairs? Encouraged to endure donating, to overlook occasional abuses, by software loaded into her mind? She remembered her scrapes and bruises from the rock climbing contract, and other times before that when a donation had been tough. She had thought herself strong for keeping on doing what she needed to put herself through college. Or was that what she had been programmed to believe?

Who knew about this? Was Jackson aware that his donors were being modified? Was Jil? Sig was supposed to be tech-savvy. Did that mean he was part of the conspiracy? Or were they all line workers, too low level to realise what was being done?

Why had this never been news? Everyone said that the megacorps controlled the A/V. but most people believed that the important stuff still got out to the public.

How many people donated these days? More than admitted to it later. Were all of them reaction-modified, assisted to compliance? What percentage of the one-percenters visited from time to time? Jaz didn't know the statistics but she guessed it was a lot. Who with the money for it would not take the chance to be young, fit, and beautiful for a while? Who wouldn't want to be an athlete, a stud, a model?

All of them had been adjusted too. Every client thought a little bit more like BodyRack wanted them to.

The company had already mastered putting things into their subjects' minds. Now they could pull thoughts out of there too. Subject Alpha was only the first.

How could anyone fight a megacorp that could do that?

During the time that Jaz dealt with those questions the group discussion moved on. Eventually someone dragged it back to the action points they were supposed to address.

"We could do more market modelling," Coreno insisted. "Right now we just roll out a list of hot topics that we want our visitors to trend. Whatever schedule comes down from the Investment boys and girls, really. We could be much more aggressive in picking the winners before they're big. Especially with the intel we'll be getting from this new thought sifting thing."

Jaz got back in the game. Life questions could come later if she survived the day. "We could do almost real-time updates to the lists," she suggested. "How often could we amend them?"

"More than the daily revisions?" objected Solomon. "Sounds like a lot of hard work for minimum gain."

"No, Viv has a point," Coreno cut in. "Instead of one five p.m. update, why not make it a continuous rolling list? Mesh it with the market projections coming from Assessment and go big!"

"Because it's stupid, is why," Kenner snorted. "It takes weeks of reinforcement, multiple visit uploads to really embed a subconscious desire. Change the message too often and it'll never bed in. Make it any more strident, and clients will spot that something has been plugged into their thoughts. The system works. Don't reinvent the wheel."

"Well we need to come up with something from this workshop, darlings," Solomon warned the group. "Now that Vampire Vasquar's toys are proving useful and Assessment is riding high, our little division is going to slide right down the food chain if we don't up our profile."

There was mutual agreement about that, if nothing else. Office politics was vicious at AllenCombeChou.

Coreno produced a data pad and pulled up a screed of files. Each one was numbered and named with a brand to be promoted. Jaz recognized every big label. "Let's review the stack," the Andalusian delegate offered. "I hate to admit that Kenner has a point, but he does. Or *she* does today," he added in slightly-mocking reference to the officer's skin choice. "We can't make big sudden register changes, it's true, but maybe we can do something with priority and get a more dynamic aggregation of preference engineering? Now, this is today's list, due to roll out in about ninety minutes..."

Jaz looked up. "That's going out today?"

"Well, it's not signed off yet, but once the Top Floor agrees it, this will be the stack. Why?"

"No reason. Carry on."

Jaz desperately tried to memorise the URL of the folder. She needed to find it again on Capelli's data-stick.

The workshop dragged on towards Jaz's four o'clock presentation.

———— • ————

The group session overran. Logging each focus team's action points took far too long. Jaz was not alone in getting restless as the activity stretched past its allotted time and gobbled into coffee break. Unlike the other delegates though, Jaz felt a growing desperation about what was to come next.

At last the session facilitator finished her summary and dismissed the department. "Sorry we went a bit over. If you hurry you can still grab a cake and beverage from the table in the foyer before the plenary commences in the main atrium. Don't forget to leave your feedback sheets on your seats."

Jaz had feedback: don't mind-control people. Don't put things into my head without my consent, so that I don't know if my choices are really me. Don't make me wonder if you programmed me to be more reckless, more cavalier, more slutty, more willing to donate myself another time. Don't drag out my private thoughts and memories and dreams to sift through for marketing or to blackmail me later. Don't be this overwhelming, terrible, unstoppable force that I can't do anything about because you're just too big, too awful.

She wrote something about more discipline in the focus group discussions instead, circled a few score numbers, and hastened out.

She ignored the queue for the tea and coffee table and looked for Mik. She couldn't see him.

Had they caught him already? Was the plan stopped before it began?

Jaz retreated to the bathroom again. She found a stall and checked Capelli's data-stick. After struggling with the unfamiliar operating system for a moment she got into the company drives and was able to find the files that Coreno had shown the group.

That was only a copy, of course. Finding the master required a bit more pushing. It was lucky that Viv had the clearances for that category of information.

She located the folder. It was approval-flagged now, ready to go out in an hour's time.

She had access. "We could do this," she whispered to herself.

The PA system announced the start of the day's last session. Everyone was to move immediately to the atrium on level one.

Jaz considered hiding in the toilet for the rest of her life. Instead she checked her appearance in the mirror—Jaz playing Capelli wearing Jaz—and appeared in the foyer to mill with the rest of the delegates towards her inevitable discovery.

The atrium was an elaborate circular hall with a domed glass roof. The place had an equatorial feel. Walls were lined with tropical plants, even small trees. There were no tables this time, only a semicircle of chairs four rows deep focused towards a plinth and speaker's podium. Mr. Shore was already there, consulting with a secretary and flicking through some notes.

Seats were not designated. Solomon from Brisbane waved for Jaz to come over and sit beside him. She shook her head, trying to mime that she needed an end seat because she was due to present; or so that she could flee the hall in desperation when she was discovered.

Mik hastened into the hall at the last moment and had to take one of the unfilled front-row seats.

Shore began. "A little bit of housekeeping. We're in a controlled communications environment. A number of you have attempted calls out on your regular comm nets. That won't work. You need to file your message through the house system so it is logged before it's forwarded. We're discussing some pretty sensitive stuff here, ladies and gentlemen. We screen. Remember too that all personal data systems will be scrubbed and detoxed before leaving."

He flipped a paper over. "A reminder that if you want the rafting for tomorrow's team-building exercise you need to sign up by six tonight. If you are bungee jumping and abseiling, then you, not the company, are responsible for any deposit losses due to skin damages. If you're going to the wine tasting make sure your rental contract includes the alcohol waiver. It's a liability condition that the tasters insist on."

He checked another note. "Those of you shuttling out at close of session tomorrow will need to get your skins to the hotel return point by 7.30 p.m. to be transferred back. If you want to extend your visit after Monday morning you'll need to make a private arrangement with your vendor."

Shore set aside the nag-sheet and leaned onto his podium to project authority, just like the manuals taught. "Now, I know you've had a pretty packed afternoon and you're bursting with ideas for our discussion, but before we get to that we've neglected the presentation from Product Placement and I'm not going to bump it again. So without further ado let me call Viv Capelli from our Rome office to come up and..."

An alarm went off.

At first Jaz though she had been caught. Someone had finally detected that she and Mik were impostors—or was that the real thing? Direct Operations would burst in to hood and cuff them, to drag them away to be disposed of where they would never be heard from again.

Shore held up his hand for calm. "Fire drill, folks. Nothing to worry about. Proceed to the checkpoint following the yellow hologram lines. Wait in the designated areas until everything is clear and you are instructed to return. You know the routine. Let's go."

He sighed exactly like a conference-runner whose schedule had received another setback and joined the file that formed at the exit routes.

Mik pushed his way over to Jaz. "You okay?"

"Yes. What did you do? Is this you?"

"I said I'd arrange a diversion to get you out of your talk—Capelli's talk."

"You set off a fire alarm? Aren't they monitored?"

"That was my plan, yes. But then I thought about all the cams and stuff and I had a better idea." He held up his wrist. The Cartier watch that had adorned it before was gone. "I bribed a houseboy to break the glass instead."

"Good work. Very timely. I might overlook you sexing me while I was being visited."

"What? Why is that different from being friends-with-benefits at home? Or Viv wearing you to sleep with Hec Alotto?"

"Don't know, but it is. Like I'd passed out drunk and you... oh, never mind. All this body-loaning politics is so screwed up anyhow. We pretend it's not like prostitution so we can look ourselves in the mirror, because we don't know for sure what we did last night. We don't have the detail, we didn't make the choices except for the big one to agree in the first place..."

Mik laid a cautionary hand on Jaz's arm. They were in the press of delegates exiting the atrium. This wasn't the place for moral conflicts and soul-searching.

"Bad luck about the alarm, Viv," Coreno called as they crushed past him. "Your moment of glory, under Shore's eye! I bet you get bumped to a coffee break tomorrow now!"

"Aw, damn!" Jaz responded.

The crowd was herded out onto one of the open terraces. Facility staff were there to guide them to designated waiting areas. The black-uniformed security staff that swarmed from nowhere to check the conference centre were more alarming.

"There are an awful lot of them," Mik murmured nervously.

"The D.O. blocks?" Coreno asked disdainfully. "They always seem to come by the busload."

Jaz decoded the acronym. "Direct Operations?"

"Who else would run security at this thing? What, you don't have them in Italy? They crawl all over us in Spain."

"We have them. Just not so... there."

Coreno snorted. "I hear you. We had one guy in our IT office, he tried to install some kind of personal software. A puzzle game, I think. *Hoverfrog*, maybe? Then the door crashes open, in come the blocks in black. They wrestle him to the ground, no caution, clamp him in those plastic cuffs, literally carry him out of there. Less than a minute. No warning, no explanation, no apology. Just gone. Never saw the guy again."

"What happened to him?" Mik ventured.

"Terminated. That's what we were told." The Andalusian delegate considered for a moment. "They probably meant 'fired'. With D.O. who can tell?"

Jaz pushed back panic. Neither fight nor flight could save her here. She had to be smart.

"I need a few moments," she told Coreno. "I'd better recheck my, um, my notes for the presentation. Shore might want a shortened version so I need to be ready. I'll just go over there and check my bullet points. Will you help me, Alotto?"

"He's Assessment," Coreno pointed out.

"Just a critical friend thing," Mik replied.

Coreno evidently caught on that the rumors about Capelli and Alotto were true. He smirked and filed the gossip away for later. "Enjoy yourselves."

Under the watchful marshalling of the centre staff and oversight from D.O., Jaz and Mik couldn't stray too far from the delegate herd. They edged to the rear balcony with its spectacular view over the waterfall and the tree canopy of the valley below.

"Did you get it?" Mik whispered.

"I think so. There's a file that is supposed to go out today to all the visitors. In less than an hour."

"Do you remember its location?"

Jaz fumbled out Capelli's data-stick and pulled up the holographic screen. She navigated through the systems, past the secure data warnings that required user identification, and found the update package that had been signed off by the Top Floor.

"What happens to it?" Mik wanted to know.

"That is what they call daily revisions. It updates a program that pushes things into the heads of visitors as they transfer into donors—into us! Little suggestions, like what holiday they would like, what brands they should wear. But soon it might include more than subliminal advertising. It might suggest what jobs to take, what contracts to sign, which people to date; a whole lot more."

"That's mind control! Is that possible? It's got to be illegal!"

"But is it? What law is there that says you can't program someone's mind? Can't read their memories electronically and sift them for useful data? The law hasn't caught up with this, Mik. Why would there be a law against something nobody knows is possible?"

"Like how there were no speed limits for cars when they were first invented and no laws about where planes could land."

"Except people at least knew about cars and planes. This is… I don't know what. But everyone *has* to know. Needs to know."

"This as a lot more than illicitly installing *Hoverfrog*. If we do this, those serious men in black uniforms will come for us."

Jaz shook her head. She'd been giving this a lot of consideration. "Not us, no. They'll come for Viv Capelli and Hec Alotto, whistleblowers. Jaz and Mik, we were just skins, shut down inside our minds while visitors did what they wanted. Nobody has ever woken up during a contract like this, remember? That's our escape from this nightmare. We wake up back home!"

"And Viv and Hec face the music."

"Viv and Hec and everybody here are part of a conspiracy to brainwash the world. I can live with them suffering."

Mik glanced at the stewards. The first people were being directed back into the building. The false alarm had evidently been identified. He hoped that the youngster he had bribed had been sneaky enough to avoid the security cams.

"We need to do this fast, then," he told Jaz. "I've got the Vasqar report and all the Skeller data. Everything on Assessment's mind-skimming stuff. Add in your recording of your afternoon's Product Placement workshop."

"None of this could ever be messaged out past the IT comms screens."

"Sure. Except we're not messaging it out, are we? We're packing it right into that upload file that's been Top Floor approved, that's going to get sent to every transfer centre across the globe to be plugged into every visitor who contracts a skin from this evening onwards."

Jaz remembered Kenner's gloomy warning about how too much information dumped too blatantly into the percenters' brains would be obvious to them. What she and Mik were about to imprint on them was as blatant as could be.

"We doing this?" she checked.

"Now or never," Mik replied. "But if we don't then someone's going to have questions about us at this conference."

"And if we do then we might end up like that IT guy in Spain. Or worse."

"They're calling us back inside."

Jaz shut her eyes and thumbed the "send" button.

---

Direct Operations came for Jaz and Mik by night, overriding the lock on Alotto's guest suite and surrounding the couple in the bed they shared.

Jaz was with her roommate for comfort, not sex tonight; Mik and Capelli had somehow shadowed the possibility of any intimate exchange between Mik and Jaz. Jaz awoke as she was pulled from Mik's arms and wrestled to the ground by men who knew how to do it.

There was no possibility of resistance. Alotto and Capelli were tag-cuffed, gagged, hooded, and handled without any disturbance that might warn other delegates of any problem.

Jaz was carried, blind and restrained, unable to struggle. She felt cold air as if she was outside, then the acoustics changed to somewhere inside where echoes were clipped. She was sat on a hard chair with her arms behind the backrest. Her wrist-tags were attached to something so she was pinioned. Her ankles were fastened to metal chair legs.

Her hood and gag were removed. She saw a small windowless room lit by a cold neon bar. The only other furniture was a metal trolley with covered equipment. Three men surrounded her, two of them flanking her at the periphery of her vision.

She wished that Capelli preferred less revealing nighties.

The interrogator in front of her stared her out. The man had no nametag.

Jaz deliberately looked away, eyeing the featureless wall and the polystyrene-tiled ceiling. Now that the worst had happened she felt liberated. She was so far out of her experience that it like being in a movie. She wished that she had Mik's acting ability. He would know how to play the scene.

"*Perché?*" her questioner asked at last.

Jaz didn't speak Italian. She remained silent.

He slapped her. Capelli lost her damage deposit.

"Why?" the interrogator asked again in English.

"Because," Jaz answered.

The man scowled. "Do you know how much shit you are in? Can you imagine? Do you think we're playing?"

"No."

"Then why did you send that data?"

"People need to know."

"Who paid you?"

"Nobody. It was the right thing to do."

The face-masked interrogator at her right wheeled the trolley forward. Jaz almost squealed for them to stop, to not use their surgical instruments on her body, that this was borrowed flesh from some part-time student trying to finance her way through art college. She silenced herself in time, though her face must have betrayed her fear.

Under the cloth was electrical apparatus. It took Jaz's screaming mind a moment to recognize consciousness transfer equipment.

"You're going back to your own skin, Capelli," the D.O. officer declared. "We've got it. We've got you. When you're in your own head we can read everything you did, why you did it, who you did it for. In your own flesh we can *cut* the truth from you. Oh, we can do so many bad things to make you confess."

As he spoke, the others attached the electrode web to Jaz's skull. This equipment was smaller than any she had seen at BodyRack, more refined and featured. It didn't whine as it powered up, it purred.

Her interrogator leaned in. "You've caused a lot of damage. The Top Floor is unhappy. There will be consequences."

"I hope so," Jaz said. "You deserve them."

"Send her back."

———— • ————

Strangers stood over Jaz.

Her nerve broke. She began to scream.

She hadn't returned to her own body! She had gone back to Viv Capelli's captive form, far off in Rome, where cruel bricks of AllenCombeChou's Direct Operations division waited to dismantle her for information and revenge!

Mik held her. "Jaz? It's okay! Jaz! They're cops. Not D.O. Just cops."

Jaz checked her hands. She felt her face. She ran her tongue about her teeth.

She was herself. She had escaped being exiled into Viv Capelli after all.

She was in the Body Transfer Reserve, on her chair, suffering from the usual return disorientation of her mind returning to her own brain. Jil and Sig were watching her, flanked by observing uniformed police officers. Most of the other Chairs were empty now. BodyRack was shutting down.

Jil looked upset. She was missing getting her daughter ready for school. Sig seemed to have aged ten years since the start of the weekend.

"It turns out that the company has been doing bad things," Mik told Jaz, by way of caution and orientation. "Imprinting compliance programming on visitors, stealing memories and secrets from them as their consciousness filtered through the equipment. Maybe some mods on us too. The whole scandal broke while we were out donating."

"We didn't know, Jaz, I swear it!" Jil promised, distressed. Sig kept silent.

"They've hauled Jackson in for questioning. The A/V channels are going crazy with it. National committees of enquiry! Lawsuits of epic proportions! Hundreds of arrests across the world!"

"So… BodyRack is finished?" Jaz asked. It wasn't that hard to play dumb right now."

"As soon as all the donated bodies get returned, everything is suspended," Sig explained. "People will have to get by being themselves for a while."

"We got sent back for waking a few minutes ago," Mik supplied. "Evidently there was some delay with our return, but they won't say what. I'll still make my audition, though, if we're cleared to go?"

"Can we?" Jaz asked the cops. "Go, I mean?" She needed more than a post-donation shower this time. She needed to get away.

"You'll require a medical screening," the officer in charge at the scene insisted. "Leave your details and we'll call you in."

"They really need to talk to staff first," Mik explained to Jaz. "You know, people who can remember anything."

———— • ————

"We saved the world. Did we save the world, Mik? Or was that some sort of weird while-we-were-donating fever dream?"

Mik put down his stubble-razor and checked his appearance. "*Somebody* slammed a whole bunch of classified data into some angry percenters. Maybe it was us."

The bathroom stall in their tiny apartment was only eight paces from the kitchen counter. Jaz could chop fruit for breakfast and still hold a conversation with her roommate as he prepped for his call. "What about Capelli and Alotto, then? What happened to them?"

"I'm not going to ask Sig. Are you? Hope that they died when we woke up in our brains, so there was nothing of them to go back to what D.O. had waiting for them." He paused then added, "Hope they're not still inside our minds somewhere, screaming to get out."

"And we just... go on? I find another way of paying for my degree. You hope today is your big break? Nobody ever knows what we did?"

"We live. I'll settle for that."

"And the thoughts they put into us? How will we ever know again if we are really ourselves? That our choices, our beliefs, our relationships, our temperaments are really our own?"

"How would you know anyway? You play the part they cast you in. Borrowed lives are better than none at all."

"That's true, I guess. We were lucky to get out like we did. Stupid nobody skin-donors who know nothing. We win."

Jaz's laugh echoed back to her. Something inside her head clicked. Her hand tightened around the chopping knife.

"Ciao bella!" she whispered to herself.

Then she headed for the bathroom to kill Mik.

## About The Author

I.A Watson writes in a small study in Yorkshire, England, but the stories can take him anywhere in time and space. Research brings history to life or predicts wild new futures. Plotting offers puzzle-boxes and mazes to explore. Characterisation allows... well, being mean to fictional people who seem real. The last, best part though is communicating those stories to readers, so the journey is shared with companions. I.A Watson has authored twelve novels, two anthologies, one non-fiction book, and enough short stories to put his bibliography over the fifty mark and he has a lot more places to visit yet.

For more information, visit chillwater.org.uk/writing/iawatsonhome.htm.

# The Earth Ship

## Graham Storrs

*Editor's Note: History is a tale written in blood that stretches backward to the dawn of human awakening and forward to the unknowable end of days. Or is it? Are human beings the source of violence? Or could our barbarity be a learned behavior, pressed into each new generation by the unbroken chain of cultures that stand behind us?*

At about noon the Earth ship landed. Liddie came in and said, "They're here." Everyone looked up and stopped and the silence was electric.

Gerol went straight to the council building where Malc and Anya were discussing the situation.

"May I see the transcript again, please?" Gerol asked, holding out his hand to Malc. The old man shrugged and pushed the sheets of paper across the table to him.

"I've read it through a hundred times," Malc grumbled. "They make as little sense now as they did two weeks ago."

Gerol picked up the record of the first and only contact between Beasphor and the visiting Earth ship. It had been recorded at the Mount Snowy Radio Observatory, where astonished astronomers had heard the Earth ship hailing them and had quickly improvised a transmitter to answer with. He could easily imagine the excited scientists hunched around the microphone.

Earth ship: This is Earth ship *Resolution* of the Imperial Fifth Fleet. Please respond if you can hear us. This is Earth ship *Resolution*. Please respond.

It was repeated over and over until the transmitter had been lashed together. Then the inhabitants of Beasphor spoke to the people of Earth for the first time in so many hundreds of years. The radio engineer, Allie, spoke first.

Allie: Earth ship? Earth ship? Can you hear me? Hey, Penn, Kate, I think I've got it working!

Penn: What's the distance now? How much delay can we expect?

Earth Ship: We are receiving you, Colony FC3098-BS4. Please stand by.

There followed a long break during which the observatory team babbled excitedly. Eventually, the ship broke its silence.

Earth Ship: This is Captain Robert Cheng of the *Resolution*. To whom am I speaking?

Allie: I'm Allie and I've got Penn and Kate with me. Are you really speaking from a spaceship?

Earth Ship: This is the Earth Ship *Resolution* of the Fifth Fleet. I would like to speak to someone in authority. Is the Colony leader present?

Kate: I'm in charge of the observatory this year, does that count?

Penn: He probably wants to talk to a councillor, Kate. Would that do, Earthman? Would you like to talk to a councillor?

The transcript showed one minute and thirty-five seconds of silence from the Earth ship. Then the voice of Captain Cheng came back.

Earth Ship: We will be arriving in ten days and will make landfall shortly afterwards. My navigator requires information.

For a while the observatory staff and the ship discussed the suitability of various landing sites. Luckily Kate was able to understand the navigator's talk about coordinate systems well enough to direct them to Hundred Acre Field, which they all agreed would be a good place.

Earth Ship: Our mission is a peaceful one. We therefore must insist that no military forces come within a hundred kilometres of the landing site. We will be monitoring the movement of military equipment and personnel from space and will defend ourselves vigorously if we feel threatened in any way.

Kate: But we don't have any military equipment or personnel. Why would we want to threaten you?

Earth Ship: We also insist that there is no air traffic within 500 kilometres of the landing site at any time. I'm sure you will understand our need to take such precautions.

Kate: No. I don't understand. Do you, Allie? Penn? We won't threaten you and I know it's very exciting and interesting that you are coming and all that but what you're asking would upset lots of people's travel plans. I can't see them agreeing to that! Couldn't you just land without all this fuss?

Earth Ship: I will not repeat my instructions. Just relay them to your superiors. This mission to your colony is under the authority of Her Imperial Majesty's Ministry for Interplanetary Affairs. When we land, we will expect an immediate audience with your civil and military leaders.

Kate: But I don't understand. I don't think I understand any of this.

Earth Ship: Just pass this on. You may also wish to arrange a celebration. Our visit marks the reabsorption of Colony FC3098-BS4 into the protection of the Empire. Long live the Empress!

The Earth ship had not spoken to them at all from that moment to this.

———————— • ————————

The landing craft ticked and sighed. Its engines cooled and its framework relaxed after the tensions of the descent from high orbit. Four other landers stood in formation around it. Above them, ten sub-atmospheric fighters circled like hawks.

Captain Robert Cheng stood in front of the viewscreens and surveyed the crowd of gawking civilians. They were coming in ground cars and buses to see the spectacle. There was no sign of military activity and no sign yet of an official welcoming party. Well, he would wait a while longer.

"There is no interruption to the civil air traffic, sir," said a young officer.

"Recommendation?"

"Shoot a couple of planes down sir, just to let them know we mean it."

"Wang?"

Another officer snapped to attention. "Yessir!"

"Your assessment of the threat this crowd poses."

Wang relaxed a little. "None whatsoever sir. A scan reveals no weapons or energy sources of any kind. Their vehicles are primitive and low-powered. No armor. We could eliminate them in a few seconds if we wished to."

Cheng paced the deck. "Why would they expose themselves like this? Is it a trick, do you think, Mr. Lee?"

Principal Officer Lee Ping Ya of the Imperial Secret Police, looked at Cheng's tall, broad-shouldered figure and smiled. "You are the military man, captain. I am only a cultural affairs consultant."

Cheng turned and looked him in the eye. Principal Officer Lee, in the usual manner of the secret police, was attached to his mission under an assumed role and title. Only Cheng knew his real affiliation—only Cheng and the entire crew. Lee was an ascetic creature, sinuous and sharp-witted, with insolent eyes. "Then perhaps you would give me the benefit of your thoughts on this culture, Mr. Lee."

Lee smiled again. "They are a puzzle, are they not? To listen to their radio chatter, you would guess they were a simple, rural people, thinking only about their families and their potato crops. Yet our observations reveal high levels of organization, a manufacturing capability and technical infrastructure well beyond any rural economy we have ever seen, and evidence of scientific awareness many advanced societies would be proud of."

"And their tactics?" insisted Cheng.

Lee just shrugged and turned away as if he was bored.

The Captain clenched his teeth in silent anger and whirled on the young officer who was now staring fixedly at his displays. "Shoot down the next aircraft to enter the exclusion zone. No warning. Then shoot down every single one that enters our airspace until they get the message." His angry gaze darted round to fix the marine colonel attached to the mission. "McGregor. I want your troops out there. I want a cordon around these ships. Got it?"

"Yes sir!" The marine snapped into action.

"Patel!" The Communications Officer yessired him smartly. "I want to talk to someone in charge. If they think I'm going to sit here playing diplomatic games with them, they're mistaken. McGregor! I want an armed guard ready to escort a delegation into that city."

Gerol was explaining his research to the other councillors. "We hardly know what we lost when the original settlement failed. So much was destroyed and so many things abandoned."

"Barbarism," Anya said, softly.

"We have no actual records from back then, of course. Our ancestors expected the people of Earth to come to us and help us, but no one came. The writings of later ages spoke of knowledge and wisdom beyond our conception and of tremendous, terrifying power. All gone."

He was lost in thought for a moment. They all were. "Some of us have hoped that the Earth people might come back one day. Some believe it will be the start of a Golden Age."

"Thommo's New Farm," said Anya, smiling fondly. It was perhaps the best-loved poem on Beasphor.

Gerol was not smiling. "I looked up some of the words from the message, tracing them back as far as I could to get their original meanings. Dora at the University helped me. What do you think that strange use of the word 'superiors' means?"

"Well, people with greater abilities, I suppose," Malc offered. "I don't see why it's so important."

"Dora thinks the word means: people who have the right to tell other people what to do."

There was a polite titter around the room. "But no one has that right, Gerol," said Anya, reasonably.

"Not here, no. But what if they do on the Earth ship? What if the crew are trying some kind of social experiment, something based on people telling other people what to do?"

"It wouldn't work. It's ridiculous!"

"Well... It might work, if there were different ranks of people, with different degrees of authority and obedience was enforced and..." Gerol faltered, trying to conceive the inconceivable. "Look," he went on. "The words Empire, Imperial and Empress. We don't know them. They're not in any of our books but Dora says they are probably all from the same root as the word imperious, which we all know. By analogy to other words, she says Empress is a female person's title or honorific. She says that, grammatically, the Imperial Fleet belongs to or is part of the Empire and that the Empress is either also part of the Empire or is a functionary in the Empire or..." He spoke louder to drown out the scoffing noises. "If this sounds insane..."

"It's rubbish! They'd have to be mad to carry on like that."

"I'm just saying, if this is true, then to be reabsorbed into the Empire may not be something we want. It may be something we should reject."

The room erupted into angry and exasperated argument. Anya rose and waited patiently for it to subside. Slowly, people noticed her waiting and remembered their manners. When there was silence, she asked, "Why are you telling us all this, Gerol? Do you wish us to do something?"

Gerol sighed and looked down. "I don't know. I'm just worried, Anya. Why have they come here after so long? Why is their tone so... so imperious? What if they are not going to be friendly, Anya?"

Anya looked at him with great sympathy for his distress and smiled. "Well, they're here now. Why don't we go and talk to them and clear it all up?"

———————— • ————————

With the five landers at his disposal, Colonel McGregor had sufficient men and materiel to capture or destroy a small city. Which is exactly what he might be asked to do. With the fighters in the air also under his command, he was confident he could handle anything the colonists could throw at him. Nevertheless, his deployment to secure the landing site was a textbook manoeuvre. This was an alien world, his intel was minimal and he did not want to jeopardize the mission by being sloppy.

His troops moved out, cleared the area and erected a boundary fence—a series of poles between which ionising lasers carried a heavy electric charge. It took little more than a bit of pushing and shouting and the whole action was complete. The colonists, who had seemed to think they were at some sort of party, reacted with shock and horror at the soldiers' rough handling of them but they backed off and no one tried anything funny and that's all that mattered.

"All right," he told a lieutenant at his side. "Give Captain Cheng's party the green light to leave."

He watched the monitor as Cheng's armoured car with six marines on foot in full battle armor moved slowly forward. Another armoured vehicle, a missile launcher and twenty-four more marines fell in behind. Above them, five fighters hovered, one high to give long-range sensor cover.

"Get me Major Young on the *Resolution*," he growled and, within seconds, Young was facing him from a display. "Young, are those drones in place?"

"Yes sir. We've had full geographic dispersal since you set down sir. At your command we can nuke any spot on the planet—or all of it at once, sir."

"Nice work, Young. Stand by."

He watched Cheng's column moving slowly towards the city. A gaggle of colonists were trailing behind them as though it were a carnival parade.

———————— • ————————

"Look! Ahead!"

The small group of councillors spotted the approaching Earth people as they crested a rise. They had seen the slowly approaching formation of aircraft some time ago but had been unable to fathom its meaning. Now they could see that it was maintaining its position directly above this column of vehicles and strangely-dressed people.

Something about the rigid order of the Earth contingent made them nervous and they slowed and stopped.

"What does it mean that they are so neatly arranged, do you think?" asked one.

"Perhaps it is an aesthetic effect they seek, like some kind of dance," suggested another.

"It is disturbing, is it not? Almost threatening in its implication of mechanical purpose."

"We must congratulate them when we meet," said one, uncertainly. "They must have practiced long hours to achieve such precision. Why, every person is walking in step with every other!"

Malc placed himself squarely in the road and waved his arms, indicating them to stop. The lead car drew right up to him and came to a halt. The two armored vehicles swivelled their weapons towards the waiting councillors, and the marchers, looking more like machines than men in their body armor, dispersed quickly to stand rigidly around the lead car. There was a short delay before a door opened and a scowling man stepped out of the vehicle. A taller, more relaxed man followed him, and two of the marchers flanked them.

Malc was so astonished by all this that, whatever he had been going to say had gone completely out of his mind. Seeing his difficulty, Anya stepped forward.

"Welcome to Beasphor, Earth people. I am Anya and this is Malc. The others... Well, I'm sure they'll introduce themselves in due course. I must say we're very excited about all this."

———— • ————

Cheng looked sideways at Lee, noting the suppressed amusement in the man's face. "I am Captain Robert Cheng of the..."

"Oh so you're Cheng!" Malc burst out. "What was all that stuff about superiors? Young Gerol's been bending our ears about that all afternoon."

"Malc, please!" said Anya. "Where are your manners? Captain Robert Cheng was speaking. Please let him finish."

Cheng regarded the Beasphoran woman coldly. Was that sarcasm? Or was she suggesting she had the authority to decide when he spoke and when he may be interrupted?

"Who is in charge here?" he snapped. The Beasphorans looked at each other in confusion. Cheng's temper finally broke. "I said, who is in charge here?" He took a step towards Anya. "You, madam. Do you have authority here?"

"I... I really don't know..." she stammered, quite alarmed by this sudden aggression.

Gerol stepped forward to face Cheng. There was a rattling of armor from the marines as they trained their weapons on him. "No one is 'in charge' as you put it. We are members of the City Council—well, most of us anyway. We were elected to serve the people of this city. We don't tell people what to do though. If you're looking for someone who tells us all what to do, you won't find anyone. There isn't anyone."

"Interesting," said Lee.

Cheng glowered at the group of puzzled, anxious colonists. "Bring this one, this one and this one," he said pointing at Malc, Anya and Gerol. Then he spun on his heels and went back to the armored car. Behind him, invisible beams stabbed out and the three councillors fell unconscious. Marines stepped forward to push back the others while the three limp bodies were picked up by servo-assisted muscles and carried back to the vehicles. Once they were aboard, the convoy turned and began its slow progress back to the landing site.

The other councillors watched in stunned horror as their colleagues were carried off. Then they surged after the Earth people running alongside and shouting for them to stop and to let their prisoners go. Hundreds of other people had watched the kidnapping and now they too joined in the haranguing of the column. Then someone in the crowd had an idea. Shouting for others to help, he ran ahead of the column and sat down in the road. Seeing him, a great cry went up. This was a good idea. This would stop the Earth vehicles. Within seconds, scores of people had followed his example and the road was filled with silent, angry people, sitting so as to block it completely.

Cheng watched the road ahead fill with people. His staff quickly updated him on the threat status. No weapons. No signs of military activity anywhere. "Well, Lee? What do you recommend?"

"Crowd control was never my forte. Just drive around the idiots."

"What the hell do they think they're doing?"

Lee shrugged and kept silent.

"Sergeant!"

"Yes, captain!"

"Clear the road. Use extreme force. Do you understand?"

"Yes, Captain."

Six of the marines marched forward and levelled their weapons at the seated Beasphorans. Suddenly the front rows of people erupted into flame and flying body parts. The marines advanced up the road and with every step more people were blasted into ruin. Soon they were marching forward through the burning, bloody wreckage that was once a crowd of people and the rest of the convoy started up and followed them. Cheng thought he saw more people run in from the crowd to sit on the road ahead but in the smoke and confusion, he could not be sure.

———————— • ————————

All through the night, people gathered at the scene of the slaughter. Ambulances carried away the living. The dead, what could be found of them, were collected by relatives and friends. The news services came but all broadcasts were being jammed by the Earth people. A slow ripple of shock spread across the city and people came in their thousands to join the mourners. A huge crowd of silent, angry Beasphorans gathered in Hundred Acre Field to sit and stare at the monsters from space.

On the fringes of the great gathering, people talked, trying to understand what had happened.

"Someone must have said something that upset them," one suggested.

"But what would they have said?"

"Something that angered them. A mistake, maybe."

"But my friend Jorge, whose brother was there, said they didn't say anything offensive. There wasn't even an argument."

"What if they said something that violated some strange taboo these Earth people have? Something we couldn't possibly know about?"

"Yes but"—and it always came back to this—"what could ever be said that would justify what they did?"

The sun rose on a crowd swollen by thousands more. Volunteers threaded through the mourners, bringing food and drinks for those that wanted them. A few banners had also appeared saying "Go Back to Earth" and "Leave Us Alone."

In the dawn, the marines on guard looked grimly out at the solid mass of faces staring in at them. If these men felt any unease, it did not show in their expressions. They were good soldiers. So they kept their weapons ready and kept their eyes open and checked and rechecked the status of the electric fence.

At the very centre of the gathering, in the command ship, Captain Cheng brooded over his cold coffee and considered his next move. The mission was going badly and he could not understand why. He had led five other reabsorption missions and each one had gone like clockwork. He made contact with the leaders, he explained the power of the Empire and the weakness of the colonists, and then they started bargaining. Once, on someone else's mission, the colonists had put up a fight but the negotiators had simply found a faction hungry for power and backed them. The fight turned into a civil war and the Empire had control in a week. After that, it was just a matter of agreeing to the amount of yttrium to be mined and how the Empire would like it delivered.

Yet this was different. This had the makings of a monumental cock-up. So Cheng's mood was dark when Lee walked into his room without knocking. He glared at the secret police officer and thought what he might do to him if he had but a little more influence at Court. "Well?" he growled.

Lee said, "It has been a long night," and helped himself to a coffee from the machine on the table. Cheng said nothing but watched as Lee slumped into a chair and ran a hand across his eyes.

Lee spoke again from the depths of his weariness. "The old one died under interrogation. The other two are all right. They'll live anyway."

"So? Who do I need to talk to?"

Lee shook his head, his eyes closed. "There isn't anybody."

"There has to be somebody. What about this Council of theirs? Who runs it?"

"Nobody. It's a kind of anarchy, or... or something."

"What about a national government? A planetary government? There has to be something?"

"There isn't! The councils are elected to help coordinate a region—usually just a city—if they need anything wider than that, they just get together and talk it over on an *ad hoc* basis. There is no military, not even any police. No one's in charge, no one gives any orders, no one has any power."

Cheng's voice was heavy with disbelief. "Crap!" he said.

Lee lifted his eyes from the table and looked straight into the captain's. "Do you think they would lie to me, Cheng?" he asked in a soft voice.

Cheng knew they would not. Not for long, anyway. "So what about the 150,000 people sitting out there watching us? Who organised that? Who's feeding them? Who's minding the children? They've got teams of workers putting up toilet facilities for God's sake! That kind of thing doesn't just happen!"

"If the crowds are bothering you, just take off and bomb them from orbit."

"That's not the point!"

Lee slammed his hand on the table. "I know what the fucking point is, Cheng. The point is that it won't be as easy to get the Empress her damned yttrium as you'd hoped." He glowered at Cheng, eyes burning. "Well, tough! I've told you all there is to know. Now it's your problem." He shoved back his chair and stomped out of the room.

Cheng sat perfectly still for a while, controlling his breathing, calming himself. He believed Lee. Why should the man lie? But it still made no sense. There had to be something they were missing.

146

———— • ————

Lee woke up some hours later to the sound of commotion in the corridors. "...stupid bastard's out there throwing..." he heard someone say as they ran past his room.

"Come on ladies, the colonel's waiting!" a marine sergeant bellowed.

Lee made his way to the command center and scanned the displays. The duty officer scrambled to attention but Lee waved him away distractedly. There on the external visual display was what he was looking for. "Put that on the speakers," he snapped and suddenly the room was filled with shouting and scuffling.

Outside, Colonel McGregor was bellowing at the colonists and several marines had formed ranks behind him, with more arriving as they watched. The colonel had his weapon out and was holding it to a seated man's head. "Kiss them!" he shouted at the man. "You saw what I did to your friend. Now kiss my boots!" Lee scanned the scene quickly and saw a nearby group of colonists tending what might have been an injured or dead comrade. Colonel McGregor's current victim stared silently ahead of him, his face a mask of stubborn fury. The people around him were not so silent and Lee could hear shouts of "Go home, you animal!" and "Leave us in peace! Why are you hurting us?"

Looking up, McGregor fired at one of the shouting people, wounding her badly. A roar of anger went up from the crowd. He put his weapon against his victim's head again and shouted something that was lost in the commotion. Then he blasted the man's head off. In a blind rage, he grabbed at another man nearby and began shouting at him too. The colonel had clearly lost his self-control but that did not interest Lee. Instead, he focused on the colonists, watching their faces and their actions as the colonel rampaged among them.

———— • ————

"Perhaps you would explain it for me, Gerol," Lee asked, some minutes later in the peaceful quiet of the interrogation room.

Gerol, tired and drawn, was using most of his concentration just to sit upright. "Explain what?" he asked from a dry throat.

"Why no one will do what the colonel wants, even when he threatens their lives."

Gerol was confused. "I'm sure people would help him if he just asked."

"No, no, no. He doesn't want help. He just wants them to do something, some little thing, to show submission."

Gerol's head swam. He felt weak and dizzy still from the drugs and the beatings. None of these questions made sense. "Why would the colonel do that? Is he mentally ill?"

Lee smiled. "Never mind the colonel. Just tell me why no one will do what he tells them to do."

Gerol shook his head. "Why should they? I don't understand!"

Lee was patient. "They should do what he says because they know he will kill them if they don't."

Gerol was almost weeping with the effort of talking to this madman. "Surely you can see it would be stupid to obey someone like that! If people were to let themselves be bullied by people making threats, then we would soon all be slaves and life would become a nightmare of fear and violence."

And suddenly it was all clear to Gerol. The key to understanding the Earth people was his. He looked up into the eyes of his torturer and was filled with awe and pity and revulsion.

Lee too, understood it all now, although he could barely believe it.

———— • ————

Outside, the colonel threw down another body and looked around. Behind him a broad swathe of corpses lay bleeding and smouldering. He was panting and hoarse and tears streamed down his face. The crowd was still passively watching him except where the injured were being tended. Many people still shouted at him. Many, like him, were weeping. His marines, realizing there was no threat, had relaxed and were watching him with impassive faces. One of them had turned away and stood with his head down and his eyes closed.

"What is the matter with you people?" McGregor croaked, his voice almost gone. "Will you sit there and let me kill you all?" In a surge of fury he snapped up his weapon but he found he couldn't fire it again. He looked down the sights at the pale, frightened, unflinching faces that looked back at him and he knew he could not kill them anymore. Perhaps he could never kill them again. Slowly, he lowered the weapon and let it fall from his fingers. He looked again at the dead and injured all around. Then he walked back to the ship without a backward glance. The sergeant stepped over to where the colonel's weapon lay and picked it up. Then he and his men also went back to the ship.

———— • ————

"Am I surrounded by total incompetents?" Captain Cheng wanted to know. He let his eyes travel around his assembled officers. "Let me refresh your memories as to why we're here at the arse end of the galaxy. We're here because the Empire needs this planet's yttrium."

*We're here*, thought Lee, *because the Empire is going broke and getting desperate.*

The Magellanic Wars had drained the coffers. It was only a matter of time, of course, before the Empire would crush the brave consortium of planets that opposed it. Meanwhile they needed fleets of battleships, fuel and materials for the munitions factories, food and supplies for the largest army mankind had ever assembled, bribes for the petty kings who might otherwise give their support to the enemy, and on and on. Some of the technologies the Empire relied on to wage war in space depended on rare and precious elements which were in short supply.

Then someone had remembered the old Federation colonization program. Before the Federation had broken up into a myriad, squabbling territories, it had sent out thousands of cheap ships with volunteers to found colonies on unexplored worlds. No one knew now what had happened to most of them since the Federation's records were destroyed before the Empire arose and brought order back to the galaxy. But a team of archaeologists had stumbled upon the details.

Among these ancient records had been the cursory planetary surveys they had done before sending off the colonists. Some of these surveys had revealed deposits of the very materials the Empire now desperately needed. Wouldn't it be nice, the bright chaps at Court had said, if these worlds, rich in essential minerals, had been successfully colonized and therefore had a ready-made workforce for extracting and processing them? Then all we'd have to do is pay them a visit and set them to work. After all, the Empire is the natural successor to the Federation and it is only fair that these long-lost colonies be brought back into the fold.

So the reabsorption of the colonies had begun. Humans being such a tenacious lifeform, a surprising number of mineral-rich planets had been found to have surviving, even thriving colonies. By the time the *Resolution* had arrived at Colony FC3098-BS4, over fifty others had been processed. The reabsorption procedure had become almost routine, and that is why Captain Cheng was becoming so anxious about this one. A failure in such a simple task would certainly be the end of his career in the Fleet.

"You all know what a shambles this mission has been so far. Well, I want reports and recommendations from each of you right now—and they had better be good. Let's start with you, Lieutenant."

Wang, put on the spot though he was, didn't miss a beat. "We have a total comms block on the whole planet, sir. If they're planning anything, they're doing it by carrier pigeon. Monitoring shows pretty much normal activity—given the comms blackout—except in the local area. Commercial flights have just about stopped. Shipping's still OK. No signs of mobilization or any military activity at all, anywhere. They seem to be coping as best they can and waiting for our next move."

"And what should that move be, Lieutenant Wang?"

Here even the smooth lieutenant paused before he answered. "Round them up into slave gangs and set them to work mining the yttrium, sir."

Cheng appeared to consider it for a moment. "I think you have failed totally to grasp the situation, Lieutenant. I have been watching the recordings of the unfortunate Colonel McGregor's little attempt at bullying. He wasn't very successful, was he?"

"No sir but..."

"Silence!" The sudden shout made everybody jump. "Major Dubois. Your report and recommendations, please."

Dubois did not have Wang's self-confidence and stammered and fumbled his way through a report on the deployment and status of their defences and their considerable offensive capability.

"And your recommendation is?" asked Cheng when the major had finally stumbled to a halt.

"I don't have one, sir. That is, I thought we should do what the Lieutenant said."

Cheng just looked at him in silence for several long seconds before he turned to the secret police officer. "You see I am in desperate need, Mr. Lee. My officers seem to believe that reciting tactics from their first-year academy courses will do instead of thinking. What am I to do? Do you have a solution?"

Lee smiled, apparently in a good mood. "Wouldn't you like to hear my report first?"

"Yes, of course. Please continue."

Lee took a breath and began. "This is a world where people are good to one another. They work hard, they feel a sense of responsibility to themselves, their families and their communities. They don't lie or cheat, they strive to be fair, and they literally do not know the meaning of the word 'exploitation.' They have no wars, no armies and, since they have almost no crime, no police either.

"It's an unbelievable society. One that exists nowhere else in the whole galaxy. I've no idea how it came about but it may be something to do with the way the population died back almost to nothing when the initial settlement failed. The handful of people who built this society may have had strange views or even stranger genes. They believe that individual freedom and an individual's personal morality are the most sacred of all things. Not that they have any organized religions of any kind—another first—but they believe that an individual's relationship to society is..."

"OK. We get the picture. It's Shangri-fucking-La. Now tell me what to do about it."

Lee was clearly a little put out by Cheng's interruption but he brought his smile back and went on. "I believe you have two options. Either you convince these people that it is for their good that they mine their planet to exhaustion in two years and give the entire product to the Empire, or you give up and go home."

He waited for Cheng to react and, when he didn't, he went on. "Clearly, it is impossible to force these people to do anything. I believe that, if we had enough time—a decade or two, say—we could corrupt and destabilize them enough to use standard techniques for gaining their cooperation. If we try any rough stuff now, all we'll get is passive resistance and avoidance. Threatening their lives just doesn't work. They believe that surrendering their right to decide their own actions is worse than death.

"So we could try trading with them. They might go for some high tech stuff, some new food strains, or whatever, but they're pretty rational and they know it's not worth the price of wrecking their whole economy and lifestyle for faster computers or cheaper rice. To be honest, I doubt there's much that we have that they want."

He stopped talking and sat back. Captain Cheng swivelled his eyes to look at him. "So?"

"So we pack up and go on to the next colony."

"That is not an acceptable option, Mr. Lee."

In the tense silence that followed, Lieutenant Wang cleared his throat. "Why not exterminate the indigenous population and bring in mining crews from the homeworlds?"

Cheng turned away with an angry "Tcha!" and Lee took it upon himself to explain. "That would work, of course," he told the alarmed young lieutenant, "but it would be too expensive. There are plenty of uninhabited worlds out there that could be mined but we don't want to go to the cost of flying shiploads of highly-paid miners and heavy equipment out and building them houses and feeding them and so on when we could get it all for free by bullying a few unlucky colonies. Geddit?"

Wang was embarrassed. "Er, yes sir." Despite Lee's cover, everybody on board except the captain called him sir.

Cheng stood up abruptly. "This is a waste of time," he told the room. "I'll be in my office. I want the colonist Gerol there in five minutes." Then he left the room.

"Well, that was fun, wasn't it?" said Lee, rising. The others said nothing but looked at each other anxiously.

———————— • ————————

Gerol and Anya sat together in the little cell. "What did he say?" Anya asked. Gerol was still confused after his interview with Captain Cheng.

"He wanted me to rule the planet," he told her. "He said the Empire would back me, that they would take care of any opposition and that I could have anything I wanted. I think he said I could have women too, but that can't be right. I told him all I wanted was for him and his people to go away and to stop hurting us. Then he raged and shouted for a while. He hit me. Here." He pointed to the livid bruise on his left cheek, but he and Anya had many bruises and it was not an especially bad one.

"I think they must want something from us," Anya said "It's the only way I can make sense of this. They want something but they are embarrassed or afraid to ask. So they're trying to force us to give it to them." She looked into Gerol's eyes. "But how can we give it to them if they won't tell us what it is?"

Gerol's nostrils flared in disgust. "Oh, I know what it is they want!"

"So I was right! What is it?"

"Yttrium." Gerol almost spat the word.

"But what is it? Who has it?"

"It's a mineral. Very rare. Apparently there are huge deposits of it here on Beasphor."

"But why do they want it?"

Gerol smiled a bitter smile. "That's exactly what I asked him. He said it was to help the Empire wage war against another group of planets. I asked him why the Empire wanted to wage war. He said many incomprehensible things about honor and pride, incursions, disputed territories, raids, massacres, atrocities... Oh it was awful. I asked him why they couldn't just talk it over and agree to cooperate. But he just laughed and said it was like talking to a stupid child.

"I asked him why Beasphor should help the Empire and pointed out that we might be more sympathetic to these other people if we heard their side of the story. He just went off shouting again and said we would all die if we didn't help them. Then he had me brought here again."

They sat in silence for a moment and then Anya moved to sit close beside Gerol. "Hold me please. I'm so frightened." He put his arm around her, careful not to squeeze any of her bruises, and they sat in that gentle embrace for a minute or so.

"What's really scary," said Gerol, "is that there are whole worlds, perhaps hundreds of worlds, full of insane people like these."

"They are mad, aren't they? It's not just that I can't understand them, is it? I mean, I've tried and tried but nothing they do makes any sense. And their horrible violence..." She shuddered.

"No. They're insane all right, but it's a kind of cultural insanity, a sickness that has invaded their whole society."

Anya pressed closer to him. "Oh Gerol, do you think we could become infected?"

Gerol said nothing but silently he thought, "I would rather be dead than mad like they are."

———— • ————

They were still holding each other in silent misery when the guards came to take Gerol back to the city. "The woman will stay here as a guarantee of your cooperation," Cheng told them. He had been watching them on the monitor and felt he had a solid bargaining chip at last.

They took him in one of the landers to the Council building. The Earth officers, surrounded by armed marines, marched Gerol into the building. They went straight to the debating chamber, marched across the floor, ignoring the shouts of protest from the councillors assembled there, and stopped beside the mediator. Two soldiers grabbed the mediator and dragged her from her chair. She struggled and shouted but, fortunately, did not try to get back to her seat when they threw her to the ground. Cheng himself led Gerol gently to the mediator's chair. "Please sit down," he said very quietly, unheard amid the shouting, complaining councillors. Amazed at what was happening, Gerol let himself be seated. Immediately, Cheng and Lee took up positions beside the chair and the troops formed up around it.

Cheng lifted his arms and called for silence. If anything, the angry babble grew louder. At a signal, two marines raised their weapons and fired into the air, smashing the beautifully painted ceiling. In the stunned silence that followed, Cheng stepped forward and spoke.

"By the power invested in me by her Imperial Majesty Empress Hui Chui Yi, I decree that this man, Gerol, is the first imperial governor of Colony FC3098-BS4. As representatives of Her Majesty's armed forces, we will serve the governor to enforce any and all of his commands."

The noise was rising again as the amazed councillors asked each other what was going on and what any of it meant. Cheng raised his voice a little and went on. "The governor's first command is that the crowd around our landing craft shall disperse immediately. Secondly, all mining operations on the planet will be required to donate machinery and personnel to a new project to be commenced at once. Finally, this building will now be known as the Governor's Palace. A new government will be selected by Governor Gerol and his military advisers over the next few days."

Cheng looked around to see how his announcements had gone down. There was confusion and many angry faces, but nothing his troops couldn't handle. He bent to Gerol and whispered, "Say something to your subjects, governor. Not too much. Just say that they should do what I told them to do and then get them out of here." He didn't like the look of stupid incomprehension on Gerol's face and turned away angrily to dismiss them himself. Before he could speak, someone stepped forward through the crowd. It was a fat woman and, the way people were patting her and urging her on, he could see she was their spokeswoman. She walked up to him and the Council fell silent behind her. She addressed herself to Gerol. This irritated Cheng, but he had just appointed the fool governor, had he not?

"Gerol," she said, "I don't know what you think you're doing here but we're trying to have a Council meeting. I think you and all these Earth people should go and do this somewhere else, don't you?"

For a moment, Cheng was so stunned by this that he allowed Gerol to reply. "I don't know what they're doing either, Marga, but they are very violent and dangerous. I think it best that everyone just avoids them until they go away."

"Silence!" Cheng's bellow shook the room. He glowered at the councillors, looking for something other than idiocy in their faces. "Bring him!" he snapped, nodding his head towards Gerol, and marched out of the room, pushing several people over as he went.

---

Two hours later, a second lander joined the one outside the Council building. Ten marines marched out and rounded up about a hundred of the people who happened to be there. They dragged and pushed their struggling prisoners into a compound they made from the same electric fence posts they had erected around the first landing site. Many people, inside and outside were badly hurt by the charged beams before they finally gave up struggling against their imprisonment. A team of rescuers who arrived in insulated clothing were shot dead by the guards and another team that turned up with a tunnel wrapped in coils of wire were also shot as they tried to push it through the charged laser beams. Gradually, activity around the compound ceased.

Then Cheng appeared and spoke with an amplified voice that no one could shout over. "Colonists, I have a hundred of your fellows imprisoned. In thirty minutes, I will kill ten of them. In thirty more minutes, I will kill another ten, and so on until they are all dead." There was a long pause while Cheng let them digest the news. "To stop this killing, all you have to do is to send me someone who has authority to speak for you and who can ensure that my demands are met. That is all." The communications officer cut the circuit and Cheng went back into his lander. Lee was there.

"You know they don't have anybody," the secret service man said.

"They'll find somebody."

"They won't. They can't. They just don't have anybody like that."

"They'll find somebody!" Cheng growled and left the room.

Thirty minutes later, they executed ten of the prisoners. A great howl of anguish and rage went up from the crowds that now surrounded the landers. The Beasphorans, despite all they had seen or heard, had not really believed that such a monstrous thing could really be done by human beings. Now they believed. The crowd surged towards the compound. The guards, watched in horror as hundreds of people threw themselves at the faintly glowing lines of deadly charge. Too late they began firing on the advancing crowd. But the posts were down and the power was off. Yelling and cavorting in triumph, the crowd and the prisoners fled the green.

Inside the command lander, the lights flickered and dimmed as the colonists fried on the electric fence, then the power was steady again and Cheng could watch the cheering crowd rushing out of the green by every possible street, leaving scores of dead behind them. He turned in shock and disbelief to Lee Ping Ya but the man just shook his head and looked away.

Cheng imagined how Lee must be gloating at his failure. He supposed the secret policeman must be composing his report in his head, a report full of well-deserved scorn and contempt. As Cheng left the control room, he felt alone and betrayed, sickened by his own impotence. Behind him, Lee was not thinking about his report at all but about the smoking remains of the dead colonists heaped along the line of the ruined fence.

---

Captain Cheng was shaken and pale as he faced Gerol and Anya in their cell. The recording of the self destruction that had just happened outside was playing on a wall screen at Cheng's command. Gerol and Anya watched with tears running down their cheeks. Finally, the last escapees left the green with the guards picking off the stragglers.

"Why did they do that?" Cheng growled. Anya shook her head. Gerol made no reply. "Why did they kill themselves like that?"

Gerol looked at Cheng. The captain was a big man, a strong man, and Gerol wondered if he would hit them again. "What else could they do?" he asked.

"They could have done what I asked."

"No," said Gerol, sadly.

Cheng said, "Then they could at least have saved themselves."

Anya replied, almost in a whisper. "No one could have watched such cruelty and done nothing."

Cheng's frustration gnawed at his mind like a rat. "Then why didn't they attack the guards, or the landers? Why just die like that?"

Gerol looked into the captain's eyes and saw the anger there that he would never understand. "We could only kill you if we became like you. That would negate the point of killing you. Why can you not understand something so simple?"

With an inarticulate roar, Cheng smashed his fist into Gerol's face, knocking him off his chair and onto the floor. Cheng drew back a black-booted foot to kick him. With a cry, Anya leapt up and threw herself across Gerol's body, ready to take the blow for him.

Seeing her huddled in fear on top of the dazed colonist, Cheng's anger turned to confusion. He stood over them breathing heavily for a moment and closed his eyes. He felt unbearably tired. His eyes filled with inexplicable tears. He shook himself and forced himself to stand upright. Without a word, he turned and left.

In the corridor, he met Lee. The secret policeman was shocked at what he saw in the captain's face but held his own expression rigid. "Captain Cheng, sir!" he said, saluting.

The surprise of this alone was enough to bring Cheng back to his senses. His chin came up and he returned the salute. "What is it, Lee?"

"I need to talk to you captain—in private. I think I have the answer to your problem."

---

The next day, all five landers lifted off and, with a roar of engines, disappeared into the wide skies. Communications around the globe suddenly worked again and radar screens cleared to reveal the mighty Earth ship moving slowly out of orbit. On the green outside the Council building, Gerol and Anya hugged each other with the joy of a freedom neither had expected ever to know again. People emerged timidly from the streets and buildings around them to collect their dead and to ask the questions for which no one had any answers.

High above them, the Earth ship gathered speed as it pulled out of Beasphor's gravity well. Captain Cheng sat in his room completing a message to Fleet Command. "In short," it said, "the colonists, either through inbreeding or environmental effects, were imbeciles who were incapable of being efficiently driven to provide the services we need for economical exploitation of the planet. Scientific study of their peculiar mental retardation is recommended at such time as the exigencies of war allow it. Meanwhile, it is my view, endorsed by Principal Officer Lee Ping Ya, that our efforts would be more profitably spent in the absorption of other colonies with less degenerate human populations."

He added his ID and sat back with a sigh. "Carpenter!" he called and a comms line opened to his adjutant. "Ask Cultural Affairs Consultant Lee if he would care to join me for drinks in my cabin. Tell him... Just tell him I'd be honored if he could."

---

"Will they come back?" Anya asked.

"Not for a long time, I hope," said Gerol.

"Do you think we should prepare? Build defences?"

Gerol smiled at her and shook his head, despite the pain. "Perhaps you didn't notice, but I think we defended ourselves pretty well."

A slow smile spread over Anya's bruised face as she turned over in her mind what Gerol had said. "Yes, we did, didn't we?" But there were tears in her eyes all the same.

"Come on," said Gerol. "Walk with me to the infirmary. There must be so many people who need help. Let's see what we can do."

## About The Author

Graham Storrs is a former research scientist who now lives in the Australian bush and writes science fiction. He has published short stories and twelve novels, covering all the major sci-fi themes, including time travel, dystopian futures, transhumanity, alien invasion and space opera and, within each theme, he likes to mix it up, writing thrillers, adventure and comedy. Keeping the science real is as important to him as keeping his characters real and his books and stories are heavily researched. He does most of his writing outdoors, in the mountains and gum forests that surround his home.

For more information, visit www.grahamstorrs.com.

# Digital Commander

## JS Morin

*Editor's Note: Technology has always offered us new chances at immortality. From the cave paintings of Lascaux to the golden record in the belly of Voyager, each of these captures the expressed essence of individual humans and carries them beyond time to touch the lives of unknown beings in some vast and murky future. And when that day comes, when the quapods find our artefacts and flap their puzzled questions, they will get no reply. They will be left to puzzle us out from the static hints embedded in the message. But it doesn't have to be that way.*

What had appeared to be a modest proving-ground facility nestled against the Sierra Nevada Mountains turned out to be anything but. Flanked by a pair of US Army soldiers, Commander Brent "Skip" Harrison limped up to the security station and stepped into a glass booth like one of the old-fashioned airport screeners. Beams of green light swept over him, top to bottom and back again. On the far side, a technical sergeant tapped away at a workstation.

"Am I cleared?" Skip asked.

The sergeant didn't look away from his monitor. "Not yet, sir. Most of us just have a few dental fillings and an ID chip. I'm going to have to ask you to be patient a minute."

Skip gave a nervous chuckle. "Not everyone comes through with robotic limbs?" He flexed his right hand and heard the faint whirr of actuators, though the doctors swore it was below the human auditory range.

The sergeant glanced up. "No, sir."

Past the security desk, a familiar figure approached wearing a white lab coat over desert camo. He was flanked by a pair of soldiers wearing body armor, toting M4 rifles. But despite the intimidating escort, Dr. Augustus Cliffton grinned ear to ear. "Decker, give Commander Harrison the all clear. Punch it in under code 403."

"Yes, sir."

A soft tone chimed and the far side of the glass both slid open. Skip lurched out and Dr. Cliffton met him with a hand outstretched. Skip compromised and held out his left. "Gus, it's been forever. What... twenty-two years?"

Gus hesitated then switched and shook Skip's non-bionic hand. "Hey, Skip. Welcome to Sand Lion Base." The years had treated Gus like a rechall punching bag. His face was weathered and wrinkled with a scar running along his jawline, interrupting the spread of stubble. But he had the energy of a cadet and the grip of an infantryman. "Don't mind the PsyOps stuff up front. We're pretty casual here."

Just past the entrance, Gus swiped them through a keycard-security station and took off his glasses for a retina scan that opened the elevator doors. Even on that short trip, four soldiers stopped to salute and address him by name.

"Commander Harrison, good to meet you, sir."

It was endearing to hear a bunch of army grunts going out of their way to remember naval rank. But the words rang true, not like some project-wide PR stunt to blow smoke up the new guy's ass. Even if the limp didn't, the hiss of the balancing pistons in his feet would have given away the cybernetics. Probably hard to give a Purple Heart winner grief after losing three limbs in battle. His finger actuators were dexterous enough for a crisp salute in reply.

But once they were in the elevator, it was just him and Gus once more. "What is this place? I've been in some pretty modern facilities, but this elevator looks like something from DARPA."

"Facility's EMP shielded, these walls are made of some material even I can't pronounce, and this whole shaft is rated to withstand antimatter ordinance. How are Madison and the kids?"

"They're great. Maddie's getting used to the..." Skip cleared his throat. "...new equipment. Meg and Kenny think I'm turning into a robot." He knocked on the white paneled interior wall with his bare knuckle. "So, you're telling me we're someplace important?"

The elevator doors opened and Gus swept a hand toward the underground cavern beyond. "Something like that."

Skip followed Gus onto the catwalk in a daze. The cavern had to have been a dozen stories tall, carved out of the mountain's heart; they were at the mid-line. Below, electric vehicles whirred, air wrenches jackhammered, and welders sparked. Above, cranes and power conduits dangled.

But in the center of it all was a giant metallic statue, waist-high to their vantage. Its enameled surface caught the light from overhead LED spotlights, giving it a factory-fresh gleam. The articulation pistons at the joints reminded Skip of his own prosthetics, scaled up to titanic proportions.

"What the hell is that? An infantry suit for King Kong?"

Gus clapped him on the back. "No. For you."

———— • ————

By the time Skip settled into his assigned quarters back in the innocuous base on the surface, his mind was spilling out his ears. Gus had shown him around the operations center, the control and monitoring stations, the programmers' cubicles, and the maintenance bay. But the mindblowing capstone to the tour had been the mech itself—the Beowulf. It wasn't just an infantry mech suit, which was little more than medieval armor with muscular amplification actuators. This was the dawn of a new age of mechanized combat: weapons that acted directly on their own initiative, possessed of a human mind.

For on-base accommodations, the little apartment he had been assigned was state of the art. Ice-box air conditioning instantly began to cool the sweat that plastered Skip's uniform to his skin. The furniture smelled of new plastic and leather. Everything had a whiff of ammonia from a recent cleaning. Next to the door, there was a wall panel with temperature and light controls. With a shiver and a chuckle that the army was still using Fahrenheit, he did some quick math and bumped the temperature up to 70 degrees.

Desert dust had coated Skip in a fine layer during his forays between buildings. His muscles ached from the longest day on his feet since rehab. He needed sleep, but more than that he needed a shower. The apartment's bathroom was equipped with a hybrid tub/shower, and for a moment he was tempted to give in, get off his feet, and soak. But if there was one thing today had proved, it was that there was still a pilot inside him. And Skip Harrison would be damned if he would let a decorated navy pilot soak in a tub like an old geezer.

Taking off his clothes used to be something he had never given a second thought. Now it was like trying to unbutton a shirt with a winter glove on one hand. The doctors and therapists all told him that his manual dexterity would improve with practice, as his neurons continued to integrate the new sensations, and he knew he was getting better at daily tasks. It was the lack of tactile feedback that got to him. It would never be the same as having real fingers again.

Skip tried to pull his legs out of his pant legs. All he accomplished was getting stuck as the leg refused to slide along the path he needed. This used to be the simplest of daily tasks; now it was a puzzle. After five frustrating attempts, he pounded a fist on the incompetent knee joint. His fleshy hand throbbed and he had to flex the fingers to make sure he hadn't broken anything. After that, he treated his legs like dead weight once he had bent them enough that he could reach his feet. At that point he slid the pants down to his ankles and yanked them off.

Seated on the cold tile of the bathroom floor, he stared at his bionic legs. Flesh and bone ended at interface sockets halfway up his thighs, grafted permanently in place. Inescapable. Part of him, but alien. Below the socket, the support struts and actuators were eerily reminiscent of the Beowulf. One of those struts was the bottom half of a titanium femur that ran inside him all the way up to the hip joint. Hard to tell sometimes where the man ended and the machine began. Well, that wasn't going to get any easier to tell, the way this mission was aiming.

*You will be the future,* Gus had said. The words echoed in Skip's mind as cool water cascaded over him. *No more human pilots. No more maimed limbs. No more lost lives.* If anyone had told him a week ago that they wanted to map his brain, he'd have told them to go screw themselves. But there were only two ways to pilot a vehicle: by remote or with a live, human pilot. And between signal security breaches, jamming, and latency issues, the military was leaning farther and farther from remote-operated vehicles.

In the back of his mind, Skip worried about getting electrocuted by a short circuit every time he stepped into the shower. The doctors had promised everything was completely safe, but it wasn't their asses on the line. Still, he couldn't just go on stinking with sweat from the short ride topside to his barracks. The paltry coolant systems built into his new limbs kept them from overheating, but the rest of him was on its own.

Skip leaned against the shower wall. One hand felt smooth tile and rough lines of grout between them. The other gave a vague impression of solid resistance and nothing more. The difference between man and machine. Even if this project were a pipe dream. Even if Gus and his colleagues could never pull it off. Even if this was the worst idea in the history of mankind—and Skip had read enough science fiction as a kid to realize it might be—they were going to try it anyway. If someone's brain was going to be the baseline of autonomous military AI, Skip would rather it was him than the next name the Army pulled out of a hat.

———— • ————

The next morning, Skip reported to work. His own retina scan now gained him access to the underground bunker, and the soldiers who accompanied him felt more like bodyguards than a security escort. Since agreeing to the piloting program, he was a VIP. He had met General Keith Kogane, who had flown in from Washington for the occasion. Gus introduced him to more techs and junior officers than he could possibly have hoped to keep straight. Skip imagined that this was how Alan Shepard got treated the day before he went into space.

But once the pomp and celebrity treatment died down, and the onlookers drifted back to their assigned posts, Skip was left in the hands of scientists and techs. Gus left him for the time being, having overarching aspects of the project to supervise. Skip wasn't sure he'd have wanted Gus right there, anyway. It was easier getting manhandled by strangers.

He had lain awake imagining the process. He had pictured a cockpit, a few electrodes, and maybe some vital-sign monitors. And he had certainly had all his clothes on—a flight suit, even. But as a pair of army corporals helped lower him into the pod, he was glad they had left him his skivvies. They even shaved his head.

Once seated, Skip's participation no longer seemed to be required. His legs were clamped in place, followed by his ams, locking him into the seat. Something one of the techs attached interrupted the signals to his prosthetics, rendering them dead hunks of metal. "Hey! I'm not going anywhere."

The tech continued to work, opening a plastic toolbox and withdrawing an IV needle. "Sorry, sir. We don't want stray signals in the pod." He raised a vein in Skip's good arm and stuck the needle in, taping it in place and hooking up a tube that disappeared into the pod's internals.

Trying his best to relax as needles, probes, and God-knew-what other devices were attached to him, Skip craned his neck and looked up. Right above him were a gantry and crane that would transfer his pod to the Beowulf once he was done being turned into a pincushion. Out of his peripheral vision, he saw a dome filled with spikes and wires swinging slowly down from behind him.

Firm hands covered in latex took hold of him behind the neck and under the chin. "Look straight ahead, sir."

Skip took a slow breath and complied. This was what he signed up for after all. No use being a pansy about it when he was probably closing in on the final stages of the prep drudgery. The edge of the dome came into view, stopping when it overhung his brow like the brim of a baseball cap. Servo motors whirred, and several rubber-coated tips pressed against his skull from all sides. The hands remained in place, and Skip kept his neck muscles slack on the assumption that if he tried to position himself, it would just take longer.

But the rubber tips kept on pressing. The motors kept whirring. Skip gritted his teeth, but a grunt of pain escaped despite his best efforts. "Gah." The motors stopped and reversed. The pressure backed off, if only slightly. The latex-coated hands retreated.

"Turn your head left, then right."

Skip tried, but all he got for his efforts was a set of rubber-tipped rods digging in all the harder. "Nothing."

"Good. You'll be glad of that in a second."

A pinprick. Then another. Skip stopped trying to count after a few minutes. Everything was taking place outside his field of view, and so far, everything only seemed to get worse once he knew what was going on. So he kept quiet and let his inadequate imagination fill in those unpleasant details.

The first familiar thing about the whole process was when they brought over a mask that looked like ones Skip had used all his career. It had that fresh-from-the-box rubbery smell, but before they placed it over his face, someone smeared it with a clear paste all around the gasket. When it pressed over his face, there was a whiff of pumped-in oxygen.

"Just breathe normally, sir."

Skip grinned beneath the mask. "I've worn these things before, soldier. Standard issue in my part of the sky."

"Please try to hold still until the sealant cures." So much for injecting levity.

There were pinching sensations of needles at either side of his neck. Something small and plastic tickled the inside of his ear canal, and then again at the other. The techs pressed something directly against his eardrums and he felt something warm being trickled in from either side. "Hey, what are you—?"

"Please hold still, sir. Those are just your comm system." The words came through muddy, as if he had swimmer's ear.

The hands came off his oxygen mask and the straps were snugged behind his head. He tried instinctively to wiggle it into a more comfortable position, but it was glued in place, plus his neck muscles had gone completely slack.

*"Testing. Testing. Commander Harrison, can you hear me?"* It was Gus's voice, crisp and plain as if he were standing in Skip's head.

Since Gus was keeping things professional, he replied in kind. "Affirmative, Dr. Cliffton. Loud and clear."

*"Good. We're almost ready to begin. Just hang in there."*

The briefing had mentioned goggles, but they weren't what Skip had pictured. These were better suited to swimming, and again they were smeared with adhesive. Skip squeezed his eyes shut while they were held in place. When he opened them, the world was blurry and warped. "Not much field of vision through these, doctor."

*"Bear with us."*

The techs backed away, though Skip felt it more than he saw or heard. A minute later, the canopy of the pod was set into place. Everything went dark. "Hey, what's going on?"

In response, a dull glow lit the interior. Between the cheap plastic goggles and the lack of features on the inside of the canopy, it wasn't much different from the darkness. There was a thump that echoed in the interior, followed by a churning, chugging that Skip guessed was a pump. The pod had filled to his waist before Skip realized that some viscous liquid was being injected in with him.

"What is this stuff?"

*"Non-Euclidean fluid. Specs are classified. Great stuff, though. Shock absorbent. Like a full-body air-bag at the ready."*

"Thought this was just a test run. I didn't even have anything like this flying combat missions."

*"And look where that got you? Besides, the stuff is dense as motor oil. Can't take that weight in a jet. The Beowulf hardly notices the difference."*

Skip waited as the level climbed, the glow from the emergency lighting reflecting off the surface as it rose until the fluid covered his goggles. He kept his breathing as steady as possible to prevent a rising panic that was threatening to well up and take over. He was trapped in a cockpit. The last time he could have said that, he was on fire and plummeting toward earth, fumbling for the eject lever in his F-54. This time would be different.

The pump stopped, and the pod was jarred. A sudden sense of heaviness came, followed almost instantly by a feeling of weightlessness. Something jarred the pod once again, then all was still. He had to be inside the Beowulf.

Excitement and fear warred inside him, quickening Skip's breath. He watched intently through the swimmer's goggles, waiting for some sort of futuristic heads-up display to appear. All he saw was the continuous dull red glow of the emergency lights.

"Ready when you are." Maybe if they knew he was raring to go, Gus and his lackeys might speed things up. There was no place he had to be, but breakfast was hours ago, and he couldn't imagine they'd be stopping for a lunch break.

"*All right. Now commander, this is going to be a little disorienting.*"

"Hit me with your best—"

Skip's boast was lost in vertigo. The emergency lighting disappeared. He wasn't in the cockpit anymore. He stared into the glassed-in control booth at eye level. The periphery of his vision was filled with status and tactical information, arranged in an unfamiliar configuration but unmistakably a heads-up display. Each time he glanced at one of the readouts, it centered itself in his field of vision and magnified. There was no Beowulf. He *was* the Beowulf.

"*Commander Harrison, report. We show successful interface. Please confirm.*"

"How'd you do this?"

"*The system bypasses your optic nerve. The distributor node in your brain that controls your prosthetics made you an ideal candidate. Anyone else would have needed surgical alteration prior to interfacing. But our system is based on the same tech they used at Bethesda to put you back together.*"

"This all looks so real…"

"*It's better than real. Your visual cortex is showing a light strain under the effort of resolving an image with more data than it's used to. I'll dial it back slightly. No point wearing you out on the first day. We've got plenty of work on the docket.*"

Gus wasn't kidding about that part. Skip spent the day running through calibration and basic coordination drills. The mech did little more than calisthenics in the underground hangar all day, never moving from that one spot. But by the time they extracted him from the probes, needles, and slime of the pod, Skip was exhausted and starving.

But he was grinning.

* * *

There was a knock at Skip's door. He turned off the shower and wrapped a towel around his waist. He was still trying to remove the last of the adhesive residue from around his face, and the odor of the shock-absorbent fluid clung to him like skunk spray. This was his third trip through the rinse cycle to be rid of both.

"Just a minute." There was decorum to consider. He gave himself a quick pat-down and struggled into pants and a shirt as quickly as he could. Mindful of not keeping his visitor waiting, he opted not to spend the time it would take to do the buttons.

He pulled the door open, expecting to see Gus or General Kogane. Instead, there was a woman in fatigues. She saluted. "Sir, I'm Captain Fiona Walsh."

Skip snapped to attention, returning the salute while doing his best to hold his shirt closed with his good hand. Then he relaxed just slightly. "Wait, you're the kind of captain that doesn't outrank me, aren't you?"

"Yes sir, just a regular O-3." She had a clipboard under one arm, and bent to retrieve a paper grocery bag that clinked with a familiar glass chime as she lifted it. "I'm here to check in on you, but I came with a peace offering."

"Peace offering?" Skip asked, stepping aside to let Captain Walsh in and keep the desert heat out. "Gus think he pissed me off or something? Sorry, I mean Colonel Cliffton."

She smiled and set the grocery bag on the kitchenette table. "Sometimes I forget that Dr. Cliffton has a rank. He rarely puts on a proper uniform. He's just... well, he's Dr. Cliffton."

Skip maneuvered around and peered into the bag on the table. Inside were a wine bottle, a six-pack of beer he couldn't identify by brand from a top-down view, some nachos, and a plastic tub of pork rinds.

"Eclectic mix."

"Dr. Cliffton didn't know if you'd developed sophisticated tastes since Kabul. The wine was..." she cleared her throat and did a fair impression of Gus. "In case you'd gone all Washington."

"Wine's good for dinner parties. I hate dinner parties."

Captain Walsh slipped up beside him and rested a hand on his lower back as she reached into the bag. "Fine. Hope you don't mind Coors. It's the best we've got at the PX."

Skip cleared his throat. "So, you drew the short straw, coming out to placate me?"

"Short straw? I had to pull rank to be the one to come check you out tonight." Her other hand slipped inside Skip's open shirt and ran along the space where he used to have abs before middle age caught up with him.

For the first time since her arrival, he allowed himself to view the captain as a woman, not a fellow officer from another branch. She was nearly his height, with her combat boots and his bare feet leveling the playing field. Her sandy blonde hair was pinned into a bun at the back of her neck. The natural bagginess of her uniform couldn't completely disguise her trim figure. And those blue eyes stared right back when he looked into them. She bit her lip.

"Captain, I—"

"You can call me Fiona."

"Captain, I'm not sure this is appropriate." Skip held up his left hand, interposing his wedding ring like a Spartan shield wall. It was the first time he could remember being grateful that it was his right arm he'd lost. "I'm happily married."

She held up a hand with a ring of pale skin where a wedding ring had once been. "I am, too. Mine's back in Arlington, making a daily commute to the Pentagon. But I'm here for a post-test psych eval, and my professional opinion is that you've had a stressful day. I'd be derelict in my duties if I didn't stay until I was certain you were... de-stressed."

Skip retreated a pace, running a self-conscious hand over his shaved head. "I'm a mess. I mean, I'm fine. Yeah, sure, it's been a long day. But I'm tired. I'm... I smell funny. I'm bald as a—"

"It looks good on you. Listen, Commander—can I call you Brent?"

"Skip's fine." He should have told her to stick to Commander Harrison. He knew as soon as the words escaped his lips.

"Skip, I can only imagine what life's been like for you on the outside. Hospital gowns instead of uniforms. Getting treated like a civilian. Must have been hell. But right here, right now, you're a hero, doing work no one else can do. And right here, right now, it's just you, me, and this cozy little apartment where I promise you, no one will bother us until 0600 tomorrow." As she spoke, Fiona slowly undid the buttons on her uniform shirt. She was still wearing a khaki T-shirt underneath, but it was pulled tight against her skin and dark at the collar with sweat.

"This is against regulations." Lame excuse. Regulations hadn't stopped fraternizing in the history of organized militaries.

Fiona dropped her shirt to the floor and slid her hands under Skip's. "Everyone here values your emotional health. I have permission from General Kogane to be here. And as for the outside world, well... what happens in secret military base *stays* in secret military base." She slipped Skip's shirt off his shoulders and pressed herself against him.

But the shirt never hit the floor. Catching the garment around his wrists, Skip hobbled backward, stumbling against the wall as he shrugged back into some semblance of being in uniform. "At ease, Captain Walsh. Stand down." Mental images of Maddie flashed before his eyes. Her smile on their wedding day. The exhausted euphoria holding Grant for the first time. Their second honeymoon in Fiji.

Captain Walsh complied without a hint of protest, scooping up her own uniform top and retrieving the clipboard he had forgotten she had even brought with her. "I think that will conclude my psych eval for the post-interface check. Thank you for your cooperation, Commander Harrison."

"Wait. This was all a test?" What kind of place was this? Wasn't it enough that they'd put him through the ringer mentally, running signals through parts of his brain he barely knew existed? Now they wanted to dangle bait in front of him to see if he'd take it?

"Yes and no. I'm here to evaluate your mental state after spending the day plugged into an experimental computer. You're aware, alert, in full possession of your mental faculties, and behaving within the bounds of your latest psych eval we acquired from the Navy." She rattled off her reply as she buttoned up her uniform—an actress backstage after playing her role.

"And if I'd gone along?"

"I'd have known you were in a compromised mental state. I really am a trained army psychologist, even though we play with expanded ethical standards this side of top secret. We both know it wasn't going to happen. That wife of yours is a lucky woman."

With a salute, Captain Walsh took her leave. Skip headed right back to the shower to see how cold the water could get in this desert.

---

In the morning, Skip once more found himself jabbed, clamped, probed, and immersed in the pod. While not a bit of it was pleasant, the prospect of experiencing the mech in the field was more than enough to keep him focused through the process, and knowing what was involved kept his nerves from fraying. When his natural vision blinked out to be replaced by the computer feed from the Beowulf, he felt a thrill of ecstasy.

He was sixty feet tall and indestructible. And today, Gus promised Skip that he'd be allowed to take the Beowulf through its paces.

"So, Doctor Cliffton, you gonna let this baby off its leash for me?" High-tension cables anchored the Beowulf to the walls and ceiling of the cavern. He could twist a few degrees, but the force feedback made him feel the resistance of lines that were stronger than the mechanical muscles of the vehicle.

*"Just a few diagnostics to complete. Your vitals are looking better today. Hope you got a good night's sleep. Today isn't going to be the cakewalk that yesterday was."*

Cakewalk was one word for it. Tedium turned out to be more like it. Raise the left arm—good. Lower the left arm—good. Now swivel the head—excellent. It was like dog training. Skip had a ten-year-old golden retriever named Daisy who could follow directions like that, and she had never been through flight school.

*"All right, Commander. We're cutting power umbilicals. You'll be switching over to internal battery power."*

"How long does the battery power last?"

*"Longer than you. Don't worry about it. Once you're on internal power, you'll have a readout for battery life."*

Army personnel swarmed the Beowulf on lifts and extendable catwalks. Images of them popped up on sub-displays as Skip directed the mech's external cameras. They were disconnecting the tethers. Soon he'd be free to operate unfettered. Once the last of the hookups was severed, there would be nothing but Skip to direct the vehicle. It took them under five minutes. As the last of the workers retreated, he flexed his mechanical muscles. "Ready to go. What's first on the agenda?"

The ground rumbled. Skip looked up into the control booth. Gus was standing there with his arms crossed and a smug grin. Whatever was going on, Gus knew, so Skip just waited to see what his latest surprise was. It was a doozy.

Skip began to sink. What he'd believed to be a solid floor beneath his feet was, in fact, an elevator platform, and it was lowering him farther below ground. Was there a test course down there? As the platform lowered, he ran through some deep knee bends and abdominal twists, exercises he couldn't have performed while tethered. The twists were mildly disorienting as they swiveled his camera view of his surroundings; it would take some getting used to the lack of direct equilibrium feedback in his movements.

The elevator ride was short, just over one mech-height down, and it ended in a long tunnel lit by fluorescent lights along both walls. He hadn't been sent down here for the view, so Skip took the initiative and started walking. The first few steps were like a nightmare trip down memory lane. He was back in his first few days of post-cybernetic rehab. His mind was fighting old muscle memory that told him one way to walk while the Beowulf refused to respond the way he imagined it should.

But having been through the process once before, Skip knew how to both persevere and adapt. The first ten steps were halting and awkward. If not for the intervention of balance-assist hardware baked into the system, he knew he'd have fallen multiple times. But the next few dozen steps smoothed out, and by the time he was halfway down the tunnel, Skip was trudging along in rhythm like a hiker caught in deep snow.

"This why I got the call on this project instead of someone with a special ops background? I already knew the learning process?"

*"It was a consideration. But the truth is, we've found that a pilot's training maps better to the controls than experience in power armor. Tactics and maneuvers are easier to teach than the sort of spatial awareness and cockpit presence you flyboys learn."*

"What's at the end of this tunnel?"

*"A door."*

So Gus wanted it to be yet another surprise. What was it with top-secret sorts? Did they not get enough excitement in their sequestered little lives? Or was this because he and Gus were old friends? No, Skip decided. This was yet another in an ever increasing list of tests. They wanted to keep him guessing, off-balance, and reacting. He had to keep reminding himself that the Beowulf was only one part of the project; he was the other. And if this was an uneven split, he would have to guess that mimicking a human brain was the harder half. After all, what was he driving but an oversized suit of power armor with a new control scheme?

The tunnel was distinctly beginning to slope uphill. He didn't need Gus to tell him that he was going to come out somewhere above ground, even if the Beowulf hadn't had an altimeter. The hangar was already an impressive feat of engineering. Duplicating it on a scale that would allow the Beowulf to run through its paces would have been impractical. His guess was proved right when sunlight peeked around the outline of the door as it swung outward.

Skip waited.

He was a robotic step from freedom, from open spaces and sunny skies. But the meter-thick slab of steel was opening at a crawl. "Mind if I give this thing a push?"

*"By all means. Give me a second to disengage the motor and it's all yours."*

A low-gear diesel grumble that Skip been ignoring as background noise suddenly ceased. He took that last step forward and reached out with the mech's right hand. He could feel the weight resisting his efforts, but there was no exertion on his part. The door swung out of the way, and Skip looked up into a clear blue sky. A shimmer in the air caught his eye. "We under some kind of force field?"

Gus laughed over the radio, and in the background Skip could hear a chorus joining him. *"You're in the most advanced thing we've got. J-PAC would kill to get their hands on the Beowulf. But we're not building Hollywood magic here. You're seeing a scatter field, in case anyone's getting nosy on satellite."*

"Understood."

Skip was in another valley in the Sierra Nevadas. Mountains hemmed him in on all sides. Scattered among the rocks and scraggly desert plants were targets of various sorts. There were modular general-purpose tents arranged in a mock-up of a military base. Along one ridge line there were giant red-and-white bullseyes, one of which was being lowered into position by helicopter. Farther down the valley, there was a small cinderblock village.

*"Commander, you're going to need to unlock fire control. Look to the lower left for a manual input console. Code is eight-seven-alpha-charlie-four-four-zulu-one-November."*

Glancing at the manual input console brought it to the fore of Skip's field of vision. Of course, the "manual" part was a stretch. As Skip focused his attention on each digit and letter in turn, the system accepted that as his selection. As soon as he finished, a whole bevy of new options crowded the heads-up display. Even more strange, he could feel the weapons almost as if they were extra finger or toes. "Whoa."

*"I'll take that to mean you have access. Now, we're going to dial back the display resolution. You're going to be getting a lot of unfamiliar neural feedback,*

*and we don't want you getting overwhelmed."*

"I thought this project was focusing on signal security. Why can you still change my interface remotely?"

*"This is a prototype. The production units will have safeguards like this built in. But until then, we can't risk you getting into trouble and not being able to adjust the settings yourself. Now, your right arm is fitted with a .50 caliber machine gun. Take aim at the tent city on your two-o'clock and open fire."*

Skip took several steps and adjusted his feet into a shooting stance. "Seems a little lightweight for a weapon this size."

*"It's temporary. We've got subcontractors working on an E-M kinetic system to replace the machine gun. For now, the exercise is more important than the firepower. Proceed with target practice."*

Skip lined up a crosshair with one of the tents and just willed the gun to fire. An automated burst riddled the tent with holes from a distance of 300 meters. "Not bad. But when did you army boys start using metric?"

*"It wasn't easy getting it pushed through, but you tell enough generals that this project is more complex than the mission that missed Mars, and they eventually get the idea that we need a single set of units. Hard to build the future while stuck in the past."*

Skip shredded tents until the .50-cal ran out of ammo. It didn't have the visceral feel of shooting down enemy fighters with the same gun on his F-54, but he was getting quicker with his aim. "What's next?"

*"Think you've got the hang of walking around in that thing?"* Gus didn't wait for a reply. *"Good, because I want you to run to the mock village."*

"Run? I'm doing OK with walking, but..."

*"Walk if you have to. You'll be doing it more than once. Eventually you'll pick up the pace."*

The first trip took him twelve minutes. By the tenth time, he had it down to three. He was learning the terrain and where he had the best footing, but more than that, he was flowing more easily from one step to the next. The thinking required was drifting into muscle memory, which was weird to contemplate, since there wasn't a single muscle of his involved in the process. The prosthetics were foreign, but had become a part of him in a shotgun wedding. The Beowulf was just connected to him by a bunch of wires and probes.

*"Great job, Commander. Time for a little fun before we call it a day."*

Skip perked up. There was something of childlike glee in simply piloting a giant robot. For all his complaints about the degrading pod insertion and repetitive drills, he was enjoying himself. Was Gus promising something even better, or was this another bait-and-switch to test him?

"Whatcha got for me? I'm ready." Ready for a good meal and six or eight showers, but a grand finale could be worth the wait.

*"You're equipped with Dragonfly Mark IV missiles. Take up a position 100 meters from the mock village and pick out a building you don't like."*

That was an easy task. On his forays back and forth, Skip had developed an adversarial relationship with the nearest structure, a four-story cinderblock apartment building that had marked the end of his timed run. Every time he came up short of his time goal, part of him blamed it for not being just a little closer. Now, it was time for some payback.

The missile controls were a little more complex than the machine gun. He had to arm the missile and confirm a target before it allowed him to fire. But the aiming was all the easier for being integrated into his right arm. For whatever reason, using the left felt less natural and the mental effort was more fatiguing. But between the improved responsiveness of his right arm and the practice he'd gotten with the Beowulf's targeting system, he had the apartment building in his sights in no time.

With an act of will, he unleashed the Dragonfly. It appeared from a rack buried in Skip's right forearm and hissed away in a contrail of propellant. The twisting course was visible as it self-corrected mid-flight, and it slammed into the cinderblocks with a concussive blast that sent up a cloud of dust. Skip wanted to crack his knuckles, pound his chest... anything to let loose the surge of power he felt. He couldn't remember the last time he'd had a front-row seat for a missile impact in his F-54. Generally, those things hit from kilometers away.

*"Ha! Nice shot, Commander. But those buildings take a while to construct. Let's move on to those bullseyes."*

Skip turned the Beowulf but remained in place. What good were missiles if you ran up to your targets to hit them? His heads-up display was able to mark the bullseyes one by one before firing the first Dragonfly. That first shot obliterated the target in a fiery spray of plywood and desert dust. It made for a better pyrotechnic show than the cinderblocks, but lacked the feel of taking down a real structure. Still, this was a training and data collection exercise, not demolition. He took careful aim and fired again. And again. Halfway through he noticed that his missile count and the number of targets matched perfectly, even accounting for the initial shot on the mock apartment building.

"I notice you guys aren't expecting any misses."

*"Any intact targets at the end are points off your final score."*

"I'm getting scored on this?"

*"No. Not really. Just keep knocking them out. This is it before lunch."*

"Roger that."

Skip was in a rhythm, but that didn't mean he allowed himself to get sloppy. He wasn't just trying to hit the painted targets; he wanted dead-center shots. So every time he aimed, he zoomed in on the target and took careful aim. Often this resulted in him fine tuning the previous marker he'd lined up on the HUD. But while he was aiming in on target seventeen, he noticed a glint from behind the wooden structure.

*"Something wrong, Commander? Targeting issue?"*

"There's something moving behind that target. I caught a reflection; might be from a camera or a cell phone."

*"Negative, Commander Harrison. This area is clear and secure. There's nobody out there but you."*

"I'm at max magnification and I'm not getting enough resolution to confirm. Request increase to maximum visual clarity."

*"Again, negative, Commander. You have two targets remaining and a green light in the fire zone. Continue firing."*

There it was again. Something moved. It was over two klicks to the target, but with the mech's digital optics, he saw it as if from across a dimly lit room. Remembering the manual control console, he glanced down at the lower right of his HUD. "Need to verify. Stand by."

The menu was comprehensive, but expertly laid out for ease of use. It took Skip no time at all to locate the visual inputs and raise them to the Beowulf's maximum value. The distant target snapped into crystal focus. He could make out the wood grain, the nail heads, the drips and runs in the slapdash paint job. And more important, he could identify two civilians on the firing range, huddled for cover behind the least safe object in the entire valley: Skip's next target.

"Bogeys confirmed. We've got two unauthorized personnel on the firing range. Request MPs for collection and debriefing."

*"Negative, Commander. We don't—"*

"Did you not hear me? I have visual confirmation. This isn't a mirage." What the hell was Gus thinking? That Skip was making this up? That it was a bug in the software making him see what appeared to be a couple college kids—one male, one female—crouched in the shadow of a giant plywood target painted with a bullseye?

*"This is a top secret facility. Anyone we send out there will be to eliminate them, not bring them in for questioning."*

Skip's blood ran cold. "Commander Harrison to base, please repeat. I didn't copy that last message."

*"Like hell you didn't, Harrison. This is a live fire exercise. These are spies, whether they realize it or not. These kids get out of here with video, it'll be all over the internet by suppertime. If we bring them in, it's just more hands with blood on them when we have to make them disappear. Just take care of it, Skip. It's only you, me, and a couple of the project crew here with me in the booth that even see them out there. This is the quick way—the secure way."*

"Sorry, Gus. I'm afraid I can't do that. I refuse to murder two kids because they wandered into your top secret base. Your perimeter security got sloppy, and I don't think they need to pay for that with their lives. Bring them up on charges… fine. But I won't fire."

*"That's an order."*

Skip brought the Beowulf to stand at ease, even though its arms lacked the flexibility to actually meet behind its back. Inside the pod, the meat version of Skip swallowed hard.

*"We'll discuss this when you get back to the hangar. In the meantime, stand down."*

That didn't sound good. Gus had given up too easily. Immersed in shock-absorbent gel, Skip couldn't even tell if he was sweating. But while his awareness of his physical self was limited, he still had the feeds from the Beowulf pumped straight into his brain. He heard the helicopter coming before he saw it.

Skip hadn't been debriefed on the contingent of aircraft at Sand Lion Base. He could tell the engine whine of an F-52 from an F-54 in his sleep, but he didn't know the prop signature of the AH-95 Kestrel. It wasn't until it crested the mountains that he realized that they weren't sending a transport to take the trespassers into custody. That Kestrel was coming to do what he'd refused to. Gus had sent in a cleanup crew.

This was on him. He was either going to stand there like the robot he appeared to be, or step in and do something.

The target was two klicks away, and he was on foot. But his practice running up and down the valley had paid off. He was in between the Kestrel and the two civilians. All he had to do was keep himself interposed and get to them before the cleanup crew could maneuver for a clear line of fire. They wouldn't dare risk damaging the Beowulf.

What had been an arduous task earlier in the day, Skip now did without thinking. He ran, and instead of his own legs, the legs of the Beowulf pumped beneath him. If he fell, so be it. If he didn't try, he'd never forgive himself. But he knew the broken terrain of the valley now. He veered aside to dodge a boulder and avoided a crevice by lengthening his stride.

*"Commander, what are you doing down there?"*

"I already told you, Gus. I'm not killing those civilians, and standing by to do nothing is the same thing."

The Kestrel was closing rapidly. The Beowulf's rear-facing cameras allowed Skip a perfect view of it on approach even as he watched where he ran. It was flying chest-high to him, more like an escort than a team racing him to a common goal. Skip imagined that the pilot must have been either confused or conflicted. Could that bird have been patched in on the same frequency as Skip and Gus?

With the Kestrel not busting a rotor to beat him to the target, Skip got there first and stood in front of the cowering civilians. They must have wised up and realized that they were in trouble, because they were taking cover instead of making a run for it across open ground with a military helicopter in the air. What they thought of the fifty-foot walking robot was beyond Skip's ability to guess.

*"You've made your point, Commander. Stand down. We're sending a team in to extract the civilians."*

Skip said nothing. The Beowulf's shoulders slumped and he let out a sigh of relief that carried over the radio. The rear camera was a smaller image, so he turned to get a view of the strike team in full resolution. He saw the pilot and gunner both salute before turning their bird and bugging out. Skip's greatest worry in this whole maneuver had been that he might have been forced to fire on friendly forces to defend the civilians.

The wait was another fifteen minutes while a search and recovery team flew in and extracted the two trespassers in handcuffs. He watched them fly over the mountains, wondering what came next.

*"You still have two more targets, Commander."*

Of course. The mission. Whatever else buzzed around the periphery, there was nothing that was going to stop a multi-billion-dollar project from moving forward. It also occurred to him that by finishing off the last two targets, Gus ensured that Skip came back into the hangar completely unarmed.

---

The techs who extracted Skip from the pod acted like nothing untoward had happened out in the desert. He was unhooked, unplugged, toweled off, and helped into a military-grade bathrobe. His legs wobbled, and someone offered him a shoulder to hang onto. Someone else pressed a fresh cup of coffee into his good hand. They helped him as he headed for the showers.

But as soon as they exited the main hangar, there was a line of officers waiting for him. Time to pay the piper.

Except that it wasn't. The assembled project team saluted. Even General Kogane and one Doctor Augustus Cliffton, standing at the end of the line. Skip stared in disbelief. Was he hallucinating? A side effect of prolonged exposure to the neural connections? The strike team from the Kestrel was there, too. He hadn't seen their faces, but they were still wearing the same flight suits. And then he noticed the two "civilian" trespassers, now in uniform and saluting along with the others.

"What's going on?"

The general and Gus strode down the line of officers blocking his way to the showers. "Damnedest thing I ever saw." The general shook Skip by the prosthetic hand, heedless of the light coating of slime that the first shower would only mostly remove.

Gus circled around and clapped him on the back. "Skip, hated having to put you through that, but I knew you had it in you."

"Had what?"

"You stood up to an immoral order," the general said. "Doctor Cliffton had the legal authority to authorize that shot you wouldn't take. You could have been locked up for that. Not only did you refuse to kill Corporal Sturges and Sergeant Banks, you put yourself in the line of fire to defend them."

Gus guided Skip down the row of officers who stood in respectful silence. "Skip, the biggest hurdle this project has to overcome is the fear that when turning over control of a weapon system to an autonomous AI, it'll turn on us."

"But I did turn on you."

General Kogane walked with them, taking up a flanking position on Skip's left. "Senator Kearny on the Armed Services Committee insisted on this test. He didn't want any piloting system that could pose a risk to civilian populations—specifically our own. We haven't had much luck finding pilots, and he's been making noise about shutting down the project. I'm packing up the data from today's showing and leaving it on his doorstep like a bag of turd. We're in business."

"What the general so eloquently means is that as of today, it's official. *You* are the future of America's AI program. We can teach you any technical skill you need for various combat systems. What we couldn't replicate is this." He slapped Skip in the chest, right over his heart.

———————— • ————————

This was getting monotonous. Skip had lost track of the number of times the ordinance drones had reloaded his missiles and .50 caliber magazines. Just because this was a mental endurance test didn't mean it had to be tedious. Helicopters lowered a new set of targets into the valley amid the wreckage of the old. He idly wondered where on base they were getting all the wood, and who they'd pressed into service nailing targets together and painting them. It wasn't exactly the sort of thing an enlisted soldier would expect when he gets shipped off to a top secret base, Skip imagined.

The voices in his ear kept changing as well. Far be it for Gus to put himself through the arduous task of keeping a headset on this whole time. But at least the rotating crew came with a relaxed familiarity. Most of them didn't even identify themselves to Skip by rank. There was Kirk, Alphonse, Rick, Sam (short for Samantha, he guessed by her voice), and even Captain Walsh, who he kept trying to avoid calling Fiona. Skip had zero doubt that her offer still stood, and he didn't want her catching any hint that he might take her up on it. The fact that it sounded like she was second in command to Gus on the project made it all the more crucial to keep things compartmentalized.

Skip wanted to rub his eyes but there was nothing to rub. Scraping the mech's forearm across the front of the head would only momentarily block a camera or two. His physical arms were restrained and the muscles not receiving impulses from his brain. His eyes were closed behind the protective goggles; or if they were open, he couldn't tell. All signs of physical fatigue were absent, but he felt them the same way his foot would sometime itch, or his right hand would ache.

"*Commander, you're up.*" It was Fiona's voice on the radio. He couldn't tell if she was trying to tease him with double entendre or had just been careless.

"How many more sets of these do I have to take down? Can we maybe switch it up with some agility drills? I'm starting to get a little stir-crazy in here. How long has this even been going on?" They'd disabled all timekeeping in the software. He wasn't supposed to be watching the clock, but he couldn't help asking.

"*Sorry, Commander Harrison. You know we can't tell you that. Please just proceed. Acquire target one.*"

Skip grit his teeth and locked in on the target nearest to his position. The system would have allowed him to designate all eighteen, then rapid-fire knock them all out. But one by one at the direction of the control booth was what they wanted. "Roger that."

They crawled through the exercise at a snail's pace. Fiona had him examine each target site after impact before moving on to the next. Near as Skip could tell, it was just busy work. It must have taken half an hour to mow down the full set of targets.

While they waited for the resupply drones, Fiona got chatty. "*So, Commander, I hear you've got kids. How old are they?*"

"What are you talking about? You've got my personnel files right there, don't you? You know I don't have kids."

"*My mistake. Sorry, Commander.*"

"Hey, no problem. You can make it up to me by cutting this marathon short and buying me dinner." Why he wasn't starving was a miracle. There must have been some nutrient delivery system somewhere among all the equipment hooked to his body. And he didn't mind leading Fiona on a little if it got him out of the pod.

"*You are married though. What's your wife's name?*"

"Madeline. Come on, this is all part of my record. What gives?"

"*What's she like? Where'd you honeymoon? How does she smell in the morning?*"

This was getting way too personal. There was no way any of this was relevant to piloting a mech or any other military system, and it was none of her goddamn business. Skip told her as much.

"*I'll make you a deal, Skip. You tell me every little thing about you and your wife, I'll get you out of that pod. How's that sound? I've got the authority on medical grounds, and you're not scheduled for removal for five more days.*"

"Days? You can't keep me in here for days. I'm climbing the walls in here already."

"*I'm listening. I'll even clear everyone out of the control booth. Just you and me. Consider it a therapy session. Now... what's it like when you wake up beside her in the morning?*"

Skip hated himself. He hated that Fiona was using him as cheap entertainment. But the thoughts of Madeline were a comfort to him, and he opened up for his own peace of mind. At the start he spoke tentatively, but eventually he was answering Fiona's questions on the most intimate of topics without giving them a second thought.

An unfamiliar voice came over the radio. It was faint, not something Skip was probably meant to hear. "*Doctor Walsh, we have it mapped.*"

"What was that? Map of what?"

Fiona's voice was quieter as well, as if she were holding her headset's mic away from her mouth. "*Excellent. This time let's delete virtual synapses 32719 through 32745, and the two clusters here where he got sidetracked by sexual thoughts about me. We don't need an AI that gets distracted so easily.*"

"Hey! What are you doing up there?"

"*Oh, dammit. He heard me. It's nothing you need to worry about. You're a good pilot. We're just going to make you a better one.*"

"By deleting parts of my brain?" Skip was wrung out. He couldn't process all this. It sounded like they were planning to eliminate parts of his personality. Could all the wires, needles, and neural connectors really *do* that?

He wasn't going to take this lying down. Skip ran for the tunnel that led to the hangar. The door was closed, but he had a fresh rack of Dragonfly missiles that said he was getting through. This would be the end of the program for him. Probably get him thrown in a hole somewhere. But they couldn't take away his memories. Life in a concrete box would be better than living as a hero and not remembering a lifetime with Maddie.

"*Captain...*" The tech's voice held a note of rising worry. She'd be a lot more worried if she got in the way of them pulling Skip out of the pod.

Fiona sighed. "*I've got it. Not like it's the first time he's done this...*"

The Beowulf stopped in place, no longer responding to his commands. The visual inputs went dark. Then all sensation vanished.

———— • ————

Gus walked with him from the jeep. On the helipad, the RAH-109 Gyrfalcon waited for him, its engines quiet. It was an easier walk than the inbound trip a month earlier. The trials had been better rehab than the actual clinical treatment Skip had gotten after getting his prosthetics. And to think, all it had taken was a few billion dollars worth of top secret equipment and a team of the military's best minds. He didn't even have a noticeable limp anymore.

"You sure you boys can get by without me?" Skip asked with a grin.

Gus shook his prosthetic hand. "We'll manage. The software version of you is a champ. Hardly know it wasn't the real Skip Harrison."

Skip gave a melodramatic shiver. "Kinda glad I can't tell Maddie about all this. Not sure she'd like the idea of every mech in the US Army knowing what she looks like naked."

"US Army isn't keen on that, either. The AI is going to be based on you. It'll have your moral compass and values, mental toughness and all that jazz. But we're going to pare it back to the essentials for field use."

"Won't that compromise those values you're after? I mean, if it weren't for my wedding vows, I'd have slept with Captain Walsh in a heartbeat, regulations be damned."

"Oh, the core's still the same. But I can't imagine you wanting the AI to remember your bank account numbers, email password, kids' favorite ice cream. That's all yours, and that's stuff you're welcome to keep private. Right this minute, we've got a team working diligently to separate the personal from the professional. Hell, even if it weren't for the privacy concerns—and you and me both know that's not the Army's top concern here—we need to keep the file size manageable."

"You're telling me that giant thing can't handle all of me?" Skip grinned at the thought that his brain was too big for a machine that size.

Gus chuckled and walked Skip to his ride off base. "All this time and you still think we're going to make mechs? That project was a pipe dream. It doesn't even run."

"But—"

"We use the hangar from Project Atlas, but that pod of yours was as close as you got to machinery. This AI will get scaled down to infantry-sized models, put into fighter jets, even spacecraft. But giant, walking military robots? Jesus, Skip, what are you, twelve or something, believing that crap?"

"Still..."

"Come on, Skip. Forget the fighter-jockey crap for one lousy minute and think big picture. Digital Skip is going to be the first person to visit Mars, to see inside the atmosphere of Jupiter. If there are alien life forms outside our solar system, you're going to be the one to introduce them to humanity. I didn't drag you into this to make weapons. That's near-term thinking. That's funding. That's holding your nose and doing what's gotta be done. I needed *you* because I wanted someone I could trust to be the face of humanity."

Face of humanity? Skip Harrison? One day, decades or even centuries down the road, some unmanned probe with his personality would greet humanity's first alien neighbors. Skip Harrison, a guy who hadn't been the face of anything since his own wedding album.

Skip laughed. "You sure you should be cleaning my personal life out of that 'bot, then?"

"Yeah..." Gus replied warily. "Any reason we shouldn't?"

"Hey, without memories of being a happily married man, you might be letting a robotic James T. Kirk loose on the galaxy."

## About The Author

J.S. Morin is a creator of worlds and a destroyer of words. As a fantasy writer, his works range from traditional epics to futuristic fantasy with starships. He has worked as an unpaid Little League pitcher, a cashier, a student library aide, a factory grunt, a cubicle drone, and an engineer—there is some overlap in the last two. Through it all, though, he was always a storyteller. Eventually he started writing books based on the stray stories in his head, and people kept telling him to write more of them. Now, that's all he does for a living.

For more information, visit www.jsmorin.com.

# The Traveller

## Christopher Ruz

*Editor's Note: Speculative fiction allows its fans to escape their time-locked lives in a multitude of ways, each path crowded with kindred spirits seeking similar destinations. It's an easy thing, to fall in love with that world of shared dreaming. But underneath the dream lies a rarely spoken and uncomfortable truth: we are not all escaping from the same things.*

Sir Alastair Trant was dead, slumped across his desk with a knife jutting from his neck. I, playing the Belgian inspector, had just lit my pipe (a prop, the bowl packed with incense) and was contemplating the elaborate mechanics of blackmail as the curtains fell and house lights came up for intermission.

In the moments before the curtains closed I glanced out into the audience and saw him: hunched, a huge, floppy-brimmed hat casting his face into shadow, the tangled mop of his hair curling from beneath the brim. As I watched, he took a small paper packet from inside his coat and popped something into his mouth.

The Traveller. Somehow, I knew he'd come for me.

Act Three was a blur. I arrested Doctor Pennyworth, the curtain fell, and we slipped into the dressing rooms to half-hearted applause. Ann was already making accusations, *you came in too late, remember the beat* and *if you'd put out the flyers like you were supposed to—*

I pushed past. Phillipe grabbed me by the arm. "Not staying for nibblies?"

"Got someone to see." I pulled free and ran through the backstage tunnels into the foyer of the Radcliffe Civic Theater. The crowd was already dispersing, but I saw the peak of a felt hat bobbing by the double-glass doors, and I wriggled through to grab the man's sleeve.

"Traveller?"

He turned, one brow raised. Middle-aged, big-nosed, smiling with his eyes. The curly hair was undoubtedly a wig but it was easy enough to squint and believe in the costume. "Yes?"

"You're the Traveller, aren't you? I mean, you're dressed—"

"Yeah, that's me. Hey, you were Inspector Guillaume. You weren't bad." He grinned, showing big buck teeth. "I've seen that play before. Doesn't Sir Trant get shot, not stabbed?"

"It's only community theater. We couldn't get a license for a replica revolver." I squinted inside his coat: the lining was patterned with tessellated triangles. The mark of the Traveller. "Damn. You even got the fabric right."

"You like the threads? Did them all myself. Learned how to use a sewing machine and everything. Hey!" He grinned maniacally as he reached inside his coat. "Been wanting to say this for ages. Would you like a peppermint humbug?"

———— • ————

We went to the Bridge Tavern overlooking the river. I paid. The water was speckled with candy wrappers and bottle caps. He said, "Is the moustache real, or do you stick it on?"

"All real." I tweaked it to demonstrate.

"And the belly?"

"Also real. Unfortunately."

His name was Steve, and he was in town for a Traveller fanclub meet. Except, in what he assured me was typical Steve fashion, he'd arrived a week early. "It's always that way. Or sometimes a week late. Mum used to say I just didn't get time. Which is ironic, I suppose." He pouted. "This was Dad's coat, before I changed the lining. He thinks it's all ridiculous. Grown man dressing like a poofter, he says."

I was on my third pint and the world was beginning to fizz around the edges. "What would he know?" I drained the glass. "I mean, how is this any different? Being Inspector Guillaume, I mean." I fell into the exaggerated accent that was more French or German than actual Belgian. "This is murder most foul, my friend! Most foul!"

Steve grinned beneath the foam of beer. His coat dragged along the floor, flapping around the legs of his barstool. "So, why?"

"Why what?"

"Why'd you grab me? You one of the fanclub?"

"You could say that." I pushed my empty glass aside and waved to the bartender for another. "I've been waiting for you since I was a boy. You see, I have a mystery."

———— • ————

When I was eleven years old I took my little sister exploring. Elizabeth was eight, and smart; she knew her times tables up to twelve, and spent her nights reading her children's Bible with the diligence of a monk.

I didn't share her thirst for words. I was in the fifth grade and books were a chore. Instead, I lived for afternoon television. It was 1978, and every day after school I curled inside my fortress of blankets and watched grainy black-and-white BBC serials until my eyes ached.

*Rescue Team Six* filled my days. After that came *Doom Squad*, and *Adventures Beyond the Border*, and even the occasional imported *Buck Rogers*, although the accents confused me. But of all those shows, my favourite was *The Traveller*. A hero set adrift in time by a nuclear explosion, gifted with great intellect and dubious morality. With his scientific instruments and his fierce scowl, he battled evil across time and space.

I cheered as he and his female companion, Elementary, chased down the villainous Chau Terriform. I cried when the Traveller abandoned Elementary in the Ice Vaults of Candor Prime. I ate peppermint humbugs by the bucket.

Elizabeth wasn't allowed to watch with me. Father said she was too young. Such things would only distract her from reading. But, from time to time, when my parents were out, I'd summon Liz down from her room and set her before the television, just to watch her squirm and cry whenever Chau Terriform appeared on screen.

Liz was a limpet. She followed me up the hill behind our house when I went to meet my schoolmates outside the Tesco, and would burst into tears when she fell too far behind, or when I didn't meet her eyes, or when I bought a bag of humbugs and refused to share. She cried a lot, those days.

It was November that year when I took her to the Bonehouse.

The Bonehouse sat at the end of a quiet cul-de-sac about a mile from our school, backing onto an old orchard where the trees grew wild, unpruned branches scratching at grey skies. We called it the Bonehouse because of the white wooden pillars framing the door, tall and knurled like femurs.

It'd been empty as long as we'd known it, and was haunted in all the ways that mattered. If *The Amityville Horror* had been released a year earlier we'd have told stories of bleeding walls and demonic voices booming in the night, but all we had was *The Traveller*. So the Bonehouse became a place where ventriloquist's dolls crawled on broken legs down the halls, and creatures with tunnels of teeth coiled in the basement, and assassins from the lonely corners of space hid in cupboards waiting to devour whatever fat-cheeked children were bold enough to wander inside.

An unspoken treaty kept us from going inside; to be eleven years old without a haunted house is a poor thing, and a haunted house only stays that way until one boy is brave or stupid enough to knock out a window and find the halls empty of monsters. Instead we ate apples in the orchard, and talked of the hundreds lost inside the Bonehouse, and sometimes Liz came with us and sat silently in the shade, soaking in all our horror stories.

She never told Mum and Dad. I never told her how grateful I was for that. I never had the chance.

The Bonehouse was a tumor. When Mum drove us to church on Sunday morning I pressed myself against the glass, searching for a silhouette of a steepled rooftop against the sky. It filled my dreams with black corridors.

Even as a child, I knew the only cure was to cut it out. After all, it was what the Traveller would have done.

So I left one Saturday morning, torch and Arnotts chocolate digestives in my pack. I passed Mum in the kitchen and waved goodbye.

Then, as I was halfway out the door, she said, "Be a dear and take your sister with you, otherwise she'll sit inside all day."

I should've seen the shape of the story already. The older brother, plans in tatters, dejectedly dragging his little sister up the street, pouting and kicking at stones. The Bonehouse looming over the horizon, slumbering, expectant. The perfect introduction to a Wednesday night Traveller broadcast. We took the long way, climbing a fence into the disused orchard, and picked apples for the better part of an hour. They were hard and sour but I ate them anyway, because I didn't want to tell Liz why we were really there, or how much I resented her presence. But she was a smart girl. She circled the meadow twice, collecting acorns in the pocket of her blouse, silver bracelet winking on her wrist, and she said, "You want to go inside?"

It was Liz that found the back door unlocked. I shoved her aside, not wanting her to steal my glory, but I hesitated at the threshold.

Maybe I knew that, after that day, the Bonehouse would only be another number on an abandoned street. That mysteries were only mysterious until they were solved.

Or maybe that's just me looking back through the lens of decades. Maybe I was just a boy, and scared of the dark. But, in time, I let go of the doorframe and stepped through.

The Bonehouse was cold, and when I breathed it felt as if I'd taken water into my lungs, heavy and clotting. I dropped my pack, fumbled for my torch and thumbed the big rubber button frantically. The circle of light it cast was unbearably thin, and I had to fight to keep from turning and running out the door, back into the safety of the trees.

I made out a small laundry with a porcelain basin, skinned over with cobwebs. A door at the rear opened into a thin hall, and then an expansive, echoing foyer, abandoned to dust and rats. The foyer rug was faded yellow by decades, tassels rotten and black. In the corner, a pedestal that had once held a vase was now empty, draped in a ghost-white sheet. A great two-pronged staircase enveloped the foyer like hungry, grasping arms. The windows above were choked with vines and what little light came through was worse than darkness. It felt greasy on my cheeks.

If Liz wasn't there I would've run. But she was already pressing in against my back, hugging me, whispering, "It smells bad. I want to go home," and if she wanted to leave there was no way I could do the same. So I went to explore.

There was a small green door tucked beneath the arc of the staircase, slightly ajar, but the thought of pushing it open made me feel as if I were falling from a terrible height. Instead I took the stairs two at a time, torch-beam bouncing across the polished rails. On the landing were armchairs draped in dust sheets and floorboards stained by sunlight and time.

Liz didn't follow.

I don't know how long I was upstairs. Three bedrooms came off the upper landing, each with old oak closets hung with wooden coat hangers and ensuite bathrooms with rust locking the taps tight. I explored each with the methodical nature of a true adventurer. I looked beneath the beds, and fiddled with the locks on the leather suitcases I found there. The empty coat hangers made me feel sad, although I didn't know why.

There were no ghosts hiding in the chest of drawers, or behind the curtains. No killer dolls with mouthfuls of human teeth waiting behind the bathroom door. I was relieved and disappointed in equal measure. As an adventure for the Traveller, the Bonehouse was a poor story.

A thud echoed up the stairs, like someone tripping over their own feet. A shriek of panic. I froze in place. A caretaker? The police? I squeezed the torch in both hands until my knuckles ached, unable to move, unable to blink. Then I remembered Liz, still waiting by the back door, and I thought of Mum's anger.

My paralysis broke, and I thumped down the stairs. The torchlight was fading, batteries already spitting their last, and when I reached the bottom I passed the light over those cold, quiet statues, those aching walls.

Liz was gone.

I called her name. My voice boomed back at me from the walls. I ran to the front door and pressed my face against the filthy windows, expecting to see her tossing acorns in the noon sun, but the street was empty. Then to the back door, still open, hoping she was out in the orchard. The trees were still; nothing moved in the wild grass.

I turned back to the little green door beneath the stairs. It had only been open a finger's width before but now it yawned wide enough for a man to slip through. A man, or a little girl.

I could barely breathe as I nudged the door open with the toe of my shoe. Beyond was a dark staircase leading down into a cellar. The air that floated up smelled of damp and turpentine. I called, "Please, Liz—"

From the black came the thump of heavy feet. The echo of a man's voice. Someone in the darkness said, "Grab her!"

Most nights I hate myself for what happened next. Other times, I remember I was only a child, and selfish, and afraid.

I ran.

The front door popped open, spilling me out into the street. Then I waited in the bushes outside the Bonehouse for an hour, trembling and gnawing my nails bloody.

Liz never came out. The house was silent and the doors stayed open.

I eventually found the courage to stand and creep out from the wilted rhododendrons, half expecting the Bonehouse to blink with broken windows, for the whole rotten structure to peel lazily from the concrete and shamble away over the meadows.

Something beyond the shadow of the doorway shifted, slow and lizard-like, and was still.

———————— • ————————

Steve stared into the dregs of his pint glass. He licked his lips. "Never found her?"

"There's only so long you can look," I said. "Police treated it like a kidnapping right from the start. Mum and Dad did alright. Never had another baby, though."

"Jesus," he whispered. "What do you think—"

"I don't know. Never had the guts to go back in the house. " I shrugged. "You get used to the silence. I looked for clues. I read a lot of detective stories."

"And so—"

I tweaked my moustache. "You read enough and you start to love them. I've done seven stage productions of *Murder by Candlelight*, one student film adaptation of *The Killers Wore Suede*—even though Inspector Guillaume isn't in the book—and I go to the children's hospital every other week and do a little show. I can tell a murderer by how he laces his shoes. I can smell blood on the wind. I am the famous Belgian detective, and I am a servant to the people."

Steve smirked. "Does it help?"

"What?"

"The detecting." Steve's cheeks were red and his nose was beginning to glow, and I thought he looked more like Alan Pearsdale in his last days of Travelling, the stumble-drunk actor pushing away the photos and pens proffered to him at conventions, burning up in the glare of his fame. "Did it help you find her?"

I ducked my head. "There are stories. Ghost stories. People say if you stand outside the Bonehouse at night, you can hear her crying. She says *help, help*. But I went and listened, and I heard different." I clutched at an empty glass. "She's saying, *Harold*. She's calling my name."

Maybe he pitied me. Maybe he thought it was all a joke, a piss-take between two grown men. Maybe, in that moment, he understood exactly what I needed.

"You want to go back," he said.

"I couldn't go alone."

"Would the Traveller abandon a friend in need?" As if by magic, he produced a silver tuning fork from his coat pocket—the Traveller's Fork, the ancient and cursed device through which he tuned time and reality to suit his needs.

"Let's get going," he said. "Before I get sober."

———— • ————

The Bonehouse squatted at the end of the cul-de-sac, scowling with broken windows, gutters choked with leaves, paint peeling from rotten boards. The wind sobbed around the steeples. If I closed my eyes, I could hear Liz's voice in the breeze.

Steve hugged himself beneath his brown coat. A sudden breeze whipped wet leaves from the asphalt and stuck them to the brim of his floppy hat. The walk seemed to have woken him up, and he twisted his hands. "God, it's cold out. You know, I have coffee at the hotel—"

"Can't you hear her, my old friend?"

"Just the wind. Look, Harold—"

"Call me Guillaume." I tried to look apologetic. "It helps me think."

"Fine, Guillaume. You know a way in?"

I did. When I told him I'd never come back to this place I'd lied. I'd stood in the shadows of the Bonehouse many times over the past years, watching the gaping black mouth of the front doors, waiting for them to spring to life and drag me in, screaming, fingernails gouging strips from the dirt. I'd circled the house and found all the weak windows, the points in the wainscotting where the boards peeled back, but I'd never been able to work up the nerve to pry them apart.

But today, I had the Traveller with me.

The Bonehouse doors were closed with a heavy chain and a Yale padlock the size of my fist, but the second window along had been cleaned out long ago and boarded over. I wriggled the nails loose. "You see, there is always a way for the thinking man."

"Christ." Steve wiped his nose on his sleeve. "You first."

The boards came away easily. Steve helped me up, and I climbed through into the shadows of the Bonehouse for the first time in thirty years.

All went silent. The noises of taxis and grey owls on the hunt was dimmed, leaving only the murmur of breath. The air was thick and treacly and when I said, "Traveller?" my voice was muted in the stillness. Everything outside the Bonehouse had ceased to exist; air didn't travel that far and there was nothing left to echo.

Steve was close behind. "Bastard thing..." His hat was caught on a nail and the brim tore as he tugged it free. He stared at the ruined fabric forlornly. "No chance I can get this mended by Friday."

I took my penlight from my coat pocket and let it wander. Mold and rat droppings, the vague odor of marijuana. At my feet was an empty bottle of Lucozade with a section of rubber pipe jutting from the plastic, yellow bong-water collecting in the bottom. Orange carapaces of cigarette butts strewn across the carpet. A pair of underpants draped carefully over the banister. The twin staircases loomed.

Steve said, "I think I cut myself. God, I've got a splinter the size of a truck."

"Quiet! How will we be able to hear her with you prattling?"

"Mate," he said. "I'll go, if you want me gone. This is your show. This place creeps the hell out of me."

I ducked my head. "Sorry. Got carried away."

"Beer talking, is it?"

"No. Just the years."

The staircase made mourning noises beneath our feet as we went up to the bedrooms. "They searched the place, right?"

"On the first night. I remember the police calling her name. She didn't call back. They looked in the cupboards, the bathrooms—"

"But you heard them in the basement. The kidnappers."

I froze, one hand resting on the balustrade, the other gripping the torch so tight it ached. I remembered that green door, and the voices beyond. "The police took me down there. There's a cupboard, and an old sink, and a space under the stairs." I closed my eyes. Police in blue uniforms. The slow sweep of torch beams. The silver buttons on their jackets shimmering in the gloom. A chorus of voices, *Elizabeth, Elizabeth! Come out!*

"There was nobody there," I finished.

"Couldn't have just vanished."

"Well, one of the neighbors saw a car. A blue rover. And some men, said they looked like immigrants. So they gave up on the house. I guess they'd call Interpol these days. Hunt for sex traffickers. All they did back then was knock on doors. Never found anything." I thought about what would have happened if the Traveller had been with me that day. We would've chased them down using the Traveller's Fork and de-materialized their car. In the closing scenes, the kidnappers would be unmasked as shell-bots operating under commands from a nearby hostile consciousness. Or symbiotes collecting intelligence prior to a planet-wide invasion. Or acid-spitting flesh-golems directed by the malevolent god Ra-Sut-Three, scouting a new location in which to hide their rotten master, and they'd taken Liz as collateral...

"Did they sound like immigrants?"

"Accents are hard."

"You didn't say they had accents. Sure they said 'grab her?' "

"Maybe I misheard. Maybe it was something foreign. Fuck, I don't know." I sucked my lower lip and tried to calm myself. Inspector Guillaume never said "fuck." Inspector Guillaume was always poised. He saw what others didn't see.

Steve followed me into the bedrooms. A four-poster squatted beneath a plastic sheet. A closet in the corner draped in white, the hatstand like a solitary ghost. A painting on the wall of a placid stream winding through proper English countryside.

Steve said, "Why didn't they tear this place down?"

"Family history? It's hard to let go of grand things." The bathrooms were grey with dust. A skylight choked with leaves, a cracked porcelain tub. Wrought iron valves in the shape of children's hands. I imagined them grasping back, and shivered. "This is no place for a modern gentleman."

"You really like the detective thing, eh?"

"It grew on me."

"Yeah. I understand. Like this." Steve tipped his floppy-brimmed hat. "The guy who played the Traveller, you know him? Alan Pearsdale? He always looked like a kid on a trip to the zoo. Everything was exciting. Like the world was a big adventure playground." He sighed. "I met him once, you know."

"How was he?"

"Angry. Pissed off at everything he wasn't." Steve kicked a suitcase and it slid away into the farthest corner of the bathroom. "Where else then? The basement?"

I remembered those voices in the depths. But that was years ago, and anyone waiting down there was long gone or dead themselves.

"Basement."

We crept back down the coiled staircase, across the detritus of bongs and used condoms, to the little green door. It wasn't locked, but a thick patina of dust coated the doorknob; even the local teenagers had better sense than to descend into that darkness.

Steve tugged it open. "Heavy door."

"So?"

"Thick enough to muffle voices. Maybe you misheard."

"Since when were you the detective?"

"Sorry, mate. Just thinking out loud. Shit, maybe it was her."

"What?"

"The shouting. Could've been your sister, and you—"

"I know what I heard." My voice quavered as I waved my penlight at the shadows. Wine crates shattered into kindling, a pile of paperbacks gorged on mildew until they'd inflated like the hairless bellies of dead rats.

Steve hesitated at the top of the stairs. "Do we have to?"

"I didn't know the Traveller was afraid of the dark."

"Piss off, Guillaume never was either."

"The famous Belgian detective holidays on the Nile and drinks blackcurrant cassis. He does not poke around in the dark and the dusty." But something else held me back. The memory of a small boy caught on the cusp of those stairs, and the banging below of angry men.

"Would you hurry up? My fingers are dropping off."

The stairs made sad keening noises beneath my weight. I swept the beam over the swollen paperbacks, the empty cupboard with the brass handles, the sink eaten through at the bottom with rust. Steve yanked the cupboard open and threw a hand over his mouth in disgust. I peered over his shoulder; a cluster of greedy black eyes stared back. Mice had built a nest in the scraps of a faded denim jacket, and now they chittered, pink worm-tails flicking to and fro.

He slammed the door shut. "This is crazy. I'm going."

"Give me a minute. Just one."

"What do you want from me?"

In the dim glow of the penlight Steve was looking less and less like the Alan Pearsdale of my memories and more like another flaccid actor in a borrowed coat and bargain-store hat. Shabby, dusty, hunching away from the light. "A minute. That's all."

Steve eyed me with something between pity and disgust. "Christ. Hurry it up, then."

I skirted the basement, kicking over empty aluminium cans, and peered into the crawlspace beneath the stairs. Concrete slab and low plastic pipes. The crawlspace extended three or four meters back before ending in a pile of red brick. The police had looked here. They'd shouted Liz's name into the darkness.

*Grab her!*

That cry still echoed. Steve was right. It could've been foreign accents. Could've been another language. Could've been the foundations settling. I was so small. An age when shadows cast by wine bottles and fruit crates grew into monsters.

Kidnappers. Of course. What else could it be? If I believed anything, it had to be that.

I crouched low and stuck my head into the crawlspace. "Hello?" My own voice came back, echoing strangely, as if reverberating off panes of ice. "Liz?"

Behind me, Steve said, "Mate, I'm going—"

I don't know why I did it. Perhaps I knew that, if I resisted the pull, I'd regret it as much as I'd regretted running out of the house all those years ago.

Belly pressed flat against the concrete slab, I left Steve behind and wriggled beneath the stairs.

The dust made my nose itch, and I sneezed so hard that tears sprang to my eyes. I could see barely a foot ahead; the penlight beam was a tiny circle the size of a pound coin, playing over red bricks spilling mortar like moss. I passed a spiderweb big enough to snare a dog, threads slick and glistening. Pebbles skittered under my palms. I whispered, "Hello?"

No reply. The crawlspace went on. The ceiling was so low that even when I wriggled on my belly the joists scratched my spine. Could Liz have gotten this far, scared little girl that she was? The light shook in my fist. Dust fell in my eyes and in my hair. A spider skittered over my ear and I almost screamed. Far behind me, dimly, Steve said, "You coming out?"

The light hit a tumble of bricks. A section of the foundations had collapsed, blocking the crawlspace. This was as far as the police had gone, all those years ago. I was about to back out when something beyond the rubble caught my eye. A flash of aluminium? "Hold on," I called. With the penlight gripped between my teeth I moved the debris aside brick by brick. It took a long time.

There was something behind. A small chamber beneath the stairs, lightless and dry.

I shuffled on, my trousers catching on the stone. A button popped from my shirt and vanished into the gloom. An inch further, one more, and I was through the heating tunnel and into that brick chamber. I stood, knees popping, took a deep breath of that stale crypt air, and passed my torch-beam across the walls.

The light caught a hint of silver.

I saw.

No. I couldn't. It was too much. I turned away and let the penlight play over the tiny chamber, the sloping dirt walls, rattling pipes running the length of the ceiling. Not a room at all, but a forgotten construction space, a gap in the fabric of the old house left to the rats and mold.

Nobody had known. Not me, not the police.

But the Traveller would've.

"I should have brought him before," I whispered. The guilt was hot in my chest, crushing the air from my lungs. "I'm sorry. The Traveller would've fixed it. He always fixes it."

Again, my penlight caught that pinprick of silver amidst the dust. It stole my breath, shimmering in time with my heartbeat.

God, it was resonating. It thrummed. It demanded.

On the edge of hearing came, faintly, the sweet tone of a tuning fork.

Without warning, the glint of silver grew.

I fell back against the brick, not knowing whether to scream, as that starburst of light expanded, growing tall, becoming a disc of light hanging in the air. Not an illusion, or a reflection of the pen-light on exposed wiring. It was a doorway, just like those I remembered from my childhood watching BBC serials, wide enough for a man to crawl through. And on the other side...

The Traveller said, "Don't touch it."

I spun. I hadn't heard him enter, but there he was, so huge and bright he seemed to fill the room. His smile was perfect and his hat was floppy and I could sense every one of his many centuries lingering behind his old, dark eyes. There was a presence to him, a looming gravity that filled every corner of that little crawlspace. I could smell the ozone on his skin, the stardust in his pores.

He was the Traveller of my childhood made flesh.

He fluffed out his coat and drew his tuning fork from his pocket. When he struck it against the wall it hummed with an alien resonance. "Time gate," he said. "In flux. Left behind centuries ago, I'd wager, and somehow it's come to rest in... 1978."

I inhaled sharply. "The year Elizabeth vanished."

"Of course. Perhaps she crawled in here playing hide and seek. These old bricks are only held on by spiderwebs. They fell behind her and there was nowhere to go but through. And where she'll end up..." The Traveller shook his head. "Poor, scared girl."

"Could we go back?"

"Goodness, no. We'd be crossing our own time-line."

"You could go alone."

"Inspector Guillaume, I just said—"

How proper that he recognised me as the famous Belgian detective. Of course. The Traveller had explored the furthest reaches of the universe. How could he not know me? "Have you been to Manchester before? In 1978?"

"Not specifically."

"So what'll you be crossing?"

He smiled, showing the gap between his front teeth. "Physics?"

"Traveller," I said. "Please."

"Well," he said, stroking his chin. "If you stepped through, you could emerge anywhere. Anywhen. But I suppose I could modulate the stream. You'll emerge at the last point of connection. Probably 1978, probably some-where in the house. But who knows? Time gates wobble. It might spit you out into space. I'd know. I've been there five times, now."

"I must try, at least. It is in my blood to try."

The Traveller nodded. "I admire that, Inspector Guillaume. Well. Shall we?"

I nodded. The Traveller aimed his tuning fork at the gulf of black, and something in that abyss shuddered and froze. Side by side, the Traveller and I stepped into the portal.

The world fluttered. Flashes of light and not-light. The walls bent around us, and the ground beneath our feet lifted and spun. I clung to the Traveller's arm and he whooped and laughed with his hat flapping around his ears, and then everything jerked to a stop and I found myself falling.

We'd appeared at the top of the basement stairs and I didn't have time to catch myself. We tumbled together, the Traveller's heel catching me in the cheek. Then we hit the ground. I stood gingerly, feeling my chest for breaks and bruises. "Anywhere and anywhen, but not on solid ground?"

The Traveller groaned. "Time travel is not an exact science, Inspector."

"When are we, then?" I hadn't seen much of the basement when I was eleven, but it seemed much the same. Empty wine crates in one corner, the tarpaulin beneath them heaped with dirt. A broken vase, a scattering of mouse droppings. The same pile of paperbacks, corners yellowed but still stacked flat. Everything as it had been five minutes before, but thirty years younger.

"I think, Inspector," the Traveller said, "that we arrived just in time."

He pointed. Pressed into the farthest corner, no more than a shadow against shadows, was a girl in a plaid dress. Her hair was tied in a single dirty ponytail. A spiderweb was plastered over her nose and brow. Her eyes were wide and terrified.

I froze, as if confronted by a startled doe in a country lane. Slowly, I went down on one knee and reached out to her. "Elizabeth? Is that you?"

Liz gathered up her dress in her tiny fists, and I remembered how scared she'd always been. It was easier to remember her as an irritation clinging fast to my arm than a shrinking eight-year-old girl, following me not out of spite but loyalty.

I swallowed hard. "I'm from the police, little one. My name—"

She turned and ran, and I called her name, but she was too quick, scurrying into the crawlspace beneath the stairs. The Traveller was close behind, shouting, "Grab her!" My fingers closed around her ankle, but she pulled free, and was gone into the black.

I cursed beneath my breath and peered into the crawlspace. "Elizabeth? Please..."

The Traveller rested a hand on my shoulder. "You can't win every time, Inspector."

I clenched my hands into pudgy fists. "I could go after her."

"And then? That time gate could spit you out anywhere. And would she know you, trust you? She'll be just as scared with you as without."

"Can you bring her back?"

The Traveller shook his head.

"So she goes alone, again. She flies through time to God knows where and the children hear her crying for a hundred years. Is that the best we can do?"

"I don't have all the answers. I'm only a scientist, detached from time. You're the master detective. Isn't this what you're best at?"

I nodded slowly, pinching my moustache between thumb and forefinger. "It is a tricky question, and one that Guillaume has never seen before. But is there not always a solution, for he that is prepared to look?"

From overhead came a creak of hinges.

I looked up to the head of the stairs, where a small boy stood silhouetted against the evening light, and I knew what I had to do.

"Harold?" I waved to the boy, smiling. "Hello? I am Inspector Guillaume, from Belgium. You may have heard of me? Your sister, she is stuck. I would get her out, but you see, I would not fit, and my colleague..."

The boy at the top of the stairs, the boy that once was me, looked at the Traveller with his jaw hanging low. "You—"

"Yes," the Traveller said. He knew the game. "And now we need you to be brave, and fetch your sister out. You're a brave boy, aren't you? Here." He took the white paper bag from inside the dusty folds of his coat. "She likes peppermint humbugs, doesn't she? Go on, take them."

The boy crept down the stairs, clinging tight to the railing. He stood before the Traveller in stunned silence, and the Traveller placed the bag in his hand and closed his fingers tight around it.

"She's waiting. Don't come out until you've found her."

He hesitated at the entrance to the crawlspace and looked back at us both for confirmation, eyes shining with tears, but in the end the boy went, the bag of humbugs crushed in his little fist. I heard him coughing, and then the sound of brick shifting, and then nothing.

I counted to five hundred, then knelt to peer into the shadows. He was gone.

The Traveller rested a hand on my shoulder. "I don't know whether that was the right thing, Inspector. But it's done."

"Where will they go?"

"There are things even I don't know. Wherever it is, they go together. Is there any better friend for a lost little girl than her brother?"

He led me up the stairs. My hands were numb on the railing. We stood together by the basement door, and the Traveller rapped his tuning fork against the doorframe, muttering, "Somewhere here, yes, a little to the left, yes, thank you. The residue of our time gate is still here. If I can find the right frequency—"

The world lurched, and ten thousand days ripped past, and I felt hungry and lightheaded and nauseous for one glorious moment and then we were back, in the dark space beneath the stairs. I took a deep breath and sneezed, twice. I still held my little torch. The circle of light it cast was dim and getting dimmer.

The Traveller hunched over to keep his head from knocking on the ceiling in that tiny room. "Job well done, Inspector Guillaume."

"And you, Traveller."

He shook my hand. "Tell nobody."

"Who would believe me?"

The Traveller winked and tipped his hat, and was gone. I was alone.

I backed out of the crawlspace in a contrail of dust and spiderwebs, replaced the bricks, blocked off the entrance to the tomb, shuffled further, and emerged into the basement. I blinked, wheezed, beat my hands on my torn dress pants and sent up cumulus clouds of grit.

Steve stood at the foot of the stairs, licking his lips. He tugged at the brim of his patchy dollar-store hat and shuffled his feet. In the gloom he looked exhausted, drooping, only a middle-aged man playing dressups. "Christ," he said, "you were in there long enough. Find anything?"

I patted my pockets, looking for a cigarette, but all I had was my prop pipe. It was flimsy and weightless in my hands.

———————— • ————————

I didn't see Steve again. We exchanged numbers outside the Bonehouse, and he said, "I hope you figure it out someday. I hope she turns up." I nodded, and said to call if he wanted to get another drink. He never did.

Our production of *Murder by Candlelight* closed after a week. The audiences grew thin, and my heart wasn't in the lines.

I went back to the Bonehouse a month after I'd met the Traveller. I sat on the pavement outside and smoked a slow cigarette and watched the windows for any sign of movement. There was none. The place was as dead as it had ever been.

I thought of Liz, crawling on hands and knees into that forgotten cavity. Maybe scared, maybe curious. Maybe trying to prove something to herself, and to me. The thunder as old stonework crumbled behind her. A cry that carried strangely off the brickwork, twisted into something terrifying. Dust in her lungs. Maybe she'd struck her head. Maybe passed out. Either way, when the police arrived and flashed their lights into that crawlspace, they'd seen only brick. They called and she never replied.

I thought of the silver bracelet on her wrist. The way it winked in the light.

But that was a different girl now, a different fiction. My sister was alive, somewhere distant and brilliant. I'd sent her to strange places with the only companion she ever truly knew or loved. I'd given her an adventure.

The wind whipped around the eaves and tore shingles from the roof. I waited to hear a little girl on the edge of the world call my name but wherever she was, she was silent, and had no need of me.

## About The Author

Christopher Ruz is an Australian author who was raised on a steady diet of high fantasy, 60's scifi and age-inappropriate horror. His work spans genres, blending magic into his space opera and Lovecraftian nightmares into his contemporary fiction. A 2017 Aurealis Award finalist and Writers of the Future awardee, Ruz aims to complete his tenth novel, *God Factory*, in 2017.

For more information, visit www.ruzkin.com.

# Afterword

Did you like these stories? Then you might be interested in following the regular reviews at ImmerseOrDie (immerseordie.com)—the site that scours the indie marketplace to find great new authors, and then promotes them to the world.

Whether it's short story anthologies like the one in your hand, a Smackdown of full-length novels like this (creativityhacker.ca/sd1-ch), or some program we haven't dreamed up yet, ImmerseOrDie is committed to celebrating the best of indie genre publishing. Tough love for a tough market.

Or maybe you're an author yourself and you think your work will stand up to our test. If so, then why not send it in and maybe get a little of this promotional action for yourself? Guidelines are available right here (creativityhacker.ca/immerseordie-submissions). All you need is the guts.

So no matter what brought you here, don't be shy. Get in touch. And by all the holy floating baubles in all the worlds, please feel free to lend this book to your friends, or send them a link (creativityhacker.ca/shiny) and let them download an e-copy for themselves.

Help us share the awesome, and we'll keep bringing you more.

www.ingramcontent.com/pod-product-compliance
Lightning Source LLC
Chambersburg PA
CBHW051507170626
46811CB00002B/698